THE RUSSIAN'S LUST

AVENGING ANGEL
SEVEN DEADLY SINS SERIES
BOOK #4

CAP DANIELS

ANCHOR WATCH
PUBLISHING

** USA **

The Russian's Lust
Avenging Angel
Seven Deadly Sins Book #4
Cap Daniels

This is a work of fiction. Names, characters, places, historical events, and incidents are the product of the author's imagination or have been used fictitiously. Although many locations such as marinas, airports, hotels, restaurants, etc. used in this work actually exist, they are used fictitiously and may have been relocated, exaggerated, or otherwise modified by creative license for the purpose of this work. Although many characters are based on personalities, physical attributes, skills, or intellect of actual individuals, all of the characters in this work are products of the author's imagination.

Published by:

** USA **

13 Digit ISBN: 978-1-951021-36-8
Library of Congress Control Number: 2022944584

Cover Design: German Creative

Printed in the United States of America

Lust is a tool, desire a trap. Wield the first, and you can take someone's soul. Fall into the second, and they can take yours.

— RILEY SHANE

THE RUSSIAN'S LUST

Russkaya Pokhot'

CAP DANIELS

1

POYEZDKA DEVUSHEK
(GIRLS' TRIP)

Washington, DC

The Russian-accented voice of one of the world's deadliest assassins wafted through the telephone as Department of Justice Special Agent Gwynn Davis pressed the handset to her ear.

"Hello to you, my beautiful friend. Is Anya Burinkova, and I have for you gift."

"You don't have to tell me your name every time you call, Anya. I'm smart enough to figure out it's you as soon as you open your mouth. Where are you?"

"That is part of gift for you. You will come to play with me on girls' trip, yes?"

"I know you don't understand this concept, but I have a real job. I can't just drop everything and run off to play with you anytime you call."

"This means yes, you will come, yes?"

The coarse voice of seasoned Supervisory Special Agent Ray White cut through the room. "Davis, who are you talking to?"

Gwynn slid a hand over the phone. "It's Anya, and she says she wants me to come on a girls' trip with her."

White held out a hand. "Give it to me."

Gwynn uncovered the phone. "Hold on, Anya. Agent White wants—"

White snatched the device. "Where are you?"

"Oh, hello, Ray. Is still okay for me to call you Ray, yes?" Without pausing, she continued. "And is good you are there. You will have Gwynn come with me for few days. You cannot come this time. Is only for girls. Maybe next time for you."

He growled, "I said, where are you?"

"I am on telephone call with you from someplace that is nothing like Washington, DC."

White pulled on the knot of his tie. "Anya, I've had less than one cup of coffee this morning, so I'm in no mood for your games. Tell me where you are."

"I am on beautiful island in Caribbean Sea, and Gwynn is coming to be with me. You will, of course, approve this, yes?"

White planted himself in his wingback desk chair and pressed his eyes closed. "Which Island, and how long?"

"Is island of Bonaire, and I think is maybe thirty-five kilometers long."

White slammed the phone onto his desk and dug his fists into his eyes. After a breathing exercise he'd seen on some old kung fu movie, he lifted the cell back to his ear. "You know I wasn't asking how long the island is. How long do you want to keep Davis?"

"I wish to keep her forever. She is my friend."

He threw the phone in Davis's general direction, and she snagged it out of the air like an Atlanta Braves shortstop. "I don't know what you said, but I think you convinced him."

"Of course I did. He cannot tell to me no. Your ticket is being delivered to Agent White's secretary. Bring little black dress. Everything else is already here."

"Okay, when is the flight?"

Anya giggled. "I will see you in only five hours, and please tell to Agent White you will do what he demands."

Gwynn glanced at Ray. "What are you talking about, Anya?"

"You will know soon. He will have one demand before he allows you to come to me."

"Whatever you say, Anya. I guess I'll see you soon."

She slipped the phone into her pocket and stood nervously in front of her boss.

"Let me guess," White said. "Your flight leaves in twenty minutes?"

Gwynn shrugged. "I don't know. She said . . ."

Before she could finish, White's phone toned, and he pushed the intercom button. "What?"

"I'm sorry to bother you, Agent White, but a courier just dropped off a package for Agent Davis, and she's not in her office."

"Bring it to me," he ordered, and seconds later, his administrative assistant slid a sealed package onto his desk and then vanished.

He slid a letter opener beneath the flap and poured out the contents onto the desk. After dropping the package into the trashcan, he stuck his glasses onto his nose and examined the airline ticket. "This is a one-way ticket, Davis."

Gwynn channeled her internal Anya. "Is only going one way. Next ticket will be also only one way."

He pointed the letter opener across his desk with a menacing scowl. "Ten days, Davis. Not ten days and ten seconds. Ten days, and so help me God, if you don't have your little Russian girlfriend with you, don't bother coming back. You can just mail me your badge and gun and play house with your little nesting doll. Got it?"

Gwynn stepped forward and lifted the ticket from his hand. "Yes, sir. I'll see you in ten days, and I'll have Anya with me. I promise."

She pulled the door closed behind her, leaving the all-boys club behind.

Special Agent Johnathon McIntyre sat staring blankly at his boss. "How? How does that happen? She gets to go off to some island for an all-expenses-paid vacation, and I'm stuck here with . . ."

"Stuck here with whom, Johnny Mac? Me?"

"No, sir. That's not what I meant. I meant . . ."

White pointed toward an empty wingback. "Relax and sit down. I'll give you a choice. You can take ten days off just like Davis and go wherever you want. You can chase her to Bonaire for all I care. But the two of them wearing nothing but shoelaces and eyepatches for ten days? You don't need that in your life. You've got enough problems without having that dancing around in your head."

Johnny Mac spent the next few seconds of his life picturing the statuesque Russian blonde and his equally fetching brunette partner, Guinevere Davis, frolicking in the sun and sand of the Southern Caribbean until White ordered, "Stop it!"

Johnny Mac collected himself. "Sorry, I was just thinking about . . ."

"I know exactly what you were thinking about, and that's not where your head needs to be."

White opened a drawer and slid a picture across his desk.

Johnny Mac leaned forward to pick up the print. "What's this?"

"What's it look like, Agent McIntyre?"

"It looks like an empty office to me."

"You should've been a detective. It's not just any old empty office. It's the office eight doors down the hall, and there's currently no name under the title supervisory special agent on the door."

Johnny Mac lowered an eyebrow. "What are you saying, boss?"

"I'm saying trips to Bonaire to play with former Russian assassins isn't the path to getting your name on that door."

Johnny Mac shook his head. "I know what you're doing, Agent White, but have you seen her in a bikini?"

"Which one?"

The younger agent's mouth fell open, and White chuckled. "Catch your jaw before it hits the floor. Eastern Europe is packed to overflowing with ten million more who look just like her. In fact, they're exporting them as fast as they can. Option number two for you just happens to involve . . . well, involvement with a few of those imports, if you think you're up to the task."

Johnny Mac leaned forward in his chair. "I'm listening."

White slid a file from the stack at the edge of his desk and flipped it open. Raising his chin to align his glasses with the contents of the file, he said, "Yep. Ten million more, just like Anya."

Johnny Mac's impatience made itself known in the form of a bouncing foot and fidgeting fingertips.

White closed the file and held it over his desk. "Relax, Johnny. I'm not going to bogart the pictures. You can have a look."

He took the file and flipped it open, but his eyes betrayed the stoic exterior he hoped he was displaying.

"I told you," White said.

"Why? Why do they all look like supermodels?"

"Who knows? Maybe God feels sorry for the Russian men who have to live where it snows a hundred feet every year."

Johnny Mac leaned back in the chair. "It might be worth dealing with a hundred feet of snow, boss."

"Trust me, it ain't. Get yourself a good Southern girl who knows exactly how to make biscuits and gravy just like her granny made, and you'll be set for life. Sixty-year-old Russian women look ninety, but biscuits and gravy never get old."

2

Davayte Potantsuyem
(Let's Dance)

Johnny Mac dropped the file onto his lap. "Are we really talking about biscuits and gravy?"

White motioned toward the file. "I'm talking about biscuits and gravy, but something tells me your mind is somewhere else."

Johnny Mac fanned himself with the closed file. "So, what's this all about?"

"Stop being a fourteen-year-old boy, and read the file instead of just looking at the picture."

Johnny flipped open the folder and thumbed through the pages. When he finished, he tossed it back onto the desk. "I'm not sure I'm tracking. What does this have to do with me?"

White bounced his pen against his blotter and pointed it at Johnny. "There's a sucker born every minute."

"Now you're quoting P.T. Barnum? This gets weirder by the minute."

White snapped his fingers. "And so I have you, lad. I'll bet you a hundred bucks you can't find any credible historical evidence that P.T. Barnum ever said that."

Johnny Mac screwed up his face. "What are you talking about? Everybody knows Barnum said that."

White leaned back and spun his pen between his fingers. "Okay, then. Make it a thousand bucks, and I'll give you until noon to find it."

"Wait a minute. This is crazy. What does any of that have to do with Russian girls and some street scam in Vegas?"

"I'll tell you exactly what they have to do with each other . . . You!"

"What about me?"

White grinned and checked his watch. "You're the sucker, and you've got ten minutes to get down to tech services. They're expecting you."

Johnny instinctually checked his watch. "Okay, but I'm still lost."

"Remember that feeling," White said. "I want you to keep that attitude and exactly that look for one unforgettable night you'll never remember."

Johnny Mac stood and shook his head. "Before I get back from tech services, would you please drink a pot of coffee so I can understand what's coming out of your mouth?"

White checked his watch again. "Eight minutes."

The men and women of the Department of Justice Technological Implementation Services Branch pride themselves in not existing. The CIA's Office of Technical Service gets all the credit when onscreen spies need new toys, but the gadget gurus in the second-level basement beneath the Robert F. Kennedy Department of Justice Building quietly go about their toils like Santa's little elves at some hidden North Pole workshop.

Special Agent Johnathon McIntyre was buzzed through the second security door and sallyport as the clock struck nine a.m.

A woman with the blackest hair he'd ever seen gave him the hang-loose sign with her thumb and pinky finger. "Cool, you're here. I'm Celeste, so get undressed."

Johnny shook his head. "What?"

"I'm just messing with you," she said. "I really am Celeste, and I do need you to take off your jacket and shirt, but you can keep your pants on if you want."

He chuckled. "You can't imagine the day I've had already, so coming to the basement to get naked seems par for the course."

She looked him over. "Naked is cool with me. I'd join you if they wouldn't fire me, but I need this gig."

Johnny suddenly decided black-haired techies might be almost as much fun as an Eastern European beauty. "Do you know how to make biscuits and gravy?"

Celeste stopped in her tracks and turned on a heel. "Biscuits and gravy? Yeah, of course I know how. I grew up in the South. Why do you ask?"

"It was just a thought that ran through my head. That's all."

"Cool beans," she said. "If you want to put my claim to the test sometime, I'd be down for that. You're kind of cute, and I'm kind of single."

"I seem to be developing a lot of new tastes lately. Maybe I'll add biscuits and gravy to the list. I'm Johnny Mac, by the way."

She blew an enormous bubble of pink gum and let it pop against her lips. When she peeled the deflated gum from her lips with her tongue, Johnny forgot all about women on the beach in Bonaire.

She led him through a pair of double doors and into what looked like a tailor's shop. Three paned mirrors with elevated stages claimed three of the four corners of the room. The fourth was a rack of hundreds of bolts of cloth.

Johnny stood in the center of the room beside an industrial sewing machine and a table littered with electrical parts, soldering irons, batteries, and spools of impossibly thin wire.

"What's all this? I don't really know why I'm here. My boss just sent me down and said I had an appointment."

Celeste giggled. "He was right. Now, give."

"Give what?"

The giggling continued, and she stepped in front of Johnny Mac with the toe of her left Converse shoe between his feet. For the first time, she was close enough for him to smell the slightest hint of perfume.

"What are you wearing? You smell great."

She blushed. "Thank you. It doesn't really have a name yet."

"Are you part of some perfume testing program or something?"

She unbuttoned his jacket and slid her hands inside across his chest and shoulders. "Yeah, you might say that. I make my own perfume. If I like it, I give it a name. If not, I don't. I haven't made up my mind yet. But since you like it, I think I'll keep it in the rotation."

"I think you should."

Celeste let her hands continue across his shoulders until she slid his jacket down his arms and across his hands. After hanging the jacket over a mannequin, she stood back to take a look at the cut, then pulled a measuring tape from around her neck. "Raise your arms over your head, G-Man."

"Do I need to take off my gun?"

She wrapped her arms around him, lacing the measuring tape over his chest. "No, leave it on. If I'm going to make jackets for you, I need to make them big enough to hide your . . . piece." She jotted down a number. "Good. Now hold your hands straight out to the side. I need to measure for the cuff."

Celeste slipped behind him and pressed the end of the tape between his shoulder blades. "You really take the Agency's physical fitness program seriously, don't you?"

Thankful for his diligence in the gym, he said, "I lift a few days a week. Sometimes we find ourselves in situations on the street that . . ."

She poked her head beneath his outstretched arm and stuck a finger to his lips. "Shh. Stop talking. You were doing just fine by letting me feel you up while pretending to measure you."

He blushed, and then she made a few more notes and slowly unbuttoned his shirt. "Okay, you can take off your gun now . . . unless you want me to do it."

He stood perfectly still and met her dark eyes.

She put on a mischievous smile. "Okay, cool. I'll do it. Do you have handcuffs, too?"

He watched her detach his shoulder holster from his belt and off his shoulders. "Keep going," he said. "You'll find my cuffs."

"I told you to stop talking." She released his belt and the button of his trousers. "Don't get too excited, big boy. I just need to untuck your shirt."

Soon, his shirt was hanging from her arm, and she pointed to a crease on the left shoulder. "See this?"

"Yeah, what is it?"

"It's a tell."

"A tell?"

She traced the line with her fingertips. "Yes, a tell. Every time you take off your jacket, this crease tells the whole world you're a cop. Only cops wear shoulder holster rigs, and all of those rigs leave creases. Except mine."

He examined her T-shirt. "You're not wearing a shoulder rig."

She delivered a playful slap to his chest. "No, silly. I don't wear a holster of any kind. I'm not a cop, but you are, and I build stuff for cops. Take a look at this." Celeste turned, draped his shirt across a chair, and pulled a shoulder holster from a drawer. "Here, try it on."

Johnny slipped into the rig, and she helped him connect it to his belt.

"I can do it myself," he said.

"Yeah, but it's more fun if I help."

"I can't argue with that."

With the new holster in place, he pulled his Glock and spare magazines from his previous holster and slipped them into place. He squirmed and twisted for half a minute. "It's like it's not even there. You've got to put these on the market."

She made an adjustment to the rig. "Nope, not yet. It's still in beta testing. But I have a provisional patent."

"Impressive."

She landed her hands on her hips. "Yeah, I know. And the holster's cool too, huh?"

"So, is this why Agent White sent me down here? To get a new shoulder rig?"

"No. Don't be silly. He sent you down here to get suited up for your mission."

"What mission?"

She rolled her eyes. "How should I know? I'm a tech-chick, not a cop. I just make cool stuff for you guys, and have I got something special for you . . ."

"I can't wait to see whatever it is."

She helped him off with his new holster and handed him a white button-down shirt. "Put this on."

He followed her instructions and stretched his arms. "It's a little bit tight."

"Yeah, I know. And it looks nice on you."

"It's a little too tight to be comfortable."

"I'm just messing with you again. Yours will fit like a glove, but this is the only prototype I have at the moment."

He chuckled. "I didn't know shirts came in prototypes."

"Shirts don't. But that's not a shirt. It's an S-H-I-R-T."

"I'm lost again."

She slid her hands across the material, pressing it against his body. "Officially, it's known as a surveillance, high-tech, identification, retention, targeting system. Get it?"

"It just feels like a regular shirt to me."

She sat on the edge of her desk and pulled a lipstick tube from her purse. With her compact mirror in hand, she applied more lipstick than Johnny thought she needed. To his surprise—but not his disappointment—she stepped against him and said, "Let's dance."

He offered his left hand, she took it with her right, and then she slid her left hand against the S.H.I.R.T. high on his chest. She hummed what

Johnny thought must've been the "Tennessee Waltz," and they swayed across the floor.

Ten seconds into the exercise, she jumped back and held out her hands. "Okay, that's long enough. Give me the shirt."

Disappointed, he shucked himself from the shirt and held it out for her.

She lifted it by the collar and draped it across a mannequin, then stepped back and presented the shirt like Vanna White. "What do you see?"

Johnny groaned. "Uh . . . a shirt that's too small for me with lipstick near the collar."

"That's not what I see at all. Watch this." Celeste pulled a wand from her desk and waved it across the fabric. The cobalt blue light cast an eerie glow against the fabric as a field of perfectly formed fingerprints appeared everywhere she had touched the cloth.

Johnny stared in disbelief. "Fingerprints from fabric without dusting? Are you serious?"

"Oh, just wait. Check this out."

She turned and stroked a few keys on her computer, and the screen came to life with an array of captured fingerprints. "My magic wand not only highlights the prints on the shirt, but it also grabs them and initiates an Integrated Automated Fingerprint Identification System search."

Beseeching the system to search faster, she rolled her fingers in waves in front of the screen. Seconds later, Celeste's picture appeared on the left side of the screen with a copy of her driver's license on the right.

Johnny Mac checked his watch. "That was crazy fast."

Celeste shrugged. "I cheated just a little. My prints are stored locally, so that sped up the search. But the concept is the same. Have you ever tried to lift prints from fabric?"

He shook his head. "I've never lifted prints except in the Academy, so I can't say I have much experience."

"Take it from me. Prints from fabric are a nightmare, but that's only one of the things this shirt can do."

She pulled a cable from beneath her computer and clipped its connector to the tail of the shirt, then she stuck a test tube in Johnny's hand. "I know this is going to sound weird, but I need you to fill that up with spit."

He took the tube and laughed. "Based on the morning I'm having, spitting in a test tube is the most normal thing I've done so far."

When he'd completed his assignment, Celeste inserted a probe into the tube and deposited it into a holder beside the keyboard. "Now, this is the part that's far out. It'll blow your mind."

A progress bar appeared on the computer screen and slowly rose to one hundred percent. Celeste entered a line of commands and struck the enter key with a flourish. "Bam! Check that out!"

Johnny leaned down and studied the indecipherable gibberish on the screen. "What am I supposed to see?"

"Okay, so it's not so impressive in its current form, but that's a boatload of DNA data collected from the saliva trapped in the lipstick stain."

She yanked a tissue from a box and wiped her mouth as if trying to remove a layer of skin. "Sorry, I forgot to take the lipstick off. I don't like makeup. I think we should all be proud of what we are."

Johnny furrowed his brow into rows of disbelief. "Are you serious?"

"Yeah, I'm serious. I don't wear makeup very often."

"No, no, not that. Are you telling me that shirt collects and analyzes DNA?"

"Well, not exactly. What it does is collect samples through microsensors woven into the fabric and creates a file to export to the computer. The computer does the actual analysis, which, admittedly, isn't great quality yet. But I'm working on it. When we do actual DNA sampling and analysis —like with your saliva—it's much more accurate and admissible in court. This, not so much, but we're getting there."

Johnny took a seat on a rolling stool. "This is fascinating. The guy who invented this must be a genius."

Celeste smiled and waved. "Hello . . . I'm that *guy*."

"No! You designed all of this?"

She brushed an imaginary spot from each shoulder. "Yep, but this is just one of my projects. I've got so many more I can't wait to show you."

Johnny felt his mouth go dry and his skin flush. "So, earlier, when we were . . . you know, flirting. Was that just . . . ?"

Celeste placed a hand on each of Johnny's knees and leaned in close. "Was that just what, Special Agent McIntyre? Are you trying to ask me out?"

He laid his hands on top of hers. "Yes, genius Celeste. That's exactly what I'm trying to do."

"In that case, I'm trying to say yes. When will you be back from your assignment?"

"I have no idea. I don't even know when I'm leaving."

She reached for his jacket and pulled his cell phone from the interior pocket. "Unlock your phone for me, please."

He typed in the code and slid the phone back into her hand. She giggled, typed for a few seconds, and stuck the phone back in his jacket. "Now we have each other's digits, and I know something you don't."

"I'm quite certain you know a *lot* of things I don't know, but what are you talking about?"

"I just happen to know you aren't leaving on your assignment before I get your new shirts and jackets made. I can have that knocked out in like two days, but if I drag my feet a little, I'm free Friday night, and date night won't have to wait until you get back."

"I never suspected you to be a foot-dragger, but Friday night sounds great."

She pointed at her mouth. "Is the lipstick gone?"

"Yes, it's gone."

Celeste leaned down, kissed his cheek, and whispered, "With any luck, maybe I can make biscuits and gravy for you on Saturday morning."

3

CHEREZ PUSTYNYU
(THROUGH THE DESERT)

Bonaire, Leeward Netherland Antilles, Southern Caribbean

The landing gear of the American Airlines 737 chirped and produced tiny puffs of white smoke as the tires kissed the runway of Flamingo International Airport near Kralendijk. Special Agent Gwynn Davis gathered her things from her first-class seat and pulled her rolling carry-on from the overhead bin. The short stroll up the gangway deposited her into the waiting arms of the woman she considered not only her mentor, but also her closest friend.

"Anya!" Gwynn squealed as she let go of her bag.

The blonde, chiseled-featured Russian beamed, but not with the practiced smile designed to allure and mesmerize targets in every corner of the world. Her smile that day was as genuine as any expression she'd ever worn. The embrace, like the smile, was pure and heartfelt in both directions.

"It is so good to see you, my dear Gwynn. You are ravishing as always. I have missed you so badly."

Gwynn tightened her embrace. "I've missed you so much. I don't like it when you go away like that."

Anya lifted the handle on Gwynn's rolling bag and motioned toward the exit. "Come. We have so much to do and even more to talk about."

The tropical sun beat down on the acres of asphalt and hundreds of parked cars outside the terminal as the pair crossed the walkway and approached the jeep that bore signage boasting Island Adventures.

"What's this?" Gwynn pointed out the ridiculous paint job. "Are you some kind of tour guide now?"

Anya slid her hand across the lettering. "You like?"

"Not exactly. What's it all about?"

"Is my company. My other job for American Department of Justice does not pay very well."

"What? You started a tourist company?"

"I did not start company. I purchased it. It is so much fun. You will see."

Gwynn climbed inside the jeep. "I have to admit, I never dreamed of you owning a company like this. How long have you been in Bonaire?"

Anya pulled from the airport parking lot as if qualifying for the Indy 500. "I have been here long enough to purchase business, learn everything about business, and send for you ticket to come play with me."

Gwynn reached across the front seat and took Anya's hand. "You know, I've really missed you."

Anya pulled down the visor against the afternoon sun and squeezed Gwynn's hand. "Did you miss me for being friend or for being police partner?"

Gwynn lowered her chin. "Both. But here's the truth that you can never tell Agent White. I'd rather be your friend than your partner. Having girlfriends isn't easy in my . . . our . . . line of work."

Without taking her eyes from the road, Anya said, "Day will come when we can be only friends and not police, and I have something you can never tell to Agent White. You can keep secret, yes?"

"Come on, Anya. You know me better than that. I'll always keep your secrets."

"Okay, so I will tell to you secret. When I am away, I miss working on missions for American Department of Justice. We are very good team, and we are doing important things. I like how this feels."

Gwynn held an arm out the window and let her hand fly against the air. "Yeah, I know what you mean. I miss it, too. Especially with you. I mean,

Johnny Mac is okay and all, but when I think about my partner, I always think about you instead of him."

Anya tapped the steering wheel and pointed toward a pool of water in the sand. "Look! Flamingos! This island is famous for them. I think they are strange, but also beautiful . . . just like you."

Gwynn chuckled. "Hey, I'm not strange. But thank you for the compliment."

"Is not compliment. Is only truth. You are beautiful woman, and you know this."

Gwynn rolled her eyes. "Next to you, no one feels beautiful. You're like, perfect, and I hate you for it. It's not fair."

Anya slammed the brake pedal, and the jeep slid to a stop on the sandy, shell-covered shoulder of the road."

Gwynn jerked her hand from Anya's. "What's wrong?"

The Russian locked eyes with the American agent. "You said you hate me. This cannot be true."

"I was only kidding, Anya. It's a figure of speech. It's like I hate you for being so beautiful. It means I'm jealous. That's all. I could never hate you."

Anya burst into uncontrollable laughter. "I know this, dear Gwynn. I am only messing with you. I stopped to put down top of jeep. Is fun to have hair blowing in wind, no?"

Gwynn pulled the ponytail holder from her head and shook out her hair. "Yeah, that's definitely fun."

With the top down and hair blowing wildly on the salty Caribbean air, the pair continued eastward until Anya pulled into the crushed shell parking lot of Island Adventures. Rows of nearly identical jeeps waited as if lined up for a race. Beyond the jeeps, two dozen four-wheelers and ATVs rested in similar formation, and a bright yellow helicopter sat on a wooden platform near the thatched-roof cabana serving as offices.

Gwynn studied the collection. "Is all this really yours?"

"Yes, is all mine. We will go for ATV ride inside desert now."

"Desert? This is a tropical island. There's no desert here."

They climbed from the jeep, and Anya led the way to a side-by-side ATV parked beneath an awning at the back of the building. "Get inside. I will show to you desert."

Gwynn slid onto the seat, buckled up, and closed the hard plastic door. Before she could ask any questions, Anya had the ATV accelerating across the parking lot and down a well-worn path.

Gwynn grabbed the handholds and drove her feet against the floor. "This is crazy. How fast are we going?"

Anya laughed. "Is not fast yet. One fifty kilometers per hour, but I promise to give to you ride of lifetime inside desert."

"Again with the desert?"

"You will see."

The engine roared, and all four tires left the rocky path as they crested a sharp hill. Gwynn squealed, and Anya gripped the wheel. After seconds of soaring through the air, the tires finally kissed the earth again, and Gwynn gasped in disbelief.

"It *is* a desert! How did I not know about this?"

Anya handled the ATV like a seasoned professional, making the vehicle slide around corners and leaving a roiling cloud of dust in their wake. She brought the machine to a stop on top of a small rise overlooking the Caribbean Sea. "Isn't it beautiful?"

Gwynn sighed and let the wind blow across her skin. "It really is. Who knew the tropics could look like this?"

Anya pulled two bottles of water from a cooler and passed one to Gwynn. "It is desert on eastern side of island because of wind and salt. Nothing can grow with so much salt water being blown ashore. Wind is always blowing hard from across Atlantic Ocean. Is no good for houses or condos, but perfect for riding machines like this."

"It's so oddly beautiful, and I love it. Let's never go back to the real world."

"This is real world, but I know what you mean. I know Agent White only agreed to let you come here if you promised to bring me back to United States with you. He gave to you two weeks, yes?"

Gwynn frowned. "Only ten days, actually. But what fun we can have in ten days, right?"

"I will make telephone call to him, and we will stay for two weeks."

"I don't think that's such a good idea, Anya. He said if I didn't have you back in DC in ten days, that I should just never come back at all."

"Ah! This is much better plan. We will never go back."

"I wish." Gwynn pointed toward the sea. "Is that a lighthouse?"

"Yes. Do you wish to see it?"

"I love lighthouses," Gwynn said. "Can we climb it?"

Anya answered with a turn of the key and pressure on the accelerator. They bounced, flew, and slid their way across the rocky terrain and passed a bevy of four-wheelers going the other direction.

"Are those yours, too?" Gwynn yelled over the roar of the wind and engine.

"No. Mine are much better. They are new and clean and always run perfectly. Those break down often because owner of company does not care. I am different. I always care."

"You're becoming quite the little capitalist, Ms. Moscow."

"Capitalism is beautiful thing," Anya said. "I can make all of money I need by giving to customers more than they expect. This is so much different from where I come from as little girl."

Gwynn gripped the handles. "Freedom is worth fighting for."

Anya brought the ATV to a sliding stop beside the abandoned stone lighthouse, and Gwynn motioned toward what had once been a doorway. "It's all boarded up. That's too bad, but it's a gorgeous old lighthouse."

Anya slid from the machine. "Is only optical illusion." She threw a powerful side kick to the thin boards covering the opening, splintering them into hundreds of tiny shards. "See? Is perfectly open for us."

Gwynn pressed a few of the splintered boards away and slipped inside. "Do you think it's safe to go up?"

Anya nudged her forward. "If we only do things that are safe, we will have very boring life, friend Gwynn."

A hundred and twenty stone steps later, Gwynn leaned against one of the openings through which light had once shone to warn mariners of the rocky eastern coastline of Bonaire.

Anya leaned against the window with her. "I thought you said you wanted to go to top of lighthouse."

"We are at the top. We can't go any higher."

Anya gave her a mischievous smile. "This is only true if you are limited by inside of lighthouse. Follow me."

The Russian sat on the stone windowsill and reached above her head. Her fingertips found the crevice she hoped for, and she pulled herself through the opening like a cat. Gwynn leaned through the opening and stared up in disbelief as Anya scaled the remaining few feet of the lighthouse and slid onto the roof.

Anya yelled, "Come on! It is easy, and you will never forget view from here."

Without hesitating, Gwynn copied her partner's movement and pulled herself through the opening. The shoes she'd worn on the flight weren't as rugged as Anya's hiking boots, so gripping the windblown stone of the structure didn't come easily.

Desperately pawing for purchase with the toe of her shoe, her left hand slipped from the narrow indention, and her heart launched into her throat. A panicked glance toward the rocky ground a hundred feet below turned Gwynn's stomach inside out.

The instant her right hand could no longer support her weight, Anya's hand encircled her wrist and clamped down like a vise. "Is okay, Gwynn. I will never let you fall. Catch your breath, and keep climbing."

"I can't," she breathed. "I want to go back inside."

Anya locked eyes with her. "Listen to me. I will never let anything happen to you. You must trust me and climb."

Anya's reassurance settled Gwynn's nerves and strengthened her resolve. Her fingertips found holds, and she finally pressed the toe of her shoe against a jaggy stone in the aged masonry. Seconds later, she slid herself onto the roof of the lighthouse and dusted off her hands.

"See? I knew you could do it."

"Yeah, I did it, but I would've died without you."

"Without me, friend Gwynn, you would not be here on island and especially not on top of lighthouse. When we are together, we can do anything. Maybe this is not true when we are alone."

Gwynn stared out over the vast Caribbean Sea and relished the wind against her face and in her hair. "It's beautiful up here."

"Yes, it is," Anya said. "This is what friends do. We show each other beautiful things we would never see without the other. You show me kindness and affection, and I show you how to live without being afraid."

4

Ubiytsa Muzhchin (Man Killer)

Washington, DC

Special Agent Johnny Mac McIntyre stepped through the door to Supervisory Special Agent Ray White's office to find his boss red-faced and gripping his telephone receiver as if he were trying to crush the plastic implement. White thrust a finger through the air toward a pair of unoccupied wingbacks, and Johnny Mac eased himself into the closer of the chairs.

"I'm going to make this as clear as possible. Davis will be back in my office in exactly ten days, and not a second later, or she'll be unemployed and brought up on federal charges."

Johnny Mac squirmed in his chair as the verbal onslaught continued.

"She's under orders to have you shackled to her ankle, if necessary, but if you decide not to join us, your little sidekick will suffer the same fate as not showing up at all. It's up to you."

The echoing clang of White slamming the handset back onto its cradle hadn't stopped when Johnny Mac asked, "What was that all about?"

White rubbed his forehead. "The Russian is trying to handle me."

"Yeah, she does that."

"Not this time," White said. "I'm not bluffing. I'll fire Davis and throw Anya in the gulag."

Johnny Mac cocked his head. "I don't think we have gulags, boss."

"Then you'll build one."

"Whatever you say. You're in charge."

White leaned back. "It certainly doesn't feel that way."

He inspected the junior agent. "Your shirt is buttoned wrong, Agent McIntyre. Get yourself squared away. What could've possibly happened down in tech services to leave your shirt buttoned incorrectly?"

Johnny Mac flushed red and fumbled with his buttons.

White drummed his fingertips against his desk. "I'm waiting."

"Waiting for what, boss?"

"I'm waiting for an answer to my question. What happened that screwed up your shirt?"

Johnny Mac chewed on his lip. "Have you met Celeste downstairs?"

"Why would I have met some random tech from the basement?"

Johnny continued squirming. "She seemed to know I was coming, and it felt like she knew a lot more about my mission than me."

White growled. "I don't have any way to know what some tech knows, but if you're finished quizzing me about what I don't know, we can get down to work on grown-up stuff."

"I didn't mean to . . . I'm sorry."

"Don't be sorry, Johnny. Be better. Now, get out your little notepad and crayons so we can brief the mission."

He slipped his pad and pen from an inside jacket pocket and caught a faint whiff of Celeste's homemade perfume.

White snapped his fingers several times. "Hey! Where'd you go?"

"Sorry. I was just thinking about something Celeste said."

White tried not to smile. "Did she show you the fingerprint shirt?"

"It's pretty amazing."

"Yes, it is," White said. "And here's how you're going to put it to work. There's a guy named Volodya Kalashnikov who owns a club in Vegas called Gedo."

Johnny looked up from his notebook. "Kalashnikov? Like the rifle?"

"Exactly. They say he's a great nephew of Mikhail, himself."

"Nice pedigree."

"Anyway, he's running a scheme out there with bottle girls. Are you familiar with the term *bottle girls*?"

Johnny shook his head, so White continued. "It's the second oldest gig in the books. Our boy, Kalashnikov, brought in a truckload of Russian girls who look a lot like our Anya. These Anya look-alikes cling onto some unsuspecting salesman from Dubuque and convince the poor sap, who just slipped off his wedding ring, to buy her a drink at Gedo, Kalashnikov's bar. In case you didn't pick up on it yet, Gedo is short for gedonizm. Care to take any guesses what that translates to in the language of freedom?"

Johnny stared at the ceiling for a moment. "It sounds a lot like hedonism from here."

"Either you've been brushing up on your Russian, or you're not as dense as Davis thinks you are."

"Maybe both."

White pulled open a drawer and tossed a small shining object across the desk.

Johnny caught the gold wedding ring and slid it onto his finger. "I guess this means I'm now from Dubuque."

White held up a finger. "Almost. Think a little farther northeast."

"Milwaukee?"

"Keep going."

"Just tell me, boss."

By way of answer, White opened his drawer again, pulled out a well-worn wallet, and tossed it to Johnny Mac.

The younger agent caught the billfold and unfolded the smooth leather. After examining the contents, he glanced up at his superior. "Toronto?"

"That's right. Because according to Eighteen U.S. Code Five Fourteen —Fictitious obligations—international forgery is a federal felony, and we're a federal law enforcement agency."

"But what if somebody tries to speak with me in French since I'm supposed to be a Canadian? I can pull off a pretty good Pepé Le Pew impersonation, but that's the limit of my French."

White dropped his chin and slowly shook his head. "Oh, Johnny boy . . . How little you know about the world around you. Over eighty-five percent of the citizens of Toronto speak only English. Besides, the girls at the Gedo Club couldn't care less about what language you speak as long as you have a stack of high-limit credit cards. And as you noticed, Mr. McIntyre, you're in possession of an Amex Centurion Black Card. That means the girls are going to love you."

Johnny pulled the card from his new wallet. "I've never even seen one of these, let alone held one. What's the limit?"

"I don't know. We're somewhere around twenty trillion in debt already, so what's another million or two?"

Johnny slid the card back into the wallet. "So, I'm supposed to put myself in front of these bottle girls and let them know I'm a high roller. Then I'm to follow them to Kalashnikov's club for a night of debauchery and top-shelf cocktails. Is that what you have in mind?"

"That pretty well sums it up. But you left out one essential element, and I'm sorry to put you through such torture, but we need you to let as many girls as possible put their hands all over your fancy new shirt."

Johnny groaned. "And most of these women look like Anya, right?"

"I'm afraid so."

He sighed. "That's a lot to ask, but I'll make the sacrifice in the name of preservation of law and order."

White chuckled. "You're such a sacrificial little lamb. Your country thanks you for your selfless service."

"Seriously, though, this all sounds a lot like entrapment to me."

"Look at you putting your quarter-million-dollar education to work. Your mommy would be so proud. This is the textbook definition of entrapment. However, we're not going to prosecute anyone based on the intel you and your shirt gather. We're merely using your work to identify a few potential targets for our own Russian bottle girl to exploit."

Johnny pocketed his new wallet. "When do I leave?"

White checked his watch. "That depends on how quickly your little girlfriend down in the basement finishes your shirts and sport coats, but I have a feeling she won't have them finished before your date on Friday night."

Johnny stood with his mouth agape. "How did you know?"

White lifted his nameplate and pointed to it. "See that? It says S-S-A. That means supervisory special agent. That means I know everything that happens in my division, and you're part of my division."

Johnny shot a thumb for the door. "I think I've got some paperwork—or something—to do."

"Close the door behind you, and brush up on your blackjack and no-limit Texas Hold'em skills."

* * *

Friday afternoon finally arrived, and Special Agent McIntyre lifted the handset from its cradle and dialed the first three digits of the four-digit tech services extension. But before he pressed the final number, he replaced the handset and pulled on his jacket. The elevator deposited him on the sec-ond-basement level, but his identification lacked the authority to permit him any farther without an escort. He hesitantly touched the call button and waited, squirming on the balls of his feet.

The buzzer sounded, followed by a pair of thuds that would've been more appropriate inside the walls of a maximum security prison than thirty feet below Pennsylvania Avenue.

The flowing raven hair made its appearance only slightly before Celeste's brilliant smile. "Oh, Agent McIntyre. Welcome back to the underbelly of the DOJ."

Johnny stepped through the door, and his favorite techy secured it behind him. She laced an arm through his and led him down a short corridor toward her lair.

He recoiled as she cozied up to his side. "I don't think this is okay at work. They frown on fraternization."

She giggled and squeezed his arm. "Relax. I'm the only one here. And besides, you and I could have a naked tea party in the main lobby, and they wouldn't fire either of us."

"What are you talking about?"

"Oh, come on. You know what's up. You're working one of the hottest cases in DOJ history, and you're Agent White's golden boy. That makes you bulletproof, and I'm . . . well, I'm me."

"You're you?"

She stood on tiptoes and planted an innocent kiss on his cheek. "Yeah, I'm me. I've got a PhD in electronic engineering, over four hundred patents under my belt, and I'm the granddaughter of Wilma Mankiller, the first and only female chief of the Cherokee Indians tribe. With a résumé like mine and a measly GS-Twelve salary, I have no fear of being tossed out with yesterday's garbage."

"I guess that explains the gorgeous black hair and perfect complexion."

She raised her eyebrows. "Did you just call me gorgeous?"

"No. I mean . . ."

"Tread lightly," she said. "I am a Mankiller, you know."

"Well, yes, you are definitely gorgeous, but I want to know more about how your grandmother got the name Mankiller."

She pushed through the second set of doors into her laboratory. "It's not as cool as it sounds. It's impossible to pronounce in the original Tsalagi

Gawonihisdi language, but it's just a military rank similar to captain. It's still a little intimidating, though, don't you think?"

"I'll be honest. I'm more intimidated by the PhD."

"What do you mean? You've got a J.D. That qualifies as a doctorate, too."

"Thanks for the confidence boost," he said. "How are the shirts coming along?"

She scanned the room for prying ears and whispered, "Don't tell Agent White, but I had them finished three days ago. I just didn't want to miss date night. So, they'll *officially* be ready on Monday morning. When are you leaving for Vegas?"

Johnny huffed. "Everybody knows more about my assignment than me."

She laid her head against his shoulder. "Aww, poor baby. You've got a hot date with a Native American princess, then you're headed to Vegas with the taxpayers' credit card in your pocket. It must really suck to be you."

"When you put it like that, I guess it doesn't sound so bad."

She took a bow. "You're welcome. Now, did you come down here just to sexually harass me, or is this official business?"

He threw up both hands. "Hey! You're the one who grabbed my arm and kissed me, Dr. Celeste. So, don't accuse me of sexual harassment."

She gave him a hip bump. "Just for the record, Golden Boy, as far as I'm concerned, sexual harassment from you won't be reported. But it will be graded."

5

BLEK DZHEK
(BLACKJACK)

Washington, DC

Ray White stared across his desk. "How was your date, Lover Boy?"

Johnny Mac blushed. "Can we talk about something else?"

"Nope."

"The date was good, boss."

White chewed on his pen. "Good enough for a second date?"

"Yes, sir."

"You do know the DOJ policy on fraternization." White's admonition didn't sound like a question.

Johnny cleared his throat. "I do, but Celeste and I—"

"Oh, so it's Celeste and not Dr. Mankiller."

"Well, I mean . . . I meant Dr. Mankiller, and I don't work in the same division, so relationships aren't technically forbidden."

White choked back the grin. "Oh, so now it's a relationship."

"Let's put it this way . . . She makes great biscuits."

The grin could no longer be suppressed. "I'll bet she does, Johnny Mac. I'll bet she does. Now, get your mind off Little White Dove and your butt on the airplane."

"Please tell me I'm booked in business class, at least. If I'm going to pretend to be a high roller, I can't show up in coach."

White tossed a sealed envelope, and Johnny had it open almost before it stopped moving. He thumbed through the paperwork inside and peered over the page at his boss. "Seriously?"

White pointed toward the door. "Yes, you're seriously on a private jet out of Andrews in two hours. Now, get down to tech services, pick up your new wardrobe, and kiss your 'relationship' temporarily goodbye. You can tell her you'll be home in time for breakfast next Sunday if you don't fall in love with some *russkaya matreshka*."

Johnny rose, headed for the door, and gave White a look across his shoulder. "Russian dolls make terrible gravy. I'll see you next week."

Downstairs, Johnny Mac didn't have to wait to be let into the tech services cave. Dr. Celeste met him at the door with an oversized piece of rolling luggage and two enormous garment bags. She fumbled with the bags, and Johnny caught the load before it hit the floor.

"It's about time," Celeste said. "I was afraid you were going to make us late."

Johnny repositioned the bags across his shoulder. "Us? What do you mean, us?"

Celeste nodded toward another heavy rolling case behind her. "Unless you plan to learn to use all this equipment on the flight to Vegas, I'm coming with."

"With me? To Vegas?"

She leaned to her tiptoes and gave him a less-than-innocent kiss. "Yes, with you, to Vegas. You didn't think I was going to let you go out there all alone with those Russian girls falling over you, did you?"

"This day just keeps getting better."

* * *

The Federal Government Hawker jet touched down at Las Vegas McCarran International Airport, and a Bellagio stretch limousine pulled to the bottom of the airstairs. Behind the limo sat a blacked-out Chevrolet Suburban.

Celeste peered out the window and pointed toward the limo. "I guess that one's for you, and I get the Suburban."

Johnny twisted from his seat and eyed the two vehicles. "Why aren't we riding together?"

"Come on, G-Man. You know we can't be seen together. You're a high roller from Toronto, and you're supposed to be all by yourself. We have to keep up appearances."

"You're at least staying at the Bellagio, right?"

She gave him a shove. "Stop worrying about me, and go play your part, Special Agent."

Johnny descended the airstairs and slid onto the back seat of the waiting luxury car. His baggage was loaded into the trunk, and soon, the driver had them heading north on the Strip. The drive to the Bellagio only took fifteen minutes, and they arrived just in time to see the world-famous fountains putting on their timeless show.

The driver opened the door, and Johnny stepped from the back seat of the gleaming limo as if he'd been stepping from limos all his life. He shot his cuffs and gave a dismissive glance at the magnificent performing fountains. "Where's my hostess?"

A young lady who should've been gracing the cover of *Vogue* magazine, and wearing a skintight blouse with one too many buttons unfastened and a pencil skirt, stepped beside him and offered her hand. "Good morning, Mr. McIntyre. I'm Carolyn LeBlanc, and I'll be your hostess for your stay."

Johnny ignored the offered hand. "Did my deposit arrive?"

Carolyn smiled. "Yes, sir. One hundred thousand dollars was wired into your casino account overnight. Simply tell your dealer how much you'd like in each draw. If you'd like, I'll show you to your suite."

"That would be nice. I'd like to freshen up. Has my valet arrived?"

Carolyn sent a barely perceptible glance toward a colleague near the bank of massive glass doors, and the man shook his head. "No, sir. She's not arrived, but we're expecting her any minute. Her suite connects to yours, just as you requested."

Johnny let himself be led to a high floor and into a luxurious suite, where Carolyn pressed a button beside the bed and the curtains slid away, revealing a million-dollar view of the most famous fountains on Earth.

"This will do nicely. Thank you. My valet will unpack for me, so there's no need to send anyone up. You'll see that Celeste is installed next door when she arrives?"

"Of course, Mr. McIntyre. And if there's anything you want—anything at all—I'm only a phone call away. Here's my card."

Carolyn slipped the card into his hand the same instant Johnny slipped a folded bill into hers.

They both said, "Thank you."

With the acting behind him, Johnny stood in awe at the massive floor-to-ceiling window, unable to keep his eyes off the fountain he'd tried so hard to dismiss upon his arrival.

A knock came from somewhere, but not the front door of the suite. Johnny listened closely as he explored the vast room. When the knock came again, he unbolted a door and swung it inward to find Celeste waiting on the other side.

She curtsied. "Good morning, sir. I'll be your valet for the duration of your stay. Unless, of course, you'd prefer someone else."

He reached for her hand, and she gave it to him so he could pull her close and plant a long-awaited kiss while there were no prying eyes.

She cooed. "Mmm, that was nice."

"Come with me. You have to see this view."

She chuckled. "We have adjoining rooms, silly. Our views are the same."

As they approached the acres of vertical glass, she gasped. "Okay, maybe not exactly the same. I've got like two windows, but this is serious."

She stepped ahead, still grasping his hand, and led him to the veranda, where the midday breeze blew through their hair as they surveyed Sin City from high above. "Have you been here before?"

He said, "I've been here a few times, but I've never stayed in the Bellagio. How about you?"

"This is my first time. It's too bad it's work and not a pleasure trip."

Johnny kissed her again. "Surely we can throw in a little pleasure over the next few days."

"*You* can, but I have to be invisible."

"There's a lot of pleasure to be had while still remaining invisible. Especially with adjoining suites."

She giggled. "Yeah, but you need to be seen spending tons of money and laughing it up. Unfortunately, I can't be part of that."

Johnny stared out over the city and watched the sun glistening off Celeste's raven hair. "I need to ask you something."

She looked up at him with fear in her dark eyes. "You're not about to get down on one knee, are you?"

"Not yet. But the day is still young."

She gave him a playful slap. "Stop it. What do you want to ask?"

"Agent White knew about our date before it happened. Did you tell him?"

"No, I didn't tell anyone. I spend most of my time alone. Who am I going to tell?"

"I wasn't accusing you or anything. I'm just curious how he found out."

She cocked her head. "Beats me. But he is one of the old guard. There's not a lot that happens in the building that the old guys don't know about. I think they develop some kind of ESP after they've been there twenty-five years. It's weird. My boss isn't an agent, but I think he helped George Washington cross the Delaware. I mean, he's ancient, and he knows everything."

"Are you gunning for his job when he retires?"

She put on a smile. "I've got my sights set on an OTS gig."

Johnny leaned against the rail. "Oh, really? CIA, huh?"

She nodded. "Yep, tech services for Justice is cool and all, but I'm really into spy gear. CIA and Justice are two different worlds. I'm keeping my fingers crossed, so if you know anybody out at Langley, I'd appreciate it if you put a bug in their ear about Dr. Mankiller at Justice."

"I don't know anybody at the Agency, but I do know someone you'd like to meet. She's a former Russian assassin and sparrow. She sort of stole my partner."

Celeste's eyes widened. "Are you talking about Anya, the Russian chick on the Avenging Angel operation?"

"Yeah, that's her. She and my partner, Agent Gwynn Davis, are all buddy-buddy now. They get to run the ops while I live in dumpsters and guard their six."

"This suite doesn't exactly look like a dumpster to me."

"This mission is an exception, but we ran three previous ops together, and I didn't have to worry about getting a sunburn from the spotlight. It never shined on me."

"Tell me about it," she said. "I spend my life in a dark basement where not even the sun gets in, let alone a spotlight. It looks like we're birds of a feather."

"I guess so. Anyway, back to Anya. Being a former SVR officer, I'm sure she's got plenty of stories about Russian spy gear."

"Do you think she'd really talk to me?"

"Yes, of course. She's scary when a fight breaks out, but she's pretty cool when she's off the clock."

She hooked a finger behind his belt and pulled him against her. "If you can get me an hour alone with the Russian, I promise to make you very glad you did."

"You may have to share your time with Davis. Those two are inseparable most of the time."

"Davis . . . Isn't she the one who looks like Jennifer Lopez without the hips?"

Johnny chuckled. "I've never really looked at her like that, but now that you mention it, I guess she does."

Celeste said, "Now it's my turn to ask a question. Since you're spending so much time with this Russian sparrow and J-Lo, what are you doing slumming it with a basement dweller like me?"

He didn't hesitate. "I've got a promising career ahead of me. They're already dangling SSA like a carrot, and I'm not going to screw that up by crawling in bed with my partner or a Russian cooperating participant. Besides, neither of them would give me a second glance."

Celeste ran her fingers through Johnny Mac's hair. "If that's true, they're the ones missing out. You have to tell me, though. Is the Russian really as hot as they say?"

Johnny twisted his shoe against the balcony. "I mean, she's all right, but she can't hold a candle to Dr. Mankiller."

She rewarded him with another kiss and checked her watch. "I think it's about time for your big debut. Let's get you suited up and ready to play."

* * *

Inside the private high rollers room, Carolyn stood beside a cart with four bottles of bourbon. "Which would you prefer first?"

Johnny ran his finger across each of the bottles, exposing his gold Rolex from beneath the sleeve of his jacket. "I think I'd like to give the Woodford Reserve Baccarat a try, but don't go far with the Pappy Twenty-three. In fact, have a bottle of it taken to my suite, please."

Carolyn smiled. "Of course, sir. And what's your pleasure at the tables today?"

He scanned the room. "Let's start with no-limit blackjack."

She led him to a felt-lined blackjack table and pulled out his chair. "David will be your first dealer, and he has your chips. Enjoy yourself. And I assume you'd like your bourbon neat."

Beneath the cool undercover exterior, Johnny Mac McIntyre could barely contain himself as he examined the absurdity of his situation. One hundred thousand dollars waited only steps away in the form of plastic chips on a felt table. In mere minutes, he'd be holding a tumbler of the most expensive bourbon he'd ever seen. But perhaps more unbelievable than all of this was the beautiful, dark-haired goddess waiting for him upstairs and listening to everything he said through the microphone woven into the lapel of his bespoke jacket.

His Waterford crystal tumbler arrived containing three fingers of golden, honey-colored whiskey that had spent two dozen years confined inside the darkness of a charred white oak barrel in the hills of Kentucky. The first inhalation filled his nostrils with an aroma the special agent had never experienced, but the first taste changed his life forever.

Will I ever be able to drink fifty-dollar Jim Beam again?

The dealer shuffled, allowed Johnny to cut the deck, and burned the first card. With a one-thousand-dollar chip in the betting circle only a few inches from his fingertips, Johnny waited for the cards of the highest stakes blackjack hand of his life. The deal came, and two jacks landed in front of him with a seven showing in front of the dealer.

Forcing himself to pretend as if he'd played thousand-dollar hands for years, Johnny fought the urge to celebrate the winning hand he believed he held. With a wave of his hand, he signaled the dealer he didn't want any more cards. David flipped over his hole card, a nine, giving himself sixteen and forcing the dealer to take another card. He slid the next card from the top of the deck and flipped it over, revealing a five and giving the dealer twenty-one to Johnny's twenty. David raked the cards and Johnny's thousand-dollar chip from the circle.

The game continued for half an hour, and Vegas's newest high roller was seventeen thousand dollars richer. His second glass arrived, but this time, the slightly darker Pappy Van Winkle graced the elegant glass and drew Johnny further from his old trusty Jim Beam.

As the dealer shuffled, a well-poised, leggy blonde slid onto the leather seat beside Johnny. "Would you like some company? I'm Amber."

Johnny ruffled a stack of chips through his fingers and cast an eye toward the woman. "Are you playing, Amber?"

She ran a hand down his arm and leaned in. "No, I just like to watch handsome men play, and right now, you're the most appealing man in the room."

"So, tell me, Amber—or whatever your name is—is it me or the stack of chips in front of me that you find so attractive?"

She drew a fingernail lightly across the back of his hand and smiled. "Maybe both. What's your name?"

He pulled his hand from beneath her and slid five thousand dollars into the circle. "Thank you for the flattery, Amber, but I prefer to play alone."

She pulled a compact mirror from her purse, checked her makeup, and stood. "You don't know what you're missing, sweetie."

Johnny won the next five hands, including a blackjack and two double-downs, and increased his stack by forty thousand dollars. He tossed a thousand-dollar chip to David.

The dealer tapped the chip on the rail and dropped it into the tip jar. "Thank you, sir. I'm sorry about the lady. If you're not into blondes, there are plenty of brunettes about."

Johnny self-consciously glanced down at his jacket and imagined Celeste hearing every word he said in perfect clarity. "Blondes aren't my preference. In fact, I've recently developed an appreciation for raven hair. That's not why I sent her away, though. Ambers are a dime a dozen.

They're in every city on Earth, but I have a taste for a little Eastern European flavor on this trip."

David finished his shuffle and paused. "Oh, so you like Russian girls?"

Johnny shrugged. "Russian, Ukrainian, Czech . . . you know. It's the accent. It gets me every time."

The dealer slid the deck across the felt for another cut and gave Johnny a knowing wink. "I think I know some girls who are exactly what you're looking for. Their English isn't great, but they have a way of making you understand exactly what they mean without saying a word."

Johnny tossed another chip across the table to the dealer. "Now you're talking."

6

MECHI I KINZHALY
(SWORDS AND DAGGERS)

Washington, DC

Supervisory Special Agent Ray White sat staring out his fourth-floor window and across the street at the nondescript J. Edgar Hoover FBI Building and pondering how his life might've been different on that side of Pennsylvania Avenue.

I would've never found myself at the end of my career and trying to control a rogue Russian assassin and a pair of mouthy junior agents.

Just as the bottom of the fourth cup of coffee appeared and the daydreaming ceased, his intercom buzzed. "Agent White, Agent Davis and your troublesome angel are here."

White slid the coffee cup onto the corner of his desk and pressed the button. "Send them in, and pray for me."

Anya was first through the door, and White expected nothing less. "Well, the two of you look like you've had a couple weeks of fun in the sun."

Davis tapped her watch. "No, sir. We only had ten days, just like you ordered."

White leaned back and studied the women. "It makes me nervous when you two follow orders, but we don't have time to deal with that right now. I need to know how long it's been since you spoke Russian with other native Russian speakers."

Gwynn turned to Anya. "I'm pretty sure he's talking to you."

Anya lowered an eyebrow. "Why do you need to know this?"

"Just answer the question," White demanded.

Anya sent her eyes to the ceiling and hesitated before saying, "Maybe three months. Maybe some days, less."

White leaned forward and cocked his head. "Who were you talking to?"

Anya scowled. "This is none of your business."

"*You* are my business. Therefore, anybody *you* talk to is my business by extension."

The Russian planted herself into one of the two wingbacks and looked up at Gwynn. "You should sit. This will probably take long time."

Gwynn glanced between her boss and her partner before gently nestling into the second chair.

White drummed four fingers on his desk. "I'm waiting."

"And you will continue to wait. No one I speak with when I am away from this place is connected to anything I am doing here. No one knows what I am doing with exception of people you have told. I do not allow beans for spilling from inside mouth."

White squeezed his eyes closed and shook his head. "I'm going to pretend you meant *spill the beans*, but you're partially right as long as you weren't disclosing classified information to a Russian national."

"I did not do this. I spoke only with person who is important to me, and person does not live inside Russia."

Gwynn's look bore more curiosity than White's, but she kept silent as her boss continued.

"The reason I asked about you speaking Russian with other native Russian speakers is because of the next assignment I have for you."

The mention of a mission refocused Gwynn's attention, sending her leaning forward.

White held up a hand. "Relax, Davis. This one isn't for you."

"What do you mean, it's not for me? We're partners. I always work the missions with Anya."

Anya peered between White and Davis. "Yes, this is true. Gwynn is my partner."

White shrugged. "Fine, but you have to teach her to speak the language like she's fresh out of Leningrad, and make sure she knows every custom and cultural nuance of a thirty-year-old Russian woman."

Anya chewed on her lip.

White said, "Oh, yeah. I almost forgot. You've got to do all that by Wednesday of next week. So, you two get out of here and get to work turning her into a Muscovite. If you fail, Davis is fired and you're going to prison."

Anya groaned. "This is not possible. You are being unreasonable."

White sent a fist hammering against the surface of his desk. "No, I'm not being unreasonable. You're making demands you don't have the standing to make. You work for me. It's that simple. You execute the missions I assign or deal with the consequences. We are not going to start this game again! You are not going to make demands, and you are not going to dictate how I run this division. Is that clear?"

Gwynn swallowed hard. "Yes, sir."

"I wasn't talking to you, Davis. In fact, get out. Go powder your nose or whatever you do. Anya and I need to continue this conversation alone."

Gwynn placed a hand on the arm of the chair to push herself to her feet, but Anya laid a hand over hers. "No, you will stay, Gwynn."

Her tone was soft but deliberate, but Gwynn continued to her feet and pulled her hand from beneath her partner's. "I'm sorry, Anya. I can't disobey orders like you can. I have a career to think about. I'm sorry."

White pulled at the knot in his tie and unbuttoned his collar.

Anya watched every move he made and every expression he wore. She spoke barely above a whisper. "Men and women with real power do not yell. Have you ever heard me raise my voice in anger?"

Gwynn was frozen in place, terrified at the thought of what Anya would say next. To her surprise, when the Russian spoke again, her words were soft but confident.

"I am deadliest person in this city. I was trained by some of most sadistic killers world has ever known. I was taught to fight and kill until life inside me is gone. I can do things with knife that will take from you ability to fall asleep at night. I can seduce any person I choose and then kill them using only my hands. I could kill everyone inside building and walk away on Pennsylvania Avenue in front of White House. No one would catch me, and no one could stop me. You have for me little jobs like catching people making counterfeit diamonds and men making wine from tiger bones, but anyone could do these missions. They are nothing. You are using battleship for bathtub toy. Give to me mission—dangerous mission against dangerous men—and I will do this for you. But this is not only what I do. I teach Gwynn also to be battleship. Take her away from me, and I will still do mission because I said to you I will, but if you do this, you will make Department of Justice weaker. Friend Gwynn will be same as me in time, and you will have no longer need for me."

The resounding silence left the air inside Agent Ray White's office quivering, and he let out the breath that had been boiling in his chest. "Sit down, Davis."

Without a word, she nodded and reclaimed her seat as White continued to temper his rage. "Look, Anya. I know what you're capable of, but we are a nation of laws and rights. I can't dispatch you to run amok with a sword and dagger."

Anya said, "Sometimes swords and daggers are only language people understand."

"Yes, this is true, and when we have a mission against people like that, you'll be the weapon I dispatch. But right now, the fact that you're a Russian raised inside Russia who knows how Russians think, act, speak, and behave is the thing we need most from you."

"Tell me of mission."

White lifted the same file he'd shown Johnny Mac and slid it across his desk. Anya opened the cover, and Gwynn leaned closer to study the file with her partner.

After allowing them several minutes to digest the contents, White said, "Before you say it again, I know this mission is beneath your skill set, but what you see in that folder is not the real objective."

Anya closed the folder and squeezed it between her hands. "Vladimir Kalashnikov is dangerous man."

White studied the Russian's smokey blue eyes and for an instant thought he saw fear behind them. "Tell me."

Anya licked her lips. "What do you want to know?"

"Tell me about Volodya Kalashnikov."

Anya squeezed the file even tighter. "You want me to go to him in Las Vegas and become one of his bottle girls, yes?"

White cleared his throat. "Initially, yes, but ultimately, we're interested in far more than just his club. Tell me what you know about him."

Anya handed the file to Gwynn and rose from her chair, then paced by White's desk and peered through the window.

Gwynn caught her boss's eye and mouthed, "What?"

White pressed a finger to his lips, and Anya pressed her cheek against the cool glass window overlooking the most prestigious avenue in the Nation's capital. She said, "Of course you know his grandfather is Mikhail Kalashnikov."

White narrowed his gaze. "Grandfather?"

"You probably believe Volodya is nephew of Mikhail, but this is not true. He is grandson, but also bastard. Is terrible disgrace to family. This is why Volodya is no longer inside Russia."

White spun his chair to face the window and the Russian. "Keep talking."

Anya pecked on the window with a fingernail. "Is bulletproof glass, no?"

"It's bullet resistant. Nothing is really bulletproof, but I don't know why they wasted the money. As far as I know, we've never had anyone shoot at the building."

"This will likely change when you challenge Volodya Kalashnikov. I was wrong, and I am sorry. This is real mission against dangerous man. Is better if I do this alone."

White shot a look at Gwynn and motioned for her to sit still and be quiet. "Tell me about Kalashnikov, Anya. What do you know about him?"

Instead of delivering her report on the target, she spun on a heel. "Where is Johnny Mac?"

"Why?"

"Is he gathering intelligence in the field?"

White nodded, and Anya lifted the receiver from White's phone. "Make call immediately, and stop him."

"Stop who?" White asked.

"Johnny Mac. You must stop him now. If he is discovered, Kalashnikov will have him killed, and no one will ever find body."

White snatched the receiver from Anya's hand and pounded out a number on the keypad.

Dr. Celeste Mankiller answered on the second ring. "Yes?"

"Where's Johnny Mac?"

"He's sleeping. Why? And who is this?"

"It's White from DC. Get him up, and put him on the phone, now!"

Muffled sounds wafted through the speaker. "Johnny, wake up. Agent White's on the phone, and he's pissed off about something."

Johnny yawned, wiped his eyes, and took the phone. "Good morning, Agent White. What's up?"

"Splash some water on your face, and get your girlfriend out of the room. We have to talk."

"She's not my girlfriend."

"Well, she's answering your phone at five o'clock in the morning and waking you up without leaving the room, so if she's not your girlfriend, I have another word for her."

Johnny slid a hand over the phone. "I'm sorry, Celeste, but I have to talk with the boss, and he doesn't want you to hear it."

Instead of pulling on her robe and leaving the room as Johnny expected, Celeste slipped the phone from his hand and pressed it to her cheek. "Agent White, it's Celeste. I'm fully read-in on the mission. I have a clearance higher than yours, and my equipment is in use on the mission. That covers the clearance and need to know. My signed non-disclosure agreement is on file with the attorney general. I'm putting you on speaker. Special Agent McIntyre and I are ready for the briefing."

7

LATUNNYYE KNOPKI
(BRASS TACKS)

The necktie reached the end of its usefulness, and Ray White yanked it from his neck. It must've landed near the coat tree, but he didn't care. "Why? Why is it the singular purpose of every woman around me to make my life unbearable?"

Celeste, the brilliant technical services officer, said, "Let me guess. Special Agent Davis and the Russian are back."

"Yes, of course, they're back, and one of them is speaking in tongues."

Johnny Mac opened his mouth to speak, but instead made the best decision of his life and remained silent.

White stared down at the phone. "Good move, McIntyre. I thought I detected your desire to speak, and then you obviously exercised the better part of valor."

Johnny remained silent, but Celeste could not. "So, you called us, White. What's the big emergency?"

"That's Supervisory Special Agent White."

Celeste giggled. "Okay, if that's the game you'd like to play, I'm *Doctor* Mankiller."

"Enough of pecking order," Anya demanded. "Is serious telephone call. You are in much danger and must stop what you are doing, immediately. You do not understand what you are doing."

Johnny lost his ability to keep his mouth shut. "What's she talking about, boss? Everything's going great out here. We've got six sets of fingerprints and at least two solid DNA samples. That's not the good part, though. We have seven thousand dollars' worth of bogus charges for liquor and *services*."

White said, "Based on who answered your phone at five a.m., you're not in need of any of those *services* they charged you for."

Anya slammed her hand down on White's desk. "There is no time for this. Volodya Kalashnikov is not just nightclub owner with whores and bottle girls. He is *oruzheynik* and *begun s oruzhiyem.*"

White let his eyes explore the ceiling from where he hoped the translation would fall, but instead, it came from the least likely tongue in the conversation.

Gwynn gasped. "Gunrunner and murder for hire?"

Anya said, "Is *gunrunner* English word for person who sells illegal weapons to anyone who can pay for them?"

"That's pretty much the definition," Gwynn said. "But how did I do on the second half of the translation?"

Anya turned back to the window. "This is true. He is not killer anymore, but for price, he will have one of his *ubiytsy* kill anyone for price."

White sighed. "*Ubiytsy* is assassin for the uninitiated."

Anya said, "If we pursue this man and do not kill him, he will target each of us and probably kill everyone except Gwynn and me."

Johnny Mac was suddenly wide awake. "Why won't he kill you and Davis?"

"He will try," Anya said. "But I will protect friend Gwynn, and I am much better *ubiytsy* than anyone who is working for Kalashnikov."

White clicked his tongue against his teeth. "And you're just going to let him kill the rest of us? We're federal law enforcement officers. We're not exactly easy to kill."

Celeste almost yelled into the phone. "Not me! I'm a scientist, and I'm really easy to kill. I didn't sign up for this."

Anya said, "Agent White, you must bring Johnny Mac and other woman home, immediately. I understand what must be done, and Gwynn and I will do it."

Celeste's trembling voice pierced the air. "Yeah, that! What she said."

White closed his eyes and let himself drift a thousand miles away. When he came back, he said, "Everybody, calm down. It looks like we've made a small oversight in our background work. For now, I want Agent McIntyre and Doctor Mankiller to stand down but remain in place. Can the two of you handle that?"

Johnny Mac said, "Yes, sir."

But Celeste didn't share his confidence. "I don't know if that's such a good idea. If this guy is as dangerous as the Russian says, I don't want to be in the same state with him."

"Relax," White said. "He hasn't seen you. He doesn't even know you exist. He's likely not seen Johnny Mac, either. He's just let our seven grand filter into his bank account. That's all you are to him—a small source of cash. You're not big enough to get his direct attention."

Anya rejoined the conversation. "Agent White is correct. Volodya does not care about seven thousand dollars. You are, for him, only small target until he learns who you are."

Celeste said, "Can you at least get us out of this hotel?"

Anya whispered to White. "Who is this woman, and why does Johnny Mac need doctor?"

White pressed a hand against her hip and pushed her back toward the window. "All right, listen up. Johnny Mac, you're going to the inn on Nellis Air Force Base, and Celeste, you're coming home with all of your toys and data. I don't need a civilian in the field on this one. Our little scratch-and-sniff operation just turned into a bullfight."

The relief in Celeste's voice was tempered with disappointment. "I guess that means we're not high rollers anymore."

"You never were," White said. "I'll have a detail pick you up in ninety minutes. Once she's clear, Johnny Mac, I want you to get yourself to the Air Force Base and lay low until I contact you. Got it?"

"Got it," Johnny said.

White let a finger hover over the speaker button. "That's all for now." With that, he cut the connection and pointed toward the empty chair. "Put your butt back in that chair, and give me the full briefing on Kalashnikov."

Surprising White, Anya didn't protest. She planted herself back into the wingback and locked eyes with him. "How did you not know about Kalashnikov?"

White checked his watch and pulled a bottle from a lower drawer. He uncorked the Gentleman Jack, poured three fingers into a tumbler, and held up the bottle toward Gwynn and Anya.

"No, thank you," came their stereo reply.

White shrugged and replaced the bottle into the drawer. After a long inhalation of the well-aged Tennessee whiskey, he let the golden elixir melt across his tongue and down his throat. "It's like this, Anya. We don't have the freedom to crawl through the lives of everyone we suspect could be guilty of a crime like your people did when the Soviet Union was alive and kicking. We have the Constitution. Maybe you should give it a read sometime. What we know about Kalashnikov is what we've gathered through legal sources without violating anyone's civil rights."

Anya lowered her chin. "And what about rights of victims? Do you believe Volodya plays also only by rules of Constitution?"

White forced a finger through the air and directly toward Gwynn. "You never heard what I'm about to say. Got it?"

She nodded. "Yes, sir."

With his attention refocused on the Russian, White said, "Those victims are extremely fortunate to have you."

Anya smiled. "Because of this, maybe I will not read Constitution . . . yet."

White enjoyed another long swallow of his whiskey and leaned back in his chair. "So, tell me what you know about our boy Volodya."

"If you want to know history of family, I will tell you what I know, but this will be only waste of time."

"Let's save the genealogy for another day and get down to brass tacks on the gun brokering side of the business."

Anya frowned. "Brass tacks? This makes no sense to me."

White downed the last of his cocktail and stood. "Get up."

Anya recoiled and stood.

White cupped a hand beneath the bottom of her chair and turned the piece of furniture upside down. "Look at this row of brass tacks holding the upholstery to the frame."

Anya leaned down and ran a finger across the brass heads. "Yes, I see, but this has nothing to do with Kalashnikov."

White returned the wingback to its upright position. "You're wrong. They have everything to do with him. The brass tacks are the final details the craftsman puts into his work that holds the whole project together. Without the brass tacks, the upholstery would fall from the padding, and the chair would be nothing more than a wooden skeleton and steel frame. The tacks keep everything else in place. That's what I want to know about Vladimir Kalashnikov."

Anya reclaimed her seat. "I like this phrase, brass tacks. We have also in Russian—"

"I don't care. Just tell me about our target."

Anya sighed. "Brass tacks of weapons selling. He has ability to acquire weaponry of former Soviet Union and sell to highest bidder anywhere in world, even here inside United States. I have no proof for court, but I know stories."

"What kind of weaponry?" Gwynn asked.

"Every kind."

"Even nukes?"

Anya pursed her lips. "This I do not know, but I will ask him for nuke for you if you wish."

White sucked air between his teeth. "How hard will it be to get close to this guy?"

"How close?" Anya asked.

"Close enough to convince him you're looking for a job."

Anya smiled. "Suddenly, mission sounds like fun. I have only one demand."

"You don't get to make demands."

"Yes, I do. We will have my Porsche in Las Vegas, yes?"

"How many times do I have to tell you it's not your Porsche? It's the property of the Department of—"

"Good," Anya said. "When should we go?"

White poured a second drink. "Fine, you can have the car, but—"

"There is no *but* inside conversation. Is only yes. Now, to answer your question, it will be difficult to get close. I will have to earn trust, and you will help me do this."

"Keep talking," White said.

"I will first become bottle girl for him. You will have Johnny Mac fall in love with me, and I will take from him everything."

Gwynn giggled. "That should be a piece of cake. He already drools all over himself when you're around."

Anya gave White a wink. "I have this effect sometimes for men. Right, Special Agent White?"

He cleared his throat and took another sip. "I'm not going to lie. That's part of the reason you're here."

Anya put on her knowing smile. "How much money can I take from Johnny Mac?"

White said, "He's already been hit for seven grand. We can justify doubling that figure if you're sure it'll get you in with Kalashnikov."

"I think it will be twenty-five thousand. This is not too much?"

"I think we can swing that, but if it doesn't yield fruit, you'll be hanging me out to dry in front of the attorney general, and I'm not looking forward to that."

Anya nodded. "I promise to you it will be enough, and you will win medal and promotion for excellent operation."

He laughed. "The DOJ doesn't hand out medals, and I'm not interested in a promotion. But I am interested in watching you nail Volodya Kalashnikov to the floor with your very own brass tacks."

8

S TSEPI
(Off the Chain)

Dr. Celeste Mankiller stood in the center of SSA Ray White's office with Anastasia Burinkova's right hand clenched in hers. "So, you're really real. I almost can't believe it."

Anya pulled her hand free. "Yes, I am real, and you are very strange woman."

White stood in amused silence watching the initial meeting play out before his eyes.

Celeste, still refusing to blink, asked, "Can you really do all those things they say?"

"What things? I make very good tea. You can ask Agent White. I have made for him tea."

Celeste glanced between the senior agent and the Russian. "No, not tea. I mean, like the other things . . . with knives and stuff."

Anya held out a hand. "Give to me cigarette."

Celeste recoiled. "I don't smoke."

Anya frowned. "Yes, of course, you smoke. Look at skin on outside of right thumb. It is rough from rolling against cigarette lighter, and you are chewing gum."

Celeste stopped chewing. "It's nicotine gum."

"Yes, this means you wish to no longer smoke but cannot stop when you are nervous, so give to me cigarette."

Celeste sighed and pulled the pack from the pocket of her lab coat. "That's amazing. How did you learn to do that?"

"Is not learning. Is only paying attention." Anya pulled a cigarette from the pack, then turned and placed it in Gwynn's hand. "Put this between lips and pretend to smoke, but do not remove from lips."

Gwynn pressed the cigarette between two fingers and set it in her mouth. Before she could lower her hand, the Russian drew a knife that had been concealed behind her belt and spun in front of her, sending the unfiltered portion of the cigarette falling to the floor in two pieces that were nearly identical in length.

Anya smiled as Celeste stood in awe of the demonstration. "This is what you mean, yes?"

Celeste silently nodded.

"Then answer is yes. I can really do those things."

The tech services genius glowed. "I want to be you when I grow up."

Gwynn plucked the filter from her lips. "Nope! I've got dibs on being Anya."

"It must be amazing to work together."

Gwynn grinned. "Oh, yeah."

White rapped on his desk like a judge calling the courtroom to order. "Okay, that's enough. She's not a show pony. We've got work to do."

The circus wound down, and everyone took a seat.

White flipped open a file and perused several pages. "You're up, Dr. Mankiller. Let's hear the genealogy."

Anya spoke up before the scientist could begin. "This is wonderful name, Mankiller. I want this name when I grow up."

Celeste pointed toward Gwynn. "Teach me to do that with a knife, and I'll give you my last name."

Anya took Gwynn's hand. "You must first learn to trust me like my partner. Friend Gwynn knows I will never hurt her."

Gwynn made a sound no one could identify and said, "That's not entirely true. You've hurt me a bunch of times while teaching me to fight."

"Yes, this is true, but also necessary. Fighting hurts, even when winning."

Another rap on the desk. "I said, that's enough. Tell us what you discovered down in your little dungeon."

Celeste said, "Oh, yeah. It's pretty cool, actually. Johnny—I mean, Special Agent McIntyre—lifted eight cigarette butts and three discarded pieces of gum from Gedo, the club owned by Kalashnikov. He said the gum and butts all came from the four girls who were, uh, handling him."

"We get it," White said. "Just tell us what you picked up from the samples."

"The shirt I designed and built didn't work as well as I'd hoped in the field, but the gum and butts were gold. I was able to separate usable DNA from every sample. I guess Johnny had his hands full, because either two different women chewed each piece of gum, or there were more than four. I got six distinct individuals, but they're not entirely distinct."

"What do you mean?" White asked. "They're either distinct or they're not."

"Without getting too deep into the science, I'll just say that five of the samples I tested have a common marker."

"They're all related?"

"Not exactly, but they're likely all from the same area. There are unique markers that show up in certain regions around the world. The particular common marker I discovered puts them in or near the city of Saransk, which is the capital of the Republic of Mordovia."

White threw up his hands. "You'll have to do a little better. My geography isn't great."

Instead of waiting for Celeste to answer, Anya said, "I have also this marker. My mother is from Saransk, five hundred kilometers east of Moscow."

Celeste snapped her fingers. "I knew it! It's the nose."

Anya instinctually reached for her face, and Celeste said, "It's the perfect nose. If a plastic surgeon could learn to build that nose, they'd make a billion dollars."

White said, "Hey! Focus! Why does any of this matter?"

Anya said, "This detail matters because I look like the girls Volodya chooses to be his bottle girls. This gives to me first key to unlock his doors."

"I like it," White said. "But after what you told me about him running guns and operating a murder-for-hire ring, I no longer care about what happens in his club. He's a much bigger fish now."

"This is true, but I cannot walk up to this man, stick out hand, and say, 'I am KGB-trained assassin. Who can I kill for you?' This will not work. I must first have subtle approach to build trust. We have wealthy mark who has lost only seven thousand dollars so far. I have perfect nose. And we have also secret weapon."

White cocked his head. "What secret weapon?"

Anya pointed to her partner. "Friend Gwynn, who has perfect every-thing except color of hair."

"Hey! What's wrong with the color of my hair?"

"It is not blonde," Anya said. "This is good thing, though. You will soon understand."

White listened to the exchange and steepled his hands. "All of this is great, but I have to run it up the flagpole before we make any moves."

"How long will this take?" Anya asked.

White lifted the handset from its cradle. "If it goes badly, it'll take a few seconds, but if she says yes, this is going to be a long phone call."

He tapped a few keys and stuck the phone to his ear. A few seconds later, he said, "Hello, Sylvia. It's Ray White. Is she taking calls?"

Less than a minute later, the voice of a second woman rang through the line. "What now, Ray?"

"You're going to like this one, General."

"Don't call me General, Ray. We're not in the Army. I'm a busy woman, so talk fast."

"Yes, ma'am. There's been a development in the Vladimir Kalashnikov case in Las Vegas, and we need—"

"Come on, Ray. Surely, you know I'm always in the loop. I know everything before you know it. You recalled Dr. Mankiller back to DC and stuck Agent McIntyre at Nellis. None of this is news to me."

"Of course not, ma'am. But it turns out that our boy, Volodya, is into a lot more than international forgery and credit card fraud."

"Let me guess. He's smuggling supermodels in from Moscow. Trust me, Ray. We're not going to get a meaningful conviction for the crime of taking beautiful women to a place they're begging to go. Stick with the credit card forgery and fraud. That's our case. And stop bothering me with your petty . . ."

Before she could finish scolding him, White said, "He's an international illegal weapons distributor, and he's running a murder-for-hire ring."

The line was silent for a few seconds, followed by, "Get up here, now. And bring your Russian."

The line went dead, and Supervisory Special Agent Ray White lifted his tie from the floor and his jacket from the coat tree. "Let's go, ladies. We've got an appointment with the attorney general of the United States."

After a short elevator ride, the quartet was escorted into one of the city's most elaborately adorned offices outside the West Wing.

The attorney general waved a dismissive hand toward a sofa and a pair of chairs. "I thought I told you to bring one person, not three."

"You did, ma'am, but the truth is, you're probably going to chew me up and spit me out before this meeting is over. I'd hate for the people responsible for this get-together to miss the excitement."

She let her eyes explore the audience. "I know Special Agent Davis . . . And you must be Dr. Mankiller from technical services."

The dark-haired scientist gave a respectful nod. "Hello, ma'am. It's nice to finally meet you."

The AG ignored her and locked eyes with Anya. "And you must be Ms. Burinkova. I've heard a lot about you, but I must say, you don't look as dangerous as you've been described."

The Russian feigned shyness. "I am now Ms. Fulton. Burinkova is my name from before I became American."

The AG eyed her and then turned to White. "So, what is this I hear about Kalashnikov being a gunrunner and murderer?"

Before White could speak, Anya said, "He is probably not murderer, but he has many of them at his disposal. If someone with money wants someone else to be murdered, Volodya will have it done for a price. This makes him not murderer but still guilty of maybe conspiracy to commit murder. I am not lawyer like Agent White and friend Gwynn, but I know this is not federal crime unless this is done to federal officer or employee or inside national property. This is correct, yes?"

The AG appeared mesmerized by the Russian. "Yes, that's correct, but there are a few other caveats that can make conspiracy to commit murder a federal offense. The weapons sale and distribution are, however, fully within our jurisdiction. Tell me, Ms. Burinkova, how do you know Kalashnikov is an arms dealer?"

"Is Fulton, not Burinkova. I told you this already."

"Forgive me, Ms. Fulton, but my question remains."

Anya turned to White. "I can talk freely with her?"

White tried not to laugh. "She's the attorney general of the United States, so yes, you may speak freely, but try not to get me fired."

Anya gave no acknowledgment and turned back to the AG. "I am trained former officer of Sluzhba vneshney razvedki Rossiyskoy Federatsii."

The AG huffed. "Yes, I know who and what you are."

"Then you should understand how I know these things about Volodya Kalashnikov. Is what you would call common knowledge among intelligence operatives of Russian Federation."

The AG eyed White. "And this is your foundation for upgrading the in-vestigation of Mr. Kalashnikov?"

"Yes, ma'am. It is. I trust Anya . . . I mean, Ms. Fulton."

"You trust her?"

White stammered. "Well, I mean, I trust her in this instance with this intelligence."

The AG pulled off her glasses and glared at White, but he spoke before she could. "No, let me rescind that statement. I trust Anya without caveat. She's never lied to me, and she's never failed any task I dropped into her lap. How many of your subordinates can you put in the same category, ma'am?"

The senior law enforcement officer in the country glared at the deadliest operative under her realm. "What would you have me do, Agent Fulton?"

Anya didn't hesitate. "Unleash us."

9

DOROGA PAMYATI
(MEMORY LANE)

The C-17 Globemaster, one of the world's most capable heavy airlift platforms, left the eleven thousand three hundred feet of runway at Andrews Air Force Base only minutes before the most recognizable aircraft in the free world was pulled from its high-security hangar. At that moment, the airplane left behind bore the call sign of SAM28000, but when the airstairs were pulled away and the door closed, it would become *Air Force One*. The probability of the occupants of the mysterious C-17 positively affecting world peace was significantly greater than the same possibility of *Air Force One*'s passengers.

The gleaming paint job of the Porsche 911 convertible shone, even through the protective sheeting covering the car that Anya would always consider to be hers. Special Agent Gwynn Davis and the Russian with a credential pack identifying her as Special Agent Ana Fulton sat in specially designed airline seats affixed to a pallet inside the belly of the enormous flying beast.

As they leveled off in cruise flight, Gwynn said, "Thank you."

Anya grimaced. "For what?"

"For what you said about me in Agent White's office. It meant a great deal to me, so thank you."

The grimace morphed into a flawless smile. "Everything I said was true. You are already more capable than most men who are lawyers with guns. You can kill three or maybe four men without waking sleeping child. You are very good, Gwynn, and you are getting better every day."

Gwynn shook her head. "It doesn't feel that way. Every time I think I've learned how to defend myself, you show me how wrong I am, and sometimes it leaves a bruise or two."

"I must tell to you secret," the Russian said. "Every time we fight, you become harder to hurt. A day will come when I cannot defeat you."

Gwynn laughed out loud. "Yeah, right. You've spent your whole life training how to fight. I got a late start."

"Yes, this is true, but you have advantage I did not have."

Gwynn turned in curious anticipation, and Anya gave her a playful shove. "You have me for teacher, and I was never so lucky."

"Okay, you've got a point there," Gwynn admitted.

Anya's gaze fell to the floor.

"What's wrong?"

Anya paused before finally looking up at her partner. "I was never allowed to be child."

Gwynn took her hand. "I'm sorry about what happened to you as a child, but when all of this is over, you and I can play like little girls in the park."

Anya squeezed Gwynn's hand. "Do you really believe it will ever be over?"

"Yeah, I'm sure of it. One way or another, it will end."

Anya inhaled a long, painful breath. "Perhaps it ends only if I am killed."

"No, that's not true, Anya. I don't know everything Agent White has planned, but I've heard him say there will only be seven missions for you. For us."

"Maybe this is true, but it does not mean I will not be killed before finishing all seven."

Gwynn put on the same smile she wore as that little girl on the playground. "You just said I'm almost as good as you in a fight, so I won't let anybody kill you."

"I did not say this. I said only that you are good and more challenging now than when we began."

Gwynn rolled her eyes. "Whatever."

The plane touched down at Nellis Air Force Base four hours later, and the rear ramp slowly yawned, opening the back of the cargo space to the brutal heat of the Nevada desert. Both women shielded their eyes from the sun's onslaught while the loadmaster carefully unwrapped the Porsche. When the car had been freed from the bondage of cargo straps, the loadmaster unlocked and opened the door.

Anya slid herself between him and the driver's seat. "Thank you for opening door for me. And I like your uniform."

The Air Force sergeant froze. "Uh, ma'am, I have to drive the car off the airplane. I can't allow you to . . ."

Anya ran her hand up the front of his flight suit and squeezed the zipper pull between her fingers. She slowly lowered the zipper and smiled up at the smitten airman. "Is too bad you have shirt on beneath uniform. Maybe next time."

Before he could protest further, she slid behind the wheel and hooked the button with her fingertip, sending the convertible top into its hiding place. Gwynn gave the loadmaster a shrug and a playful wink as she slid onto the passenger seat. Leaving the flabbergasted crewman behind, Anya left the ramp, accelerating through sixty miles per hour.

Gwynn yelled over the roar of the wind and engine. "Do you know where you're going?"

Anya shook out her long blonde hair and smiled up at the midday sun. "Vegas, baby!"

The Las Vegas Strip was moving at its typical snail's pace, the blonde and brunette in the little blue Porsche stopping more traffic than the congestion. By the time they finally pulled beneath the portico at Caesars Palace, the desire to put up the top and crank the air conditioner almost outweighed their love of the sun on their faces.

Check-in was a breeze, and a bellman showed them to their adjoining rooms high above and overlooking the Strip. Anya rewarded the bellman with a kiss on the cheek, and Gwynn did so with a folded bill slipped into his palm.

"I'm pretty sure he'd rather have another kiss from you than my twenty bucks."

Anya smirked. "Perhaps, but it doesn't matter. He is gone now. We should have nap and shower. Tonight will be exciting night for us."

"What's tonight?"

"You will see. Sleep well, and dress to impress. I will see you at eight."

Gwynn took Anya's wrist. "Wait a minute. You're not going to take a nap, are you? You're trying to get rid of me for a few hours. I thought we were partners."

"We are," Anya insisted, "but what I have to do is better alone."

Gwynn huffed. "You told Agent White you would teach me to be just like you. You can't do that if we're not together. Besides, I'm not sleepy."

Anya relented. "Okay, but this will not be easy for you."

"Just name it. I might surprise you."

The Russian said, "Make yourself ugly."

Gwynn took a step back. "What are you talking about?"

Anya stepped beside her partner and motioned toward a full-length mirror. "Look at us. People remember women who look like us, and we have work to do on street before we are ready to make memorable impression."

Gwynn landed her hands on her hips. "And you were going to leave me out of that?"

The Russian sighed. "I should have known better. You have five minutes to be ready and ugly."

Gwynn emerged minutes later, well hidden behind a New York Mets hat and a pair of sunglasses that could double as beach umbrellas.

Anya ran a finger across the bill of Gwynn's cap. "This is baseball team, yes?"

"Yeah. When I was in college, I had a boyfriend—well, more of a play-thing to be honest—and he was a huge baseball fan. We went to every Mets and Yankees game he could score tickets for. We even went to Boston to see the Red Sox a bunch of times. Apparently, Fenway Park is some kind of big deal."

Anya's smile grew as the memory replayed in her mind. "I remember first time to see baseball match in University of Georgia. Chase had job of catching when he played there. He was very good, and I have baseball shirt with his name. Is also my name, but is on shirt for him, not me."

Gwynn stood, watching her friend stroll down memory lane. "You know, you're never going to be happy with a man until you stop comparing them to Chase. There's no way he was as good as you remember."

"This is true," she said. "He is even better than I remember. There is sign in baseball stadium with his name. We had chili dog and beer. You have had this, yes?"

Gwynn giggled. "Yeah, everyone has had chili dogs and beer at a ball game. It's part of being an American."

"I will tell you more of story about first time at baseball match later."

"It's called a game, Anya, not a match. And I thought we had work to do."

"We do, but I was having pleasant memory. Is over now, so come with me."

From the street, the pair was nothing more than two tourists with base-ball caps and oversized sunglasses, but from behind those glasses, nothing went unnoticed.

"Where are we going?" Gwynn asked as they strolled south on the Las Vegas Strip.

"Russia," Anya said. "And I can see it from here."

Gwynn peered through the throngs of tourists, gamblers, and hawkers. "If I remember my world geography, I'm pretty sure you're looking in the wrong direction. Russia is about four thousand miles west of here."

Anya laced her arm through Gwynn's. "Rodina may be across ocean, but we are going to Red Square."

She led her partner through the grand entrance of the Mandalay Bay Resort and Casino. The palatial property was spread out before them, and they took in every inch.

Anya motioned toward a long corridor. "I think it is this way."

Gwynn offered no resistance, and soon, they were standing in front of the Red Square—Las Vegas's only Russian-themed restaurant.

Gwynn pointed toward a headless statue standing beside the impressive entrance. "Well, that's weird."

"This is Vladimir Lenin. Or *was* him before removing his head. This is what happens inside Russia when things go wrong."

"If this new mission of ours is as dangerous as you seem to think it is, good ol' Vladimir may have gotten off easy."

10

SOBESEDOVANIYE
(JOB INTERVIEW)

After two and a half hours on the street, learning every inch of the Las Vegas Strip, Gwynn and Anya arrived across the street from Gedonizm.

Anya stared at the club. "This is where it will begin."

"It doesn't look like I expected."

"What did you expect?"

Gwynn shrugged. "I don't know. I guess I thought it would be seedier. That place looks really nice."

"It would be terrible idea to expect wealthy men to come inside cheap-looking club."

"Yeah, I guess you're right. Do you have a plan to get inside yet?"

Anya wouldn't look away from the entrance of Gedo. "I have plan for me to get inside, but for you will be very difficult. You are not Russian."

"Surely they have some girls who aren't Russian."

Anya motioned toward the club. "I do not think this is correct. We will look inside."

"Now? But we look terrible."

"We will not go inside yet. For now, we will only look. Maybe you are correct. Maybe not everyone is Russian."

They crossed the Strip, weaving their way through the ocean of stopped cars, and arrived immediately in front of Club Gedo. Just as they stepped onto the sidewalk, a pair of ravishing blondes emerged from the club and lit up cigarettes.

Anya leaned toward her partner and whispered, "Keep walking, but do not go far."

Gwynn turned north and found a waiting bench that provided the perfect vantage point from which to watch her partner at work. Anya pulled off her cap and sunglasses, shaking out her long, blonde hair as she did. She motioned toward the cigarette of the closer woman, and in her native Russian, said, "May I have one of those? It has been a long time since I have Russian cigarette."

The woman pulled a pack from her pocket and held it out toward Anya. She pulled one from the pack and leaned in for the woman to light it.

With the pack returned to its pocket, the woman cupped her hand around the lighter and touched the flame to Anya's cigarette. "You are new here. I do not recognize you."

Anya took a long drag and exhaled, allowing the rising stream of smoke to encircle her head. "Yes, I am new in town, and I need job."

The two women examined Anya. "You will have to go shopping."

Anya frowned. "What are you talking about?"

"Your clothes," said the first woman. "They must go. Look at us. If one hundred men walk by right now, all of them will look to us and never see you, but you are pretty enough. We will teach you to do hair and makeup. You are not *prostitutka*?"

Anya bowed her head. "I do not want to be *prostitutka*."

The second woman reached for Anya's hand. "It is okay. You do not have to do that. You will make more money here than inside bordello. You will learn how to make men give to you all of money without taking off clothes."

Anya raised her eyebrows. "You will teach this to me?"

The first woman said, "You are Russian woman. You already know how to do this, *dorogaya devushka*. This comes naturally for Russian woman."

Anya allowed a smile. "When can I begin job?"

The second woman placed a hand on Anya's hip and encouraged her to turn around. "You have already started, my pet. Now, look onto street and find rich man."

Anya pointed out several potential marks.

"This is good. You are going to be wonderful for this job. Now, go back to your place. You do have a place to live, yes?"

Anya nodded, and the woman continued.

"Good. Go there and take shower. You are sweaty. Make hair and face beautiful, and wear nice clothes to show off legs. You have very long legs. This is good."

Anya pretended to take notes in her head, then asked, "Then do I come back here?"

"Yes, you do, but do not come alone. Bring man. Bring rich man with credit card. When you come inside, I will see you, and I will show you what to do."

"This is all I must do to make money?"

"There's a little more to it, but you will do hard part first. This is getting man to come into club."

Anya's smile broadened. "I can definitely get man to come with me to club. I will show you."

The woman patted Anya's shoulder. "Go now. If you come back, you will be amazed how much money you will make, but you have to split money with me as long as I am teaching, yes?"

"Sure. If you say so."

Anya crossed the street, leaving Club Gedo behind.

Gwynn remained on the bench until the two women finished their cigarettes and headed back inside. After she was certain they were no longer watching through the window, she abandoned the bench and headed north on her side of the street. She caught up with Anya about halfway back to Caesars Palace.

"The two women were betting on whether or not you'd come back."

Anya laughed. "Which one said I would come back?"

"The taller one said they'd never see you again, but the other one says you'll definitely come back. At least that's what I think they said. My Russian still isn't very good, but I'm learning."

"Yes, *dorogaya devushka*, you are learning."

Gwynn thought for a moment. "Darling girl?"

Anya smiled. "*Da*."

"So, what's the plan?"

The Russian chewed on her lip for a moment. "My part of plan is working perfectly. In fact, is working better than I expected, but I am still working on plan for you. It will come to me. Just be patient."

"Okay, Anya. I trust you, but don't leave me in the dark on this one. We're a team, remember?"

"Yes, I know this, and we need third member of team for tonight."

"Third member?"

"Yes, we need Johnny Mac. I will take him to club with me tonight."

Gwynn winced. "I'm not sure that's a good idea. He's already been there once. Won't they get suspicious if they see him again?"

"No, I do not think this is what will happen. I believe they will think I am very good at picking man to bring inside since he is same man they picked before. Also, they will know he is not afraid of spending thousands of dollars to be with beautiful Russian women."

Gwynn chuckled. "Yeah, I think most men fall into that category."

"Men think money makes them attractive to women," Anya said. "But this is not true. Money is attractive—not person having this money. If man is good-looking, nice, kind, respectful, and also has money, he is attractive, but this is also true even if man is not rich. You would agree with this, no?"

Gwynn considered her theory. "I guess you're right, but it would be nice to not have to worry about having money. I know it's not everything, but life is easier when you don't have to worry about paying the bills."

"Yes, of course, but this is not most important thing. You should be also happy."

Back in Anya's suite, Gwynn made the call while Anya took the shower the Russian bottle girl had recommended.

"Agent White, it's Davis. Everything is going perfectly, and Anya already made contact."

"With Kalashnikov?" White asked.

"No, not yet, but she got a job at Club Gedo, and she starts tonight. That's why I'm calling."

"You're calling because it's your job."

"Well, yes, of course, but I'm also calling to get Johnny Mac back in the game. Anya thinks it would be a good move to bring him back to the club with her tonight."

White groaned. "I'm not so sure. What's her logic behind that decision?"

"She wants to impress the folks at the club by choosing a man they've already chosen. She thinks that'll reinforce their trust in her. It also gives us a chance to hit his credit card nice and hard a second time. That will definitely win Anya some points with these guys."

"I'll give it some thought. Where is she now?"

"In the shower. Why?"

"Because I'm in charge, and I want to know where my assets are. Is that okay with you, Special Agent Davis?"

"Yes, sir. I'm sorry. I thought you meant . . . Never mind. I'm sorry."

"Don't be sorry, Davis. Tell me what you thought I meant."

"I thought maybe you believed I'd left her alone at the club. I wouldn't do that. She's my partner."

"No, I wasn't thinking that. You're a good cop, Davis. Don't forget that. I trust you, and I trust Anya when it comes to operational details. I'll send Johnny Mac to your hotel. Do you think you can brief him without screwing it up?"

"I don't think it'll require much of a briefing, boss. He just has to drink and enjoy being fondled by beautiful women all night. That's good work if you can get it."

"You know something, Davis? You're right. Forget Johnny Mac. I'll be right over."

Gwynn giggled. "I don't know, Agent White. Johnny Mac might fight you for Anya."

"Fair enough," he said. "I'll let the young guy have all the fun tonight, but don't let it get out of control. You're in charge."

"Don't worry, boss. I won't let you down."

"You let me down constantly, Davis. Just don't let anyone get dead."

Anya emerged from the bathroom with a towel wrapped around her head and another around her body. "You will help with hair, friend Gwynn?"

Three minutes into the drying process, Gwynn dropped her brush and turned off the dryer. "Now I really hate you."

Anya stared up at Gwynn in the mirror. "Why would you hate me?"

"You're a natural blonde."

"Yes, of course, just like you are natural brunette. But why would this make you hate me?"

Gwynn reclaimed the brush. "Just look at you. It's not fair for you to have all of *that* and naturally blonde hair."

"It was not my choice. Is only genetics."

Gwynn huffed. "Yeah, well, your gene pool must look a lot like the Caribbean. Next to you, mine is more like a mud puddle."

11

MOYA SVIDANIYE
(MY DATE)

With hair, makeup, and wardrobe complete, a tone chimed inside Anya's suite.

Gwynn hopped from her seat. "That must be your date."

"You think he will like?"

Gwynn rolled her eyes, "Really? He's going to drool all over himself."

Anya ducked her chin. "I have small confession."

"Oh, this ought to be good. Let's hear it."

"As you know, I have been trained to make men do for me what I want, but tonight it feels different."

Gwynn furrowed her brow. "Different how?"

"Is silly, but having date with Johnny Mac feels like date with brother . . . if I had brother."

Gwynn giggled. "I get it, but maybe you can pretend he's Chase."

"You are terrible. This is not nice. I thought you were my friend."

Gwynn reached for the doorknob. "I'm just messing with you. I have a feeling Johnny Mac will enjoy the night enough for both of you."

Anya gave her a wry smile and turned for the bedroom. "Tell him I am not ready yet, and I will make grand entrance."

Gwynn twisted the knob and looked up to see a man she didn't recognize. Behind him stood her other partner in jeans and a T-shirt. "Uh, hello . . . Two things. First, who's this, and second, why aren't you dressed?"

Johnny said, "Captain Tom Elsmore, meet Special Agent Gwynn Davis."

The man extended a hand, and she shook it. "It's nice to meet you, Tom. Call me Gwynn. Come in."

Tom stepped through the door and gave Gwynn a look. "I'm charmed. Are you the . . ."

Johnny laughed. "No, she's not. She's my partner."

Gwynn looked around the man who stood several inches taller than Johnny Mac. "What's going on here?"

Johnny closed the door behind him. "Let's get inside, and I'll tell you about it."

Gwynn led them to the sitting room and motioned toward the sofa. "Have a seat, and let's clear this up. No one is supposed to be here except DOJ."

Tom took the floor. "I'm not DOJ. I'm on loan from another alphabet soup agency. I'm a special agent with the Air Force Office of Special Investigations. I'm temporarily assigned to SSA White for tonight's operation."

Gwynn turned to Johnny. "Why am I just now hearing about this?"

Johnny shrugged. "I don't know. You can take that up with Agent White. For some reason, he didn't think it was a great idea for me to go back inside so soon."

Before Gwynn could protest, Anya floated into the room, and Captain Elsmore leapt to his feet.

Anya eyed Gwynn. "*Kto oh?*"

Before she could answer, Tom spoke in flawless Russian. "You must be Anastasia. I'm Tom Elsmore, your date for the evening . . . And obviously the luckiest man in Vegas."

Anya did a passable job of hiding her surprise, but Tom's sharp jawline and piercing blue eyes made him almost impossible to ignore.

Gwynn pulled out her phone. "I'm on it."

SSA Ray White answered almost before it rang. "Calm down, and tell your little girlfriend to do the same. I made a command decision. Special Agent Elsmore is going in with Anya because we can't afford to have pictures of Johnny Mac's corpse splashed across the front page of the *Las Vegas Review-Journal*."

Gwynn said, "What are you talking about?

"Just tell Anya what I said, and she can explain it to you."

"What is he saying?" Anya demanded, but Gwynn held up a finger.

White said, "Trust me. I know what I'm doing."

The line went dead, and Gwynn stared at the phone for a moment before saying, "He said to tell you that we can't afford to have pictures of Johnny Mac's corpse on the front page."

Anya's shoulders sagged. "Of course, he is correct. This was terrible mistake in plan. I will kill *him* instead."

Tom recoiled. "Kill me? What are you talking about?"

Anya waved him off. "Do not worry. I will probably not have to really kill you, but we will see."

Tom smiled at the Russian. "It might be worth the risk."

Anya said, "Tonight, you are to call me only Ana." She emphasized the ahh in Ana.

"I can do that. Is there anything else I need to know?"

Anya said, "Yes. Do not speak Russian, and do not react when anyone else does. You can do this, yes?"

He said, "*Da*."

"You have credit card with large limit, yes?"

He patted his hip pocket. "I've got it covered."

"Give to me wallet."

Without protest, he pulled the wallet from his pocket and laid it in her palm. She thumbed through the contents and pulled his driver's license from its slip. "This says New York. This is not real?"

"It's real enough," he said.

She returned the license and slid the wallet back into his hand. Before her fingertips slipped from his palm, she dragged a fingernail across a silver wedding band. "And this?"

"It's a real ring," he said. "But there's no Mrs. Elsmore."

"This is nice touch. You are also police officer, yes?"

"I'm with Air Force OSI, but I've only been here in Vegas for two weeks. The last decade of my life has been spent overseas."

"This is why you know Russian, yes?"

"Not exactly. My mother was from Ivanovo, and my father is from Berlin, so I grew up in a house with three first languages—English, Russian, and German."

"If this is true, why are you in American Air Force?"

"My father moved to the States with his parents when he was nine or ten."

"That would have been during Cold War. Coming to America was very difficult in that time."

Tom said, "It was way before my time, so I don't know. My grandparents have been gone for thirty years, and my mother passed away a few months ago."

"I am sorry to hear this."

"Thank you."

Johnny Mac said, "I hate to break up this courting ritual or whatever it is, but we've got work to do. Davis and I will move out and get into position outside the club. Tom's watch is a transmitter, and we'll each have an earpiece. What's the abort code?"

Anya said, "*Persik.*"

Tom frowned. "Peach? Why?"

"I had for snack earlier, and it was bitter. This will mean we do not like it, and we are coming out."

"Okay, *persik* it is. Let's go, Davis."

Gwynn rose and pointed to the Russians. "You two be good. Give us thirty minutes, and let us know when you're headed our way."

Anya slid her hand into Tom's. "We will be very good. He is perfect gentleman. I can tell these things. But I will not be gentlewoman. Tonight, I am terrible person taking advantage of maybe happily married man from New York."

Gwynn and Johnny left the suite, and Anya said, "You must have drink. Vodka?"

"I prefer bourbon, but if vodka is what you have, I'll take what's available."

"I will make for you, drink."

Anya returned a minute later with a flute of champagne and a tumbler of golden liquor.

Tom took the glass and raised it into the air. "To first dates with beautiful women."

Anya touched the rim of her flute to his tumbler. "To not killing handsome Air Force officer."

Tom chuckled. "Indeed."

* * *

Thirty minutes passed like seconds, and the most beautiful couple in Vegas hit the street.

"You understand what will happen tonight, yes?"

Tom said, "Agent McIntyre talked me through it, but I'd love to hear your expectations."

"You have security clearance, yes?"

He chuckled. "Yes, a clearance, a signed non-disclosure agreement, and a need to know."

Anya gave him a smile. "You have worked with government for long time."

"You could say that. I spent four years at the Air Force Academy and seven months in flight school before I was reassigned to security police, and eventually, to the Office of Special Investigations."

Anya frowned. "Only seven months at flying school? What happened? Did you fail?"

"That's one way to look at it. I took some shrapnel to my left eye when my instructor and I had to punch out of a T-Thirty-Eight that caught on fire during a training mission. After that, I couldn't meet the aeromedical standards, so I watched my flying career fly away without me."

Anya sighed. "I think this makes us same."

"Same? What do you mean?"

I was to be gymnast, but my body grew too tall for this. You were to be pilot, but your body experienced injury, stopping this for you. This makes us same, and also same ancestors, *malen'kiy russkiy mal'chik*."

Tom squeezed Anya's hand. "I don't think I qualify as a little Russian boy. I'm red, white, and blue to my core. I guess that's why I decided to stay in the Air Force, even after screwing up my eye. Maybe patriotism isn't dead after all. How did a *malen'kaya russkaya devochka* end up working for the Department of Justice?"

"Maybe little Russian girl grew up to be also American inside, and maybe I was also injured and could not become what I wanted. My injury was not like yours, though. It was only on inside."

He eyed her for a long moment. "You're a remarkable woman, Anya. If that's really your name."

"My mother gave to me name of Anastasia, but Anya is better."

"Okay, Anastasia."

She jerked her hand from his. "No! This is name only for mother. Not for you. Do not call me this name."

He took a step away and threw up his hands. "I'm sorry. I didn't know. It won't happen again, I promise."

She bowed her head and slipped her hand back into his. "I am sorry. This is overreaction. I use only Anya or Ana. I am not angry with you."

He put on his smile again. "Good. I wouldn't want you to be angry with me. Rumor has it you're quite the swordsman."

Anya winked at her date. "Perhaps rumor is true."

They continued their walk toward Club Gedo until Tom said, "So, are you going to tell me what's going to happen tonight? That's how this conversation started, you know."

"There is no time for me to tell you this. We are almost to club. Remember only this . . . You are businessman, not policeman, and you do not speak Russian. I will take care of everything else."

"I think I can handle that."

"There is one more thing. I will try to put water inside vodka bottle, but this will not always be possible. You must pretend to be drunk, even if you are not."

He glanced over her shoulder and across the street. "Don't look now, but your partner Gwynn is camped out in that window."

"Yes, I saw her. I am very good at street work. Also, Johnny Mac is trying on hats in shop just behind us. We will be always under watchful eyes tonight. Are you ready?"

He grinned. "Ready for a date with half a dozen gorgeous Russian women? Somehow, I think I'll find a way to suffer through it."

12

Pochti Nikogda
(Almost Never)

The dichotomy of the bustling sidewalk to the elegant interior of Club Gedo was impossible to ignore. Instead of the thundering techno beats and flashing lights Anya expected, the scene that lay in front of her more closely resembled an opulent European gentleman's club. Soft music played, smoke rose from a few tables, and the ratio of gentlemen to ladies fell beautifully in favor of the men. Leggy Eastern European beauties graced the arm of every man in the room, but only one pair of eyes rose to meet the club's newest arrivals.

The elegance and grace with which the woman crossed the floor sent Anya's mind reeling back to State School Four, where she'd been trained to perfection in every detail of seduction, including the walk of the statuesque seductress drawing ever closer.

Anya whispered, "The ballet has begun. Enjoy."

Surprising Anya, the woman stepped directly in front of her while still staring at Captain Elsmore. She hissed in sensual Russian. "Look what a wonderful plaything you have brought for my kittens. Watch and learn."

Submission wasn't easy for the DOJ's secret weapon, but she swallowed her pride and stepped back as the woman she'd met only hours before slid her arm into Tom's and led him deeper into the club.

Anya took a step behind and reemerged on Tom's left, reclaiming his hand in hers.

The woman cooed. "I promise this will be evening you will never forget. My name is Oxana."

He drew his arm tightly against his side, pressing her hand and wrist into his abs. "I'm Thomas."

The woman continued enjoying the feel of his body without a hint of fat. "You are big, strong man, Thomas. I would like to have drink. You will buy for me, yes?"

Anya didn't like the jealousy simmering in her gut, but the game was afoot, and she had no choice but to play her part. "I will also have drink."

Oxana peered around Anya's date. "Yes, of course."

They crossed the room and waded through a dozen tables with a dozen men devouring the attention of three dozen adoring women. When they reached the bar, the bartender leaned toward the trio, and Oxana slid a hand across his. "Champagne for my girlfriend and me, and our man will order for himself."

Reinforce bravado, and encourage dominance.

The mantra had been poured and pounded into Anya's head every day at State School 4, and Oxana was playing directly from the book.

"Vodka . . . rocks."

The bartender nodded. "Stoli?"

Tom took a moment to admire the two beautiful women at his side. "Tonight seems to be turning out to be a special night. Maybe you've got something a little more top-shelf back there."

The bartender gave Tom an appraising eye. "You look like man with means to enjoy finest things in life." He paused, eyeing Anya and Oxana. "I think I have bottle just for you, but is not cheap."

"Neither am I. Can we open a tab?"

The bartender held up a pair of fingers forming a V, and Tom stuck a credit card between them. When he returned, he poured the champagne for the ladies first and slid an unlabeled bottle of clear liquid onto the bar. He poured an ounce into a glass and slid it toward Tom.

The Air Force cop stared down at the glass. "I asked for rocks."

The bartender smiled. "Try first before we defile with frozen water."

Tom lifted the tumbler, touched the rim to each of the lady's champagne flutes, and asked, "What's the Russian word for cheers?"

"*Budem zdorovy,*" came the two women's reply.

Tom gave it his best false American attempt. "*Boooh din ziddy voy ah!*"

"Perfect!" Oxana declared, and pressed the flute to her lips.

Anya did the same and let the champagne pour across her tongue. Shocked, she swallowed the sweet sparkling juice, obviously containing exactly zero alcohol.

Oxana laid a hand across Tom's broad shoulders, steering him away from the bar and toward a darkened corner of the room.

Touch excessively, and gently lead your target.

How many hours had Anya spent perfecting the dance in the forest outside Kazan on the banks of the Volga River? Could Oxana be a graduate of the school? Could she be a sparrow like Anya?

She reached for the unlabeled vodka bottle, but Oxana glared at the bartender, who snatched it from Anya's fingertips.

The skilled seductress directed her prey into the booth and ordered, with only her eyes, that Anya slide herself onto the horseshoe seat opposite the choreographer of the delicate dance. Anya obeyed and slid onto the supple leather until her exposed thigh was pressed lightly against Tom.

Instead of mirroring Anya's action, Oxana slid onto the seat with her knees folded delicately beneath her. She leaned toward the OSI special agent, exposing her burgeoning cleavage from the low-cut dress she wore perfectly.

Show surrender by giving your target unexpected access to your body.

How much more proof did Anya need? Was Tom really the target, or had she been discovered and fallen into the same honeytrap she'd set and sprung through the years?

Tom, whether playing his role perfectly, or simply surrendering to his libido, refused to take his eyes from the offered prize. Oxana leaned in and pressed her delicate lips against his earlobe, whispering something Anya could neither hear nor read. Tom's reaction told her the whisper had only been part of the seduction and nothing sinister.

Anya raised her dress, fully exposing her right leg, and laid it across Tom's thigh. Watching his Adam's apple rise and fall in his throat reminded the former sparrow of the power she held over every man.

Oxana's eyes drifted to Anya's thigh, and she turned, allowing her body to slide against Tom. In one motion, she accepted the bottle from the bartender, who'd followed them to the table and poured the crystal-clear vodka into the waiting glass.

Oxana's finger followed the liquid until the elixir was dripping from her manicured tip. Pressing her moistened finger against his mouth, she painted the vodka across his lips until his tongue could no longer resist. She teased the tip of his tongue with her finger until Tom's eyes fell closed, and Anya felt the muscles of his leg tensing beneath hers.

Explore fixations, beginning with audible cues whispered, while kissing the flesh of the neck or earlobes. Continue exploration for oral fixation with fingertips or a probing tongue.

Oxana could have written the textbook and flawlessly demonstrated each technique. Not only had she been a student of State School 4, but she must have also been an honors graduate.

"Forgive me," the siren whispered. "But I find myself uncontrollably drawn to you, and I cannot withdraw."

Flatter your target, leaving him believing you are powerless against him. This not only softens resolve, but also fortifies the ego.

Any lingering doubt that Oxana had been a KGB- or SVR-trained sparrow crumbled, and Anya chose to reveal her secret.

She slid from the booth and tilted her head toward the restroom. "*Ne ukhodi bez menya.*"

Oxana stiffened and locked widened eyes with Anya, her sister sparrow.

Tom's command of the Russian language and his well-trained investigator's ear caught and catalogued the exchange, but he had no way of knowing what the phrase "Do not leave without me" could possibly mean beyond its literal translation.

Anya watched him and secretly celebrated his ability to withhold physical reaction to a language he knew so well. Observing Oxana's reaction to the phrase every sparrow knew all too well, solidified their common history, but in doing so, had she also revealed too much too early?

The ladies' room was small, cramped, and bare, but it provided the one thing Anya wanted at the moment—a place to send a text message without attracting attention.

OXANA IS TALL BLONDE AND ALSO SPARROW. ALL IS GOOD. CONTINUING MISSION.

Gwynn replied with a single period, and Anya returned to the table to find the vodka bottle further depleted and Oxana further involved. Tom's eyes bore the glisten of a man thoroughly enjoying his situation.

Anya slithered back into the booth, ran one hand through Tom's hair, and landed the other inside his thigh. The tightening she'd felt earlier at Oxana's touch returned, but with significantly increased intensity.

Not all sparrow's touches were the same.

Oxana slid her fingertips across the back of Anya's caressing hand, and she continued up the delicate flesh of her arm. Anya sighed a luxurious groan from deep within her stomach. As intended, Tom noticed both Oxana's caress and Anya's cooing. The teacher and student, with secrets shared, now had their prey striding confidently into their snare.

Oxana leaned in and moved her hand from Anya's arm to the curve of her dancer's neck, encouraging the assassin-turned-agent to also lean against their target. Anya followed her encouragement and let the skin of her cheek press against Tom's, with her lips only inches from Oxana's.

The teacher whispered, "Look at her. Isn't she beautiful?"

Tom answered with an animal's groan, perfectly defining the lustful hunger any man would feel in such a moment.

Oxana continued. "We will move someplace where all of us can enjoy this even more, yes?"

Anya breathed, "Yes, this is wonderful idea."

Oxana let her lips brush against Tom's as she stood, and Anya drew his earlobe between her lips, giving it a gentle bite.

She whispered, "If you feel uncomfortable at any time, pinch my thumb, and I will get you out. You understand, yes?"

He turned and pressed his lips to hers, and after a long kiss neither had to force, he said, "Oh, yes."

Oxana led them through a pair of doors separating the gentleman's club atmosphere into a world that shared only one similarity with the first: the body count remained solidly, with beautiful women outnumbering the men.

Before their eyes had adjusted to the darkness and flashing lights, the second woman Anya had previously met at the club entrance emerged from the throng of pulsating bodies and grabbed Tom's shirt with both hands. His dark hair stood in stark contrast to her pale skin, and tiny beads of sweat rolled across her flesh.

She pulled Tom against her. "You are beautiful man. You will dance with me."

It wasn't a question, and Tom didn't resist. Anya watched her date being led to the dance floor by yet another Russian seductress, leaving her alone with Oxana the sparrow.

They situated themselves in another booth well away from the dance floor, but the pounding rhythm from the massive speakers still made conversation difficult.

Above the thudding beat, Oxana spoke in her native Russian. "Is rare to encounter sister sparrow. I clearly have nothing to teach you."

Anya peered through the crowd, searching for Tom, and Oxana laid a finger beneath her chin and turned her face back into the darkness of the booth. "You are sparrow, yes?"

Anya swallowed hard as the memory of what she'd been forced to endure at State School 4 flooded her mind. The endless hours of sweaty seduction and copulation with smelly old Russian men, who'd likely been lifelong members of the Communist Party, hacked away at pieces of her diminishing soul with every lustful, disgusting touch, taste, smell, and horror.

She cast her gaze to the pit of darkness beneath the small table. "No, I was removed from school before becoming sparrow."

Oxana's eyes widened with interest. "How were you removed from school? I have never heard of this. Surely, you mean you failed."

Anya shook her head. "No, I mean I was removed because I killed man I was required to . . ." Anya paused as if reliving the shame of being removed from State School 4.

Oxana's smile turned cold. "I am envious. You must tell me why you killed him, and also how."

"It was terrible thing to do, but I remember having no other option. He tried to force me to do something I could not do. Something I would never do, even with romantic lover."

Oxana seemed to block out the noise of the club and focus singularly on Anya. "What were you forced to do?"

"I was not forced to do it. He only *tried* to force me to do this despicable thing. I said to him I will not do this, and I warned him many times, but he would not relent. I broke his neck and set his body on fire so he could taste hell before arriving."

Oxana narrowed her gaze. "And for this, they removed you from school?"

"Yes."

"Why were you not killed?"

The hook was set, and Anya smiled with greed in her eyes. "SVR does not kill person who is capable of such violence. They train her to become even better killer than seductress. I cannot be whore because I am murderess."

Oxana continued swallowing the baited hook. "You are now SVR officer?"

Anya allowed her eyes to once again fall to the floor. "No. I have terrible flaw inside me."

"What flaw?"

She feigned disgrace. "I detest what is called inside America, micro-management. If someone will tell to me mission, I will always accomplish it, but if I am told mission and exactly how to do it, I will always break rules. SVR cannot accept this."

Oxana smiled with the expression of a woman on the verge of striking gold, but the dark-haired dancer made her second appearance with Tom in tow. Sweat poured from his skin as if he'd just emerged from a sauna.

She said, "Sorry, girls, but I believe I have worn him out on dance floor. He probably needs water instead of vodka now."

Tom wiped his brow and poured himself onto the seat. "Yeah, water would be a great idea."

Oxana waved a hand, and a girl still in her teens appeared. "Bring for him water. Very very cold water."

The girl vanished and reappeared with a tall, clear glass of ice and what appeared to be water.

Tom took the glass from her hand and caught his breath. "I don't know the Russian word for *thank you*."

The girl said, "Is *spasibo*, and you are welcome."

She lingered for a moment too long, and Oxana waved her away. The girl vanished as Tom took his first tentative sip of the glass's contents.

Apparently satisfied it was, in fact, water, he downed the glass and sucked a chunk of ice into his mouth. "I've got to tell you. I love to dance, but I've never done it like that. You Eastern European chicks know how to get it done."

Anya took his arm. "Yes, we are sexiest women in all of world. How is it you do not know this already?"

He shrugged. "I guess I've lived a sheltered life, but I sure am glad I met you. And you're sure you're okay with all of this?"

"What do you mean?" Anya asked.

Tom motioned toward Oxana and then to his dance partner. "All of this. You know . . . them."

Anya kissed him again. "Of course I am okay with this. I would not bring you here if I were jealous woman. Maybe now you will dance also with me, yes?"

Tom squeezed his eyelids closed and shook his head. "Yeah, that sounds great, but I'm a little lightheaded right now. Give me a couple of minutes to cool down."

Oxana waved again, and the young girl who delivered the water reappeared. "You have our vodka?"

She produced the bottle and a fresh glass.

Oxana poured and slid the glass toward Tom. "Vodka will help. You probably need another drink. This will make you feel better."

Tom wrapped his fingers around the tumbler and slowly lifted it from the table. As the rim of the glass touched his lips, his arm lost the ability to support the weight of the drink. The dancer caught the glass and helped Oxana lay Tom onto the seat.

The young girl collected the glasses and bottle before disappearing into the darkness.

Anya stared down at the Air Force officer and took his hand. "Is he okay? What is happening?"

Oxana gave Anya a wink. "Do not worry. He is just fine. Is only small tranquilizer in water. He will have wonderful dreams mixed with wonderful memories. This is what every man loves—crossing tiny line between reality and fantasy."

As his body relaxed, Tom gave Anya's thumb a barely perceptible press, and she gave him a reassuring squeeze of his hand.

Oxana stood. "Take from him wallet, and come with me. Work is finished, and is now time for paying."

Anya did as she was told and said, "But what about him?"

Oxana said, "Do not worry. He will be fine, and you will return him to his hotel soon."

"How? He is two hundred pounds."

"You will see, but we must go now. Natasha will care for him."

Anya followed Oxana through a series of doors, down a corridor, and into an office with two small desks holding a collection of credit card machines.

"What is all of this?"

Oxana pushed the door closed behind them. "This is how we make more money than *prostitutki* without taking off clothes."

She fingered through a collection of credit cards and pulled Tom's from the stack.

Anya held up the wallet. "Why did I have to bring this if we already have credit card?"

"Take from inside wallet driving license and study signature. Then practice making signature. They taught you this skill, yes?"

Anya smiled and grabbed a pen. "*Da.*"

Sixteen thousand, four hundred dollars later, Anya had signed seven credit card slips. She examined her work and rolled the pen back onto the table. "Not bad, yes?"

Oxana thumbed through the receipts, lifted Anya's hand to her lips, and kissed the back of her wrist. "You are natural, but I think maybe there is more for you than only this."

Anya let the woman embrace her hand, making no offer to pull away. "You said I would be paid. Is this true?"

The woman pressed a six-digit code into a keypad on the door of a tall, thin safe. The door swung away, and she pulled a stack of bills from inside. She counted out the stack in front of Anya. "Four thousand, one hundred dollars."

Anya let her eyes linger on the cash as if she'd never seen that much money. She spread it across the table and played with the bills as if she'd just won the lottery. "All of this is for me for only one night?"

"It is all yours," Oxana said. "Usually, new girls are required to take only half and give to me half for teaching, but you do not need my teaching."

Anya cut the cash in approximate halves and slid one toward the woman. "I insist. Is not fair if I do not pay you. We are sparrows, and we must always care for each other."

Oxana pushed the money away. "I am sparrow. You are murderess. You will tell Volodya I would not take your money, yes?"

"Who is Volodya?"

Oxana looked around as if there were someone to overhear. "You will soon meet Volodya. He is very generous man, but also man who does not tolerate betrayal. I think you will like him."

"What about Tom? You said I would take him back to hotel. I still do not understand how I can do this."

"Follow me, and I will show you."

They tread back down the corridor and through a door Anya hadn't noticed, to find Tom sitting somewhat upright in a semi-reclining wheelchair.

"Is he okay?"

Oxana laid a hand on Anya's shoulder. "I told you he will be fine."

She withdrew a hypodermic needle from a cabinet near the back of the room and inserted it into Tom's thigh through his pants. She depressed the plunger and removed the needle from the syringe.

"More drugs?" Anya asked.

"Yes, but this time, it is only epinephrine. It will act against tranquilizer, but only enough to allow him to walk without falling down. He will remember nothing of this when he wakes up tomorrow inside his hotel room."

"But if he is waking from shot, he will remember me and maybe push me away."

Oxana pressed a small capsule into Anya's palm. "No man would push you away, my pet. You are irresistible. When you get him back to hotel room, you will dissolve this into water and give to him. He will drink and fall asleep in minutes."

"What am I to do after that?"

Oxana handed Anya the credit card receipts. "Wrinkle these, and put them separately into his pockets. Then go home or go to party and spend four thousand dollars. This is all. There is no more to do."

"But what if—"

"Do not worry about what if. There is no what if. We do this every night, and there is never trouble."

"Never?" Anya asked.

"Almost never."

13

SLEDUYUSHCHAYA ZHERTVA (NEXT VICTIM)

A cab—one Anya had not called—was waiting when she led USAF OSI Captain Tom Elsmore from the back door of Club Gedo.

An enormous man with arms the size of telephone poles and the shiniest head she'd ever seen shoved a fistful of bills through the driver's window and Tom onto the back seat. He caught Anya's arm as she stepped toward the open door. "You know what do to, yes?"

His heavily accented English was challenging to understand, so she answered in Russian. "*Da.*"

Obviously relieved, the giant spoke in the only language he truly knew. "I have not seen you before. What is your name?"

Anya looked down at the bear paw encircling her bicep and back up into the face of the man.

He squeezed. "I asked for your name."

She caught his thumb and twisted the wrist in one swift motion, sending the enormous man to his knees. She looked down into his agony-filled eyes. "My name is Do Not Ever Touch Me Again, and if you do, I will tear off your arm and beat you to death with it."

She cast his hand away and slid onto the seat beside her date. The bruiser with the broken thumb kicked the door closed, and the driver hurried from the alley.

"Where are we going?"

Without looking up, Anya said, "Caesars Palace, but take long way. My boyfriend needs time to feel better."

The cabbie removed his right earbud and eyed her in the mirror. "Boyfriend? That's a new one. The man paid me for a direct fare, Natasha. If you want anything other than that, it's going to cost you."

Anya glared into the mirror. "Did you see what I did to the man who paid you? If we arrive at hotel in less than twenty minutes, you will regret becoming taxi driver."

The man let out a huff, shoved the earbud back in place, and turned toward the Strip.

Anya leaned down, placing her face only inches from Tom's. "Are you okay?"

He nodded.

"Okay. We will be at hotel in twenty minutes. Your breathing is good, yes?"

Again, he only nodded, and she pulled out her phone. "Gwynn, is Anya. We are inside taxi, and I made time for you to arrive before us. You must wait inside doors of side entrance number three, but go into hotel at main entrance. Someone will be watching when I take Tom from cab to inside hotel, so do not let them see you. We will need probably wheelchair."

Tom pawed at her arm. "No, no wheelchair. I can walk."

She hung up and slid the phone back into her purse. After pounding on the divider several times, she finally managed to get the cabbie to remove his earbud again.

"What do you want now, lady?"

"You will take us to side entrance number three. You know where this is, yes?"

"Yeah, lady. I know where everything is in this town."

Twenty minutes later, the driver pulled to a stop outside the least conspicuous entrance to the massive hotel and casino, and Anya helped Tom to his feet.

She turned back to the cabbie and slid a folded bill through the tiny slit at the top of the window. "Thank you for not making me hurt you."

Tom leaned against Anya as she keyed her way through the door and discovered Johnny Mac and Gwynn. Johnny caught Tom's arm and hefted it across his shoulder, shifting the weight from Anya to him.

Gwynn stepped into an alcove, returning seconds later with a black wheelchair. Despite Tom's protest, Johnny deposited him onto the chair and headed for the elevator.

Once inside the suite, Anya started an IV in Tom's left arm and took a knee at his side. "How are you feeling?"

"I'm okay. Just groggy. What did they give me?"

"It was a tranquilizer of some kind," Johnny said. "And it sucks. You're going to hate the headache tomorrow."

"I already hate it," Tom mumbled.

Anya gave the IV bag a squeeze. "You will feel better soon."

Tom rubbed his eyes. "I need to go to the bathroom."

Anya looked up at Gwynn. "Take him to bathroom. I must talk with Johnny Mac."

Gwynn obeyed, and Anya turned to Johnny. "How much did you remember after having drugs at club?"

"Nothing," he said. "It slowly came back to me the next afternoon, but the night was a black cloud until then."

"Does Ray know we are safe?"

Johnny nodded. "Yeah. Gwynn checked in right after you called. He'll be on a plane tomorrow morning."

"A plane? Where is he going?"

"He's coming out here. Surely you didn't think he was going to sit in DC while we had all the fun, did you?"

"He does not like being old."

Johnny shook his head. "What?"

Anya straightened a pillow on the sofa. "Agent White, he does not like being old. He misses working in field like us."

"I don't think that's a function of age as much as rank. He's not an operator anymore. He's an SSA."

"Yes, this is true. But he was very good field agent like you when he was twentysomething."

Johnny cocked his head. "Did you just give me a compliment?"

"No, I said only truth. You are very good. You are brave, strong, resourceful, and you know basics of fighting in street. You will be someday excellent leader like Agent White."

"Thank you, Anya. That means a lot to me. Seriously, thank you."

"I miss also my youth."

Johnny recoiled. "What do you mean? You're barely older than me."

"Perhaps I mean just like Agent White. I sometimes miss doing things I was trained to do and things I am very good at."

"You were an assassin."

Anya let her mind drift back into a time she often tried to forget. "I was not only assassin. I have many skills. I miss, sometimes, being alone. In America, everyone is team. This is not always good. Sometimes, carrying only knife into dark night is better than carrying team."

"You don't like working with us?"

She frowned. "This is not what I mean. We are good team. Gwynn is very good and getting better. I am afraid I will put her inside situation that will get her killed. I do not wish to do this."

"It's the nature of what we do, Anya. We can't do our jobs and guarantee everyone's safety. We all know and accept the risks."

"Yes, I know this, but she is my friend, and I would never forget her if she is dead."

Johnny inspected a fingernail. "It's dangerous to get that close to your partner, you know."

Anya sighed. "This is why we do not have partner in SVR."

"Hey!" Tom yelled. "I could use a little help in here."

Anya was through the bathroom door in an instant to see Tom holding himself over the toilet with blood streaming from his arm where the IV had been. His convulsive retching sounded like the cries of a dying animal.

Gwynn said, "This isn't good."

Anya knelt beside him. "You will be okay. Is only reaction to drugs. I will make sure you do not die."

He convulsed again and moaned. "Maybe dying would be better."

"Is good that you are vomiting."

The next hour became an exercise in babysitting a full-grown man. Anya continued to force fluids, and Tom continued to expel them at every opportunity.

Gwynn grimaced. "I think he needs a doctor."

Anya wiped his mouth with a wet washcloth. "No. He needs only reason to feel better, and I have this reason."

Tom took the washcloth from Anya's hand and pressed the cool cloth against his forehead. "What's your reason?"

"Tomorrow, you will be rewarded with fighting big man with no hair inside club."

"Oh, yeah," Tom groaned. "That sounds like a real day at the carnival."

"You are big, strong man. You like to fight. I can see this in your eyes. Not right now, but before you were sick. You are street fighter. I feel this about you."

"Just look at me," Tom said. "I'm sure I look real imposing right now."

"You will be better soon. Your body is protecting itself from poison. This is what body is supposed to do. I do not think you need doctor. Only fluid and time, yes?"

"No doctor, but please keep hanging IV bags."

The night continued until Captain Tom Elsmore retained more fluid than he ejected, and miraculously, he even slept for a restless two-hour period.

Anya sat beside him and monitored the intake of fluids, replacing each bag just before the previous one was depleted. When their stash reached its limit, Johnny Mac commandeered extra bags from the in-house paramedics.

As the morning sun climbed the eastern sky, raising Sin City's temperature back toward three digits, Anya yawned and stretched herself awake on the sofa. "Where is Tom?"

Gwynn said, "He's in the bathroom."

Anya pushed from the sofa, but Gwynn said, "Don't worry. He's just showering. But I'm sure he wouldn't mind if you watched."

"Stop it. I am only worried because he is important to mission."

Gwynn said, "I think his part is done, and from the looks of things, he's paid his dues."

"Is only beginning. Today is real mission."

Gwynn handed her a cup of hot tea. "Real mission? What are you talking about?"

Anya sipped the steaming tea. "Thank you. Real mission is Volodya Kalashnikov, and I need Tom for this. I must kill him."

"Kill Kalashnikov?"

"No, I must kill Tom, and I think we need girlfriend of Johnny Mac for this."

Gwynn shook her head. "Slow down. You're killing me here. I'm not tracking at all."

"Is simple," Anya said. "We must make Volodya Kalashnikov believe we killed Tom. For this, he will ask us to kill more people for him. You are lawyer gun, so you understand what this means."

For the first time that day, Special Agent Gwynn Davis smiled. "Agent White is already in love with you, but for this plan, he'll fall down and kiss your feet. You're a genius. When did you come up with this?"

Anya rolled her eyes. "He is not in love with me. He only likes having tea with me. This is all."

Gwynn sighed. "Remember when I called you a genius? Well, I'm re-thinking that one. If you can't see that Agent White is head over heels for you, you're not paying attention."

Tom emerged from the bathroom in boxer shorts and nothing else.

Gwynn's eyes turned to saucers. "Wow!"

Anya giggled. "You do know you said that out loud, yes?"

"Uh, yeah, and I'm surprised you didn't say it, too. Look at him. He's like a statue or something."

Tom ignored the gibberish. "I'm sorry, but I didn't bring any clothes, and mine from last night are, well . . . not in very good shape."

Gwynn hopped to her feet. "Don't worry. I'll go downstairs and find something that'll fit you. They've got some great shops down there, but I'll have to get a closer look at you to make sure I get the right size."

"Yeah, sure. That'd be great. I'm a thirty-six waist and an XL shirt. Just some shorts and a T-shirt would be great. I just need something to get back to the base. I guess you're finished with me, huh?"

Gwynn spun a finger in the air. "Give me a little turn, would you?"

He held up his hands and slowly spun.

Gwynn bit her lip. "My god, you know you're like, perfect, right?"

"I don't get out much, so I spend a lot of time in the gym. I'm far from perfect, though. Every year gets a little harder."

Gwynn said, "From where I'm standing, it's working for you, Captain Tom. I'll be back in a few minutes with your clothes, but you don't have to be in a big hurry to put them on, okay?"

Anya gave Tom a glance. "There is difference in body from gym and body from working, but friend Gwynn is correct. You are beautiful man."

He waved a dismissive hand. "Stop it. I'm going to find a place to hide and kill some time now."

Gwynn giggled and pointed down the hall. "My room is back there. I think that would be a great place for you to wait until I get back. Oh, I almost forgot. Don't look Anya directly in the eyes. She's some sort of witch, and I'll never have a chance if you fall under her evil spell."

Anya snapped her fingers. "I am not witch, so get robe from closet and sit with me. We must talk."

Gwynn snapped, "Hey! Remember what I said, muscle boy. Don't look into her eyes. Got it?" He gave her a wink, and she turned to Anya. "Hands off!"

Tom pulled the robe across his shoulders and perched on the chair across from Anya. "What do we need to talk about? Did I screw something up?"

"No, you did everything perfectly, but I have plan that involves you. And now is time for me to do exactly what I do best."

"What's that?" Tom asked.

"I gut men like pigs. Filthy, disgusting pigs. And I play in their blood."

Tom shuddered. "That's slightly terrifying."

"This is not worst part," she said. "You are next victim."

14

VREMYA UBIVAT'
(TIME TO KILL)

Special Agent Gwynn Davis came through the door with three shopping bags and a drink carrier. "I brought coffee!"

Anya examined the cardboard contraption holding four steaming cups. "I do not drink coffee. You know this."

"That's why I brought tea for you."

"This is why you are best friend to me. Thank you."

Gwynn said, "Give me a second, and I'll let you know if you're still my bestie." She strolled across the room doing her best Marilyn Monroe walk, and Captain Tom's head turned in perfect unison with her every stride. She ignored Tom and handed Anya her tea. "Yep, you're still my girl."

Johnny Mac snatched a cup, and Gwynn slid one into Tom's hand, allowing her fingers to linger just a moment longer than necessary.

He cleared his throat. "Uh, thanks for the coffee, but did you get me some clothes?"

Instead of answering, she shook the bags and curled a finger. "Come with me."

Gwynn and Tom disappeared into her room, and Johnny Mac threw up his hands. "What's that all about? Dude takes off his shirt, and she turns into a lovestruck teenager."

Anya sipped her tea. "Do not be jealous, Johnny. You are also handsome man, but Gwynn has probably never seen you with shirt off, yes?"

He shrugged. "I mean, I do hit the gym, and I—"

"You do not have to tell me this. I see this from cut of suit. You are very fit."

"That's right, I am. But I don't go around shucking off my clothes."

Anya leaned close to Johnny. "Do you have crush on friend Gwynn?"

He recoiled. "No. I mean, she's . . . well, you know. She's all right, but I don't . . . She's my partner."

Anya slid toward him. "Do you have crush on me?"

Nervous laughter fell from his mouth. "Come on, Anya. Everybody has a crush on you, but we all know there's only one man on Earth for you, and the rest of us can't compete."

Anya cocked her head. "You are talking about Chase?"

Johnny grimaced. "What? No. Everybody knows you've got a thing for Agent White."

"This is not true. Does he think this also?"

"Who? Agent White? Sure. He's been around, and if you weren't working for him, he'd be all over you."

Anya shuddered. "This is not true. He only likes having tea with me. This is all. Besides, this is silly talk. We have serious thing to discuss."

"Whatever you say. What do we need to discuss?"

Anya spent the next ten minutes laying out her plan, and Johnny asked all the right questions.

When Captain Tom came back into the room, he was wearing designer jeans, a well-starched button-down, and loafers.

Anya said, "I do not think this is shorts and T-shirt you ordered."

He laughed. "No, Gwynn said I'd look better in this."

"Gwynn is right. You look very nice, but I need you to look dangerous."

He scowled. "Dangerous? What are you talking about?"

"Johnny will tell to you plan, and I will have shower. Maybe I will come from bathroom with only boxer shorts. This is good idea, yes?"

Tom turned to Johnny as if begging for help, and the special agent rose to the occasion. "Nobody wants to see you in boxers, Anya."

She stroked his face with the back of her curled fingers. "Okay, I will come out with no boxers. Think about this while I am inside bathroom, and tell to Tom my plan."

* * *

Darkness fell over the city, but no one seemed to notice. Between the streetlights and well-lit casino entrances, the Vegas Strip still looked like high noon.

Anya slipped through the back door of Club Gedo and slid her arm into Oxana's.

"Oh, hello again," Oxana said. "You did well last night. Do you have next man to bring into club tonight?"

Anya said, "Thank you. I enjoyed last night. You are good partner."

Oxana gave her a smile. "You are not so bad, either. We have similar background, so working together comes easily."

"Yes, this is true, but I have something to tell you about man I was with last night."

Oxana motioned for the bartender. "We need vodka. Good vodka."

Two short glasses materialized on the bar, and Oxana slid one toward Anya. "What about man from last night?"

Anya lifted the glass and poured the vodka down her throat. "He is very angry, and I think he is coming here. I tried to tell him this is terrible plan, but he did not listen. He is—"

Before she could finish her sentence, Captain Tom Elsmore kicked his way through the front door. A bouncer stepped in front of him, but the Air Force OSI officer sent him melting to the floor with a crushing blow to his throat. Two more thugs stepped up, but he swept the first man's feet, sending him to the ground and then driving a thundering jab to the second man's nose, showering blood in every direction.

He stepped in front of Oxana and stuck a finger in her face. "You! You are going to put me face-to-face with the owner, right now, or you and I are going to have a serious problem."

Oxana showed no sign of fear. "You cannot come into club and assault our employees. You will leave now, and I will not call police, but if you do not go, I will be forced to call nine-one-one."

"Call whoever you want, lady, but you'd better have the owner standing right here in thirty seconds, or I'm going to tear this place apart until I believe I've gotten my money's worth."

Oxana lowered her chin. "You do not frighten me. You are confused bully. I have never seen you before. Go away, now, and nothing will come of this."

Just as they'd practiced back in the hotel suite at Caesars Palace, Tom lunged for Oxana, but Anya reacted with blinding speed. She swept Tom's hands away from Oxana's throat and landed a pulled punch to his solar plexus. He feigned the pain a real punch would've delivered and staggered backward, but Anya's onslaught had barely begun.

Tom threw a practiced punch toward Anya, but she sidestepped the assault and grasped his wrist. Less than a second later, she had his arm twisted behind his back and his face pressed tightly against the floor.

He growled. "I'm going to kill you, you crazy—"

Anya grabbed his hair and shoved his forehead into the floor. "Do not call me this name you were going to say. I do not like this word."

He growled and squirmed like a cornered animal, but the Russian copied his every move as if the episode were a choreographed performance. Several knee-strikes to the precise spot where Tom's protective cup rested looked horrifying to every man watching the scene, and Tom played his part to perfection.

The theatrical blood capsules that had been tucked neatly between Tom's cheek and gums burst between his teeth as Anya made a show of pounding his head against the floor. The horrific sounds of the collision between skull and tile came from the palm of her free hand slapping the floor while his head landed harmlessly against the back of his hand pressed beneath his head.

The ruse worked exactly as Anya had planned as everyone in the club watched the blood pour from Tom's mouth. She forced him to his feet and frog-marched him through the club and into the alley, where the performance continued until she finally shoved her victim into the back seat of a waiting SUV. Without looking back, she climbed behind the wheel and left the alley as if out for a leisurely afternoon drive.

Inside the SUV, Tom shook off the stars encircling his head and sat up. "If that's your way of taking it easy, I never want you to be mad at me. Where did you learn to fight like that?"

She gave him a look in the mirror. "I was well trained by men of exceptional cruelty. You are not hurt, yes?"

He wiped what he hoped was all fake blood from his face. "Not hurt, yes. That's one way to put it. I'm okay, but let's never do that again. Deal?"

"Yes, this is deal. Your part of all of this will be finished soon. We have now only to meet rest of team inside desert because is now time to kill you."

He pulled a seatbelt across his shoulder. "If you pretend to kill me the same way you pretend to fight me, I'm not looking forward to this at all."

Anya chuckled. "Is lucky for you, I will not be involved in killing except to make sure your body looks like I was responsible for wounds."

As Tom imagined the gruesome scene ahead of him, he groaned. "Does it ever bother you?"

Anya met his eyes again in the rectangular mirror. "I would like to say I do not know what you are talking about, but this is not true. I am not psychologist, but I know from experience people can be made to believe any lie if it is given to them time after time. Taking life from person is terrible thing, but sometimes necessary. I was once only assassin. I did not think or feel. I only did what I was ordered to do and nothing more."

"Once? But no more? What changed?"

Anya checked the road as they left the booming city into the barren, seemingly endless expanse of desert. "Person who was very special to me showed to me kindness and freedom. These are things I never knew in Russia."

"Is that how you came to work for the DOJ?"

Anya closed her eyes for a moment as the rough asphalt passed beneath the SUV. "No, I was forced to work for government after I did something terrible because I believed it was right thing. That has now changed. I work with Gwynn and Johnny Mac because I know is right thing to do."

"You're a fascinating—and terrifying—woman, Anya. I think we could use a thousand more just like you."

"This is kind of you to say. Thank you, but one thousand like me would be too much for world to bear."

Tom laughed. "You're probably right about that. Maybe when this is all over, we could get a drink and spend some time not killing each other."

Anya smiled. "I would like this, but is wrong for me to do."

"Why is it wrong? We don't work together, so there's no rule about seeing someone who works for another government agency."

She shook her head. "No, is not written-down rule. It is rule of friendship. Friend Gwynn is very fond of you, and it would hurt her if I said yes to you. I cannot hurt her, but I am flattered by offer. *Spasibo*."

"I think that's the best shoot-down I've ever experienced. We should all be so lucky to have a friend like you. So, really? Gwynn?"

Anya laughed. "Yes, silly boy. Is not obvious? She turns to little schoolgirl when you are near. Tell to her same offer, and she will be very happy."

"Maybe I'll do that."

"No maybe. Just do. Besides, I would be terrible in relationship. Is best for me to be alone. Is what is best for everyone."

Tom studied her face. "I'd like to hear that story sometime."

"Is no story," she said. "Is only truth. But this does not matter now. There they are. It is now time to kill."

15

SVET, KAMERA, MOTOR
(LIGHTS, CAMERA, ACTION)

Tom and Anya stepped from the SUV and approached the collection of vehicles, lights, and people.

The Russian said, "This looks like set for filming movie."

Gwynn stepped in front of Tom and gently touched his face. "Ouch! Are you okay?"

"I'm fine. It's all make-believe. Well, most of it, anyway. Your girlfriend is quite the brawler."

Gwynn grinned. "Tell me about it. She's been teaching me to fight, and I'm a good student, but I'll never be as good as her."

He cocked his head. "I have to disagree with that statement. I think you're already better than her—at least when it comes to getting my attention. Maybe when we're all done here, you and I could—"

"Hey, you two! Get over here. We've got work to do, and I want to wrap it up before we attract any unwanted attention." Dr. Celeste Mankiller was undeniably in charge of the night's operation.

Tom turned. "We'll talk more later, okay?"

Gwynn took his arm. "There's no reason to talk later. The answer is yes, I'd love to."

"But I didn't even tell you what I had in mind."

She giggled. "It doesn't matter. I'm in."

Celeste clapped her hands. "Chop chop! Let's get moving here. You, big guy, get in the hole on your side."

Tom studied the set and pointed toward the shallow grave. "Uh, that looks like some kind of mafia nightmare. I'm not sure I have the stomach to get in that thing."

Anya said, "I can put you inside hole, but blood will be real this time."

"On second thought, I believe I'll do it on my own."

He crawled into the hole, rolled onto his side, and Celeste stepped into the pit with one boot on either side of the OSI officer.

She said, "I'm going to sit on your hip. Is that okay?"

"Do I have a choice?"

"Sure. I can have Anya kill you for real if that would make you feel better."

He patted his hip. "Consider this your throne."

He barely felt her petite frame as she planted herself as if riding a horse. She made several measurements. "Close your eyes, and hold your breath."

He obeyed, and she spray-painted several locations on the sand around his body. Then she climbed from the hole. "You can open your eyes and breathe, but don't move. I need to set up the shot."

She repositioned two sets of lights and a camera mounted on a rugged tripod. "Okay, close your eyes again. I'm going to get a few baseline shots." She snapped several shots and made minor adjustments to the set. "I think we're ready for the action. You can come out of the hole."

Tom climbed to his feet and dusted off the clothes Gwynn had dressed him in several hours earlier.

Celeste withdrew a pair of knives from sheaths and presented them to Anya. "These are called marking blades. As you can see, the cutting edges are dull, flat, and completely harmless."

Anya took the props from her hands and held them up to the light. "In my hands, these are not harmless."

Celeste huffed. "Okay, I misspoke. I'm sure you could kill all of us with a spoon, but my point is this. These blades aren't going to slice Captain Elsmore."

"This is much better statement. I will not hurt Tom with your marking blades, and I am very familiar with how they work. I have trained with them for many hours."

Celeste checked her watch. "I think we've probably got ten to fifteen minutes before somebody sees our lights and comes to check us out. We don't need that, so let's get this done." Everyone took a step toward her, and she continued. "I want Captain Elsmore—"

He interrupted her. "It's Tom. Just Tom."

"Okay, Tom it is. I want Tom on the other side of the hole in a defensive fighting posture."

He leapt across the grave and took the stance she directed.

Celeste inspected his position. "Good. Now, I want Anya right here."

The Russian moved into position with the marking blades at the ready.

"Perfect. Now, I want you to kill him, but make it nasty. I don't want a clean crime scene."

Anya smiled broadly. "I can definitely do that for you." She turned to Tom. "Are you ready?" He nodded, and she said, "I need you to resist and fight as if you were afraid for your life. This is only way it will appear real."

"Just try not to really kill me, okay?"

Without an answer, Anya lunged forward, crossed her arms, and placed a blade on each of Tom's collarbones. She drew the blades downward in powerful arcs as if slicing open his chest. He reacted by extending both hands forcefully to shove her away from him. Anticipating his movement, Anya drew each of the blades across his forearms and stepped into him. When their motion halted, one of the blades was pressed tightly against the inside of his right thigh, just above the femoral artery, and the other rested solidly against the side of his neck at his jugular.

"Well, that didn't take long," Celeste said. "Back up, and let's have a look at him." She shone a blacklight against his skin and clothing. The areas where Anya's marking blades had slid lit up like neon signs.

"This is great," she said. "But I've got some bad news for Tom."

Celeste paused and stared up at him for a long moment.

"What?" he asked. "What are you looking at?"

She said, "It's too bad you're just a captain and not a major because it would be really cool if you called me ground control, and I could call you Major Tom."

"Thanks a lot. Now I'm not going to be able to get that song out of my head."

Anya frowned. "I do not understand any of this. What is happening?"

"Never mind," they said in unison.

Celeste shook her head. "Sorry, I got sidetracked, but the next step is going to hurt. I need the two of you back in place where you stopped a moment ago."

Tom returned to his stance, and Anya pressed the blades back into their targets.

Celeste studied the positions and made small changes in each of their postures. "Now, I want you to imagine you've killed him with the slices to the neck and leg. I want you to force his body into the grave from that position."

Tom took a breath and strengthened his position, but Celeste said, "No. I need you to relax. All of your blood is pouring from your body at both ends. You're not going to have the strength to resist any longer. Just relax and let Anya throw you. Try not to break your fall. Just let it happen naturally, and be as limp as possible."

He nodded and let his shoulders sag. Just as the tension left the long, lean muscles of his legs, Anya thrust herself into him, lifting him from his feet. An instant later, he was on his side with his breath exploding from his lungs.

Celeste yelled, "Perfect! Don't move!"

A thousand camera clicks later, the shoot was over, and Dr. Mankiller's work had only just begun.

With Celeste's gear loaded back into the vehicles, Tom asked, "Are you sure you're finished with me for the night?"

Celeste said, "Unless we need to reshoot something—which is highly doubtful—we've abused you all we can. I'm sure the DOJ would like to offer you a free cup of coffee or something of similar value for your hard work."

"Coffee actually sounds pretty good right now. It's been a real pleasure working with all of you. Maybe we can do it again sometime."

Anya glanced between Tom and Gwynn. "I have idea. I will ride back to hotel with Celeste and Johnny Mac. I think Gwynn should take Tom back to Air Force base."

Gwynn grinned. "That sounds like a great idea to me."

* * *

Back at Caesars Palace, Celeste set up her computer and buried herself in graphic arts wizardry. Johnny Mac lingered over her shoulder, mesmerized by every keystroke and sweep of the mouse, while Anya watched the teapot with equal anticipation.

Anya knew Johnny was obviously doing everything in his power to get closer to Celeste, and the brilliant tech seemed to be loving every ounce of the attention. The thought of what Gwynn and Tom might be doing danced in her head as the kettle began to whistle its shrill cry. When she'd swallowed the last drop of tea from her mug, she pulled on her favorite pair of sweatpants and an old University of Georgia baseball jersey with the number twenty-one emblazoned across the back.

* * *

After Celeste had spent twenty hours in front of her computer, she threw up her hands like a victorious prize fighter. "I've done it!"

Anya crossed the room and replaced Johnny Mac, peering across her shoulder. "Oh, this is wonderful work. I have never seen anything like this."

Celeste stretched, yawned, and leaned back in her chair. "I knew I could do it, but I never thought it would take so long. Does it look convincing?"

"On screen, it is perfect, but I must see printed picture."

Celeste opened a zippered pouch at her feet and pulled out three squares of thick, plastic-like material. "Just wait. You're going to be amazed."

She fed the material into a device that looked like a cross between a shredder and an ancient printer. Ninety seconds later, the material landed in the collection tray at the front of the mysterious box. Celeste lifted each one and examined it closely before passing them to the Russian. "I hate to brag, but I designed and built that printer specifically for jobs like this, and I think it's pretty cool."

Anya lifted the three squares from Celeste's hand and scrutinized each one. "Is okay to brag when it is truth. They are perfect, and I would be fooled if I did not know truth. I cannot wait for our prey to take bait."

16

Kryuk, Leska, i Gruzilo
(Hook, Line, and Sinker)

Dr. Celeste Mankiller pawed at her eyes. "I can't believe I worked on that for almost twenty-four hours. I'm exhausted."

Anya, still fascinated by the result of Celeste's labor, motioned down the hall. "You have earned day off, and you must sleep. Is now up to Gwynn and me to make next step."

"Do you really think this crazy plan is going to work?"

"Yes. If I did not believe it would work, I would not ask so much of you and Tom."

"In that case, I'm going to bed, and I'll be standing by for phase three."

* * *

Gwynn and Anya pulled into a parking lot half a block from Club Gedo and climbed from the Porsche.

"Is now showtime, as you say in America."

"I think you do that on purpose," Gwynn said.

"Do what?"

"Pretend like your English is still weak. You're not fooling me, though."

Anya glanced over each shoulder, and without any hint of an accent, said, "This has to be our little secret."

"Why?"

Anya frowned. "I do not understand question. Are you asking why it must be secret or why I speak with accent?"

"Both."

"Is very simple. If I speak with Russian accent, Americans make assumption I am not as smart and sophisticated as they are. This gives to me wonderful advantage. I think English word is *underestimated*."

"You're more amazing every day," Gwynn said. "Now, let's see you put some of those language skills to work."

"This reminds me. You must say nothing inside club. You will stand behind me and never change expression, no matter what is said. You can do this, yes?"

"Yeah, I've got it. I'll just stand behind you and look tough."

"No! Do not do this. You are to stand behind me and look bored. There is reason for this, and you will understand soon."

"Whatever you say, Master Yoda."

"Who?"

Gwynn shook her head. "Please tell me you've seen Star Wars."

"I do not know of this war."

Gwynn grunted. "No, it's a movie series with Luke Skywalker and Princess Leia, and they're brother and sister. That gets weird, but it's great. Yoda is the little green dude with pointy ears, and he's a Jedi master." She paused, apparently waiting for Anya to show some sign of remembering the movies, but she still stood with a look of complete befuddlement. Gwynn threw up her hands. "Really? Nothing? No memory at all?"

"I am sorry. I do not watch television or go to movies."

"When all of this is over, we're having an all-girl Star Wars marathon at my place. We'll do pedicures and drink champagne and just veg out. It'll be great."

"This does not sound like fun for me, and I do not know how to veg out, but I will like spending time with you when we are not on mission."

Gwynn smiled. "That's what it's about. So, is it time to go to work?"

"It is."

The valet retrieved the Porsche, and the two most beautiful—and dangerous—women in Vegas drove away from Caesars Palace with the top down and their hair billowing after them.

"Driving is terrible because of traffic, but I do not want to be trapped at club if plan goes badly."

Gwynn tried to tame her hair, but it kept getting wilder with every passing minute. "I understand. What do you really think is going to happen tonight?"

"Only two things are possible. Volodya Kalashnikov will either hire us or try to kill us. There is no other option."

"That's comforting."

"We are not so easy to kill. We will put up great fight if this happens, but there will be at least four men and probably more. I think is probably better if we do not kill Volodya, but other men are not important."

Inside Club Gedo, Gwynn leaned into Anya and whispered, "This place doesn't have the same appeal it had before."

"This is reasonable. Inside our minds, this place is now arena for killing, and we are gladiators."

"I think I like that."

Anya sighed. "I think you do not know what gladiator is. They were slaves who were forced to fight until death. This is terrible life."

"Okay, maybe I don't like the thought of being a gladiator as much as I did, but . . ."

Before she could finish, Oxana came through a darkened door and immediately locked eyes with Anya. Without a word, she motioned for her to follow and turned for another door.

Anya whispered, "Is maybe doorway to coliseum where lions and chariots await."

Gwynn said, "I'm not afraid of lions. I killed one with a shard of broken glass in Miami while you were having a nap."

Anya grinned. "Yes, you did. I will never forget this. It was day I knew we would be comrades forever."

The pair followed Oxana through the door, down a short corridor, and into a grungy, poorly lit office. Anya pressed the door closed behind them and scanned the room.

Oxana leaned against a barstool. "What did you do, and who is she?"

Gwynn took a step back and tried to appear uninterested as Anya said, "I solved problem for you."

"You may *think* you solved problem, but you only made everything worse."

Anya laid the pictures into Oxana's palm, and she stared down at them in disbelief.

"You killed him?"

"Of course. This is what *we* do."

Oxana looked up, peered between Anya and Gwynn, and raised an eyebrow. "We?" In angry Russian, she growled, "You murdered a man whose last credit card transactions tie him to this club. You just delivered us into hands of police."

Anya leaned in. "You are not listening. I said I solved problem for you, and this is exactly what I have done. Search for credit card transactions. You will find nothing. I have person"—she paused and glanced at Gwynn —"who can make things disappear. There is no connection to club. I found man to bring to club. This means he is my responsibility. No one will ever find body in desert, and no one will ever know this man was inside club."

Oxana held up a finger and pulled a cell phone from her pocket. She pressed the speaker button and spoke in Russian to the woman who answered. "Search for credit card records from two nights ago, and find ones credited to new girl, Anya."

She listened as the woman typed furiously. Moments later, the woman said, "There are no records credited to her, but I processed them myself. I have electronic backup of transactions. Let me look."

Oxana waited, and Anya stood, patiently knowing there would be no record of the transactions.

Finally, the disembodied voice said, "They're gone as if they were never here. I don't understand. How is this possible?"

Oxana said, "Do not worry about this, and do not mention it to anyone, especially Volodya. Do you understand?"

"Are you sure that's a good idea? He needs to know what's going on in his club."

Oxana said, "I told you not to worry about it. I will handle it, and he will know, but not until I tell him. If I find out you have told anyone, you will be on airplane to Moscow, immediately. You understand, yes?"

She groaned, "*Da, ya ponimayu.*"

Oxana disconnected and turned to Anya. "You are not sparrow."

Through her stone-faced stare, Anya said, "I am not *only* sparrow, but also many other things."

"You are still SVR or FSB, aren't you?"

Anya hardened her expression. "I am neither of those and will never be again. I am American now, with passport and driving license. But this does not mean I no longer have my skills and tradecraft."

"You are *ubiytsa*."

Anya's tone came from deep inside her chest. "Just like sparrow, assassin is only one of the things I am."

Oxana scooped her phone from the table and slid it into a pocket. "Wait here. I will be back." She left the room and pulled the door closed behind her.

Anya and Gwynn immediately moved to the wall beside the only door into the room, and the Russian whispered, "If she comes back with men, I will take first, and you will take second."

"What if there's more than two of them?"

"You will kick door closed after second man comes into room. That will make time for us to deal with first two and prepare for more. But do not step in front of door."

Gwynn rolled her eyes. "I'm not that stupid, comrade."

As the sound of multiple footsteps approached, Anya whispered, "Get ready."

The knob turned, and the door swung inward ninety degrees. Anya waited for the first man to take his third step inside the room, then she launched from her position, sweeping his legs and sending him melting to the floor. Taking full advantage of the element of surprise, she pinned the man's face to the floor with a powerful elbow and never looked up.

Gwynn caught the second man's collar and dragged him into the room. The instant he was fully inside the office, she gave a powerful side kick to the door, slamming it to its jamb. She continued the arc, dragging the man around her body until he collided with the wall she'd been waiting at only seconds before. The blow sent stars dancing around the man's head, but the elbow strike to the base of his skull rendered him harmless and unconscious on the floor. Anya delivered a similar blow to her victim just as the door swung inward again.

"What are you doing? Stop!"

Gwynn and Anya looked up to see a bewildered Oxana staring in disbelief at the two crumpled men. "Why would you do this?"

Anya pushed a strand of hair behind her ear. "You left alone and returned with these men. There was no time for questions. We had to defend ourselves."

"Defend yourselves? Against what? These men are no threat to you. They are here to escort you to meet owner of club."

Anya looked down at the unconscious men and shrugged. "You should tell us these things before sending two big men into dark room. They will be okay, but will have bad headache. You have smelling salts?"

Oxana shuddered. "No, I do not have smelling salts. I have only cold water. This will work, yes?"

Anya said, "We should try."

Oxana produced two bottles of water from a recessed refrigerator in the corner of the office. Seconds after the water collided with their faces, the two men were back in the land of the living and shaking off the attack.

Gwynn's victim squeezed his head between his palms. "What was that?"

Staying in character, Gwynn ignored the question, but Anya did not. "That was limited reaction to perceived threat."

"Limited?" the man bellowed in heavily accented English. "I do not wish to see unlimited reaction."

Anya glared down at him. "From this, you would not wake up." She examined the man as he climbed to his feet and stood on trembling knees. "We do not need you to escort us to meet owner of club. Tell to me where he is, and give to me name. This is all we need."

Oxana shook her head. "This is how it is done. No one sees Mr. Kalashnikov unless they are escorted."

Anya said, "I know he has dinner at Red Square Restaurant inside Mandalay Bay. If you insist on sending big strong men who just lost fight with two women, we will meet you there. And, of course, we will tell Mr. Kalashnikov we did not feel safe riding with such weak men."

The two men turned to Oxana, and she ushered them out of the room with a tilt of her head. She turned to Anya. "We do not know who you are, but we will know soon. Mr. Kalashnikov is expecting you, but if you do inside restaurant what you did here, you will sleep with man you buried inside desert. You understand this, yes?"

Anya gave a nod to Gwynn and said, "We understand you will try, but we are not soft targets like these two 'men.'"

Gwynn led the way out of the club as Anya followed, constantly checking behind them. As they pulled from the alley in the Porsche, Gwynn let out an impressive scream. "That was amazing! Do we get to do that again at Red Square? Oh my gosh, I'm so pumped!"

Anya laid a hand on her forearm. "Calm down. I know is exciting, but you must be calm for next meeting. The first fish swallowed hook, line, and sinker, but Kalashnikov is not so hungry to take bait dangling in front of him."

17

UZHIN PODAN
(DINNER IS SERVED)

Anya watched a massive airliner climb off Harry Reid International Airport with its landing gear retracting into its belly and the pair of jet engines pushing the winged tube into the night. "Do you ever think about where people are going when you see airplanes taking off?"

Gwynn looked up at the target of Anya's attention. "I can't say I've ever played that game, but where do you think they're going?"

"Maybe Moscow."

"Maybe, but I'm not sure there are any direct flights to Moscow from Vegas."

Anya watched as the flying behemoth trailed off, becoming just another glimmer in a sky freckled with billions of tiny lights flickering through the hot summer night.

Gwynn studied her partner. "You miss Moscow, don't you?"

Anya instantly ceased her stargazing. "I miss home."

"Do you ever think you'll live there again? I mean, when this is all over."

"I think you do not understand, friend Gwynn. Home is not a place. It is only feeling. Sometimes I have this feeling with you."

"Aww, you're going to make me cry. That's so sweet."

"Is only truth."

"Where have you felt most at home?"

Without hesitation, Anya said, "With my mother."

"You were so young when she died. I can't imagine what you had to go through."

Anya tried to smile. "Do not be sad for me. I learned so many things after my mother was killed. I miss her, but if she was alive, I would have had boring life inside Soviet Union, and I would not have met you."

Gwynn pointed to the gleaming entrance to Mandalay Bay. "Here's our stop."

"Yes, I know. I am searching for anyone following us. We will go around block and make at least two false stops."

Gwynn chuckled. "They teach surveillance-detection routes to federal agents, too."

Anya made the next turn with her eyes glued to the mirror. "Do they teach also how to lure in follower and kill him with bare hands?"

Gwynn stopped chuckling. "No, they didn't teach us that, but I have you. That means you can teach me everything you know."

Anya pulled into the parking lot of an all-night pawn shop and slowly drove behind the building. "There are many things I know but will never teach to you. I will teach only good things—things to keep you alive when people are trying to kill you."

"Yeah, those are the things I want to learn."

Anya killed the headlights and turned the car around.

Gwynn whispered, "What are we doing?"

"Surveillance-detection route is boring. Catching driver who thinks he is smarter than me is never boring."

Gwynn beamed. "Oh, this is going to be good."

They climbed from the car and took up a position in the shadows between a dumpster and a stack of wooden pallets.

"Do you have knife?"

Gwynn slid a switchblade from her pocket and pressed the small, sliver button. The blade glistened in the dim light.

"Very good," Anya said. "When car stops, stay low and slice valve stem from back tire. Do not try to pierce tire. Is too easy to let hand slip onto blade doing this. Is always better to cut valve stem."

"Got it," Gwynn said. "But are you sure someone was following us?"

"I am sure two cars were following us. First one is very sloppy, but driver of second car is good. He would not fall for trap."

Just as Anya predicted, a brown, four-door sedan crept around the corner of the pawn shop until its headlights illuminated the Porsche. The driver threw a cigarette butt from the window, and the glowing ember bounced across the asphalt.

"Now," Anya whispered.

They sprung into action. Anya moved silently behind the car and disabled the right rear tire at the same moment Gwynn sliced the stem from the left.

With the two rear rims resting on flattened tires, Anya lifted the still-glowing cigarette butt between her fingers and pressed it into the driver's left ear. He bellowed and recoiled in pain and surprise. "What the—"

She left the butt in his ear and drove a thumb beneath his jaw, forcing his head against the seat. An instant later, the tip of her favorite fighting knife came to rest between the man's eyes, and a trickle of blood slowly oozed from beneath the steel.

Anya growled. "You are terrible driver, and this will get you killed. Perhaps tonight."

The driver froze and swallowed hard. "What do you want?"

"I want you to stop following me, and also for you to call friend in other car and tell him same. If he continues to follow me, I will find you and gut you like pig. This is clear for you, yes?"

The man tried to nod, but Anya added just enough pressure to the blade to freeze his movement.

"Good. I am happy you understand."

She withdrew her blade from his nose, stepped back, and swung her knife through the air, burying the blade in the thin metal of the car's door. The glass inside the door shattered, and the driver jumped.

Anya said, "Next time, target will be your head. Now, make calls."

They slid back into the Porsche and pulled onto the busy street.

Gwynn strained to see across her shoulder. "Do you really think he'll call his buddy?"

"I do not know, but one thing is certain. He will not follow us again tonight."

Anya made two more temporary stops and a dozen turns. "I think we are black."

Gwynn put on a puzzled look. "Why do we care if someone is following us? They already know where we're going. Wouldn't it be easier for them to put a team on the front door of the restaurant and wait for us?"

Anya pulled into a parking space and shut down the car. "You are thinking like policeman instead of spy."

Gwynn unbuckled her seatbelt. "Okay, then. Teach me, oh great spymaster."

Anya stepped from the car. "We will talk while walking." After a cautious scan for prying ears, Anya said, "Yes, they know where we are going, but they do not know what we will do on road. Maybe we will stop and collect weapons to kill Kalashnikov. Perhaps we will report back to operation center to notify SWAT team we are moving in. Knowing what we do between getting inside car and meeting Kalashnikov can tell many things about our mission. I want to appear to have no mission."

"No mission?"

"Yes. If we are who and what we are pretending to be, we will have no contact with anyone on road. We are only assassins—not policemen. This makes sense, yes?"

Gwynn sighed. "I have so much to learn. What would I do without you?"

"You would have boring life and boring job."

"Yeah, you're probably right. My world was so dry and dull until you showed up."

"I did not show up, friend Gwynn. You captured me."

"Yeah, but I didn't want to say that."

"Is always better to say truth."

Gwynn stopped and laid a palm against the door in front of them. "That's right, and I expect you to remember that next time I ask you where you go and what you do between assignments."

Anya cast her eyes to the sky. "Maybe I should make new phrase. Is most of time better to say truth."

Gwynn shook her head. "It must be nice to make up the rules as you go."

"Is very nice. I recommend trying, but for now, you must be silent again—just like inside club."

"Don't you worry, comrade. I'll stay in character. But I have a question."

Anya huffed. "Do not tell to me you have question. Simply ask question."

Gwynn slid her hand from the door. "We don't know what this guy looks like. How will we know if we're dealing with the right guy?"

Anya grinned. "You are, once again, thinking like police officer and not spy. It is impossible for powerful men to hide. They are like fat in fresh cream. The always rise to top and float."

"You're quite the philosopher, did you know that?"

Anya pulled open the door. "I am not philosopher. I am spy."

Gwynn paused for a beat before following her partner through the door.

The maître d' posted at the desk inside the door of Red Square looked like someone who'd been sent over from central casting to play the role of a flawless Russian goddess. Anya didn't seem to notice, but Gwynn was mesmerized.

The woman ran a long, slim finger down a printed page. "Do you have reservation?"

Her accent was even thicker than Anya pretended hers was, so she answered in Russian. "We do not have reservation, but we are meeting a friend. He is expecting us."

"Who is your friend?"

"Volodya Kalashnikov, and he is not patient man. If you delay us, he will not be happy with you."

Still in her native tongue, the hostess said, "I do not know if he is inside restaurant. I will talk with manager and—"

Anya took the woman's wrist and applied just enough pressure with her thumb to relieve any doubt about who was in charge. "You will take us to Volodya Kalashnikov, or I will tear hand from arm."

The woman instantly trembled, and her already-pale skin turned even whiter. "I cannot. Please do not hurt me."

"You can, and you will. I will not hurt you unless you do something stupid." Anya released the woman's hand. "We will follow you."

The woman straightened her skirt and turned on trembling legs.

Gwynn watched as she strode ahead of them, purportedly leading them to Kalashnikov. She thought, *Why? Why do they all look like that? Perfect legs. Perfect face. Perfect hair. I hate them so much.*

As they wound through the sea of tables and tourists, Gwynn tried to identify the bevy of food in bowls and on plates, or making its way into the mouths of the dozens of diners. Aside from the pickles and beets, nothing looked familiar or enjoyable.

The hostess led them through a curtained opening, and the cacophony of utensils on plates and uproarious conversation died as soon as the curtain fell closed behind them.

Anya and Gwynn scanned the long table ahead and took inventory of the most threatening of the guests. Anya picked out one woman holding her knife more like a fighter than a diner, so she would keep an eye on her. Two of the biggest men at a table of nine drew Gwynn's interest, and she noticed pistol-shaped bulges beneath their suits. Gwynn caught the eye of a third man sitting passively near the window and wearing the same expression of boredom she bore on her face.

The man at the head of the table with a pair of astonishing women flanking him raised his chin and let his eyes dance past the hostess and across the newest arrivals. In harsh Russian, he boomed, "What is this? Why would you interrupt me by bringing these people in here?"

Anya placed a hand on the hostess's shoulder. "*Spasibo.* You may go."

The woman scurried through the curtain and vanished, obviously thrilled to be anywhere except in that particular room.

Anya locked eyes with the man at the head of the table. "Oxana, if that is her name, sent us to you, so I am certain this is no surprise. Only surprise is missing men who were to report our every move."

The man's eyes narrowed, and he cast a glance down the table before saying, "I do not know what you are talking about."

Anya stepped toward him, but the two massive men slid their hands inside their jackets, so she froze in her tracks. After staring at the man for several seconds, Anya returned her exploring eye across the remainder of the dinner guests. The woman slipped her knife from her right hand into her left and spun the blade beneath her wrist.

Anya made a mental note of every detail and turned back to the man at the head of the table. "You are not man we are here to see. You are wasting our time with silly game."

She rounded the table, and every eye in the room followed her every step. She came to a stop behind the silent, bored-looking man and laid her hands on his shoulders. The two armed giants eased their weapons from their holsters and let them come to rest on their laps.

Anya glared at the man at the head of the table. "You are not Volodya Kalashnikov. You have cleft chin, broad eyes, and no cheekbones. No one who is direct descendant of Mikhail Kalashnikov could look like you."

She squeezed the shoulders of the guy in front of her. "This man, though . . . His eyes are narrow and cheeks are high, like everyone who shares blood of Kalashnikov."

The man at the head of the table stiffened and growled, "*Ty malen'kaya suka . . .*"

The man in front of Anya raised a hand. "Enough. You are obviously very skilled, but you have interrupted my dinner."

The woman palming the knife dug her heels into the floor and pushed away from the table. Before she could stand, Anya drew her knife and raised it above her head. The two armed, muscled brutes raised their pistols, and the room exploded into a storm of movement.

Anya swung the blade through a massive overhead arc and pinned the woman's arm to the table with her knife, slicing through the material of her jacket and into the heavy wooden surface of the table. Gwynn stepped behind and between the potential shooters and wrapped her hands around their heads. She drew her palms together, sending the two heads crashing together, rendering one man unconscious and the other dazed beyond usefulness. With one more blinding motion, the special agent collected the pistols and gripped one in each hand. A crushing blow to the skull of the still-conscious man sent him melting from his chair and onto the floor.

Kalashnikov didn't flinch. "I see you are as skilled as I have been told, but I do not discuss business while I am eating." He motioned toward the two felled gunmen. "Please take their seats and join us. Maybe we will have time to talk after we've had *pustynya.*"

Anya reclaimed her knife and straightened her victim's sleeve bearing the blade's wound. "*Spasibo,* comrade Kalashnikov. Perhaps you should claim your rightful place at head of table."

He lifted his napkin, wiped the corners of his mouth, and rose. With a few whispered words, the man who'd played Kalashnikov's role nodded and left the room.

18

DOLGAYA HSTORIYA
(A LONG HISTORY)

The meal dragged on for another hour, and the two beefy, would-be gunmen staggered their way out of the room.

Volodya Kalashnikov pulled the napkin from his lap, checked his watch, and waved a hand. "It is time now for business."

His heavy Russian accent reminded Gwynn of Anya's refusal to hide her Eastern Bloc speech.

Everyone stood to leave except Volodya, Anya, and Gwynn. To her surprise, Anya watched Oxana stroll silently into the room. Oxana ignored everyone except Kalashnikov and leaned down beside him, slipping an envelope into his hand. He didn't look up but slid a finger beneath the flap and emptied the contents onto the table in front of him.

Anya watched with measured interest as Volodya lifted each picture and studied it closely.

After several minutes of staring down at the pictures, Volodya looked up and spoke softly. "You did this?"

Anya stared back at him with the icy glare only Russian women can give, and nodded once but didn't speak.

He spread the picture on the table and allowed his eyes to play across them once more. "Why?"

Anya said, "Because I was responsible for bringing him to your club. When he came back into club with threats, someone had to deal with him. Because he would have never been there if I hadn't brought him the night before, I was still responsible for him. We did only what you would have done."

He placed the photos back into the envelope and slid it down the table. "Are you calling me a murderer?"

"Is not murder. Is self-defense. He was willing to fight and do harm to club. He was very angry, and he was not easy to kill. Someone taught him how to fight."

He seemed to inhale her words as if experiencing her instead of simply listening. "Someone also taught you to fight and to kill."

Anya bowed her head. "Yes, this is true. The same masters your grandfather served made me what I am."

He gave her words time to ring in the air before saying, "My grandfather, Mikhail, designed and built rifle that has killed more men than all other weapons combined. I was born into long line of men who understand and appreciate art of separating enemies from their souls."

Anya raised her head and met his stare. "I was trained to fight with AK Forty-Seven. This is weapon your grandfather created, and it is magnificent, but as you have seen"—she motioned toward the envelope containing the photos of Tom's end—"I do not prefer weapons of noise. I prefer silent weapons like your friend at table tonight."

For the first time, Kalashnikov smiled. "*She* is not like you, I am afraid. At least, I hope not. I watched her palm knife as if readying to kill you, but this is not what she was doing. She was hoping for chaos so she could kill me."

Anya frowned. "Kill you? Why would you have someone at your table who wished you dead?"

He laughed. "It was probably not Sun Tzu who first said this, but he gets credit for words . . . Keep your friends close, keep your enemies closer. Which of these are you?"

Anya motioned toward the envelope of pictures. "We have proven to be *blizkiye druz'ya*."

Volodya let his eyes fall on the envelope as a look of cautious contemplation overtook him. After a long moment, he lifted his gaze to meet Oxana's, still standing beside him. "All of this is true?" Oxana nodded, and Volodya turned back to Anya. "What do you want?"

She focused on a spot immediately between his dark eyes. "This is wrong question, comrade. Proper question is, what do *you* want?"

"All of this is little too convenient. You and your American friend show up out of nowhere and offer to me anything I want. I am man with many enemies, especially in Russia. I think maybe you are here on assignment from Kremlin to destroy me."

She said, "Like you, I have also many enemies inside former Soviet Union. I am persona non grata in real Red Square. It is up to you whether or not I am same inside this Red Square."

He drummed his fingers on the table. "You are sparrow like Oxana, yes?"

Anya slowly shook her head. "I *was* sparrow, but not like Oxana or anyone else. All women can seduce man to fall to his knees, but when I do this, he never stands again."

He licked his lips and took another sip of vodka before motioning toward the empty chairs. "Sit down and send her away."

Anya glanced at Gwynn. "*We* will sit, but she does not leave."

"Is she also sparrow? She is certainly beautiful enough."

"She is not, but she has many other skills hidden behind beautiful face."

He grunted. "Very well. She may stay."

Anya and Gwynn took seats on opposite sides of the table to allow each to keep Volodya and the other in sight.

Anya let her hand glide across the tabletop and come to rest only inches from Gwynn's. "I refused to be president's *prostitutka*, so I am marked for death inside Russia. I am not so easy to find and kill, so I came to Canada on freighter two years ago. Hiding inside ship, I was hungry and cold, but I survived by making friend of man inside engine room. He brought to me food and blankets but told no one I was on board ship."

"Why are you telling me this?" Volodya asked.

"I need for you to understand what I am."

He raised an eyebrow. "*What* you are, not *who* you are? I think maybe you have English pronouns confused."

She set her jaw and slid the envelope back toward him. "No, comrade Kalashnikov, I have words exactly as intended. I am animal. Look again at pictures, and you will see. What *we* do cannot be done by mere humans."

He laid a finger beside the envelope and flicked it back down the table. "Who do you work for?"

"This is why I am here," she said. "We are ronin."

"Ronin? This means samurai without master, yes?" She nodded, and he said, "And you want to be my samurai, yes?"

"Just like on ship, I am hungry and cold."

He shot a finger through the air and toward the envelope. "How many times have you done that?"

"For you, only once, but there could be many more if this is your desire."

He sighed. "Ah, there's the sparrow I expected. You speak of desire, and you are now seducing me."

Anya allowed her smile to come. "I would not be whore for president of Russia, but for him, I tore souls from dozens of men and sent them to Hell. For you, I can do same . . . nothing more."

"And in return, you expect food and blankets?"

She leaned forward and widened her eyes. "No, Volodya. From you, I expect caviar and warm palace."

He leaned back in his chair. "I have already many men who do what you are offering. Why would I—"

Before he could finish, she said, "Because nobody is afraid to invite two beautiful women to sit down at table, but no one would allow one of your many men to sit so close. My friend and I have keys to unlock every door, and as your men learned tonight, we are impossible to follow."

Volodya watched Oxana as she studied the two women. When their eyes finally met, she motioned toward the curtain with her chin, and Kalashnikov said, "Perhaps you would like to have drink at bar with your friend."

Anya said, "We are not thirsty."

Volodya sighed. "Wait outside while Oxana and I talk about you."

Anya leaned forward and laid a gentle hand on the man's forearm. "If we walk through curtain, you will never see us again. This is what you want?"

He pondered her ultimatum and turned to Oxana. "Tell me what is happening inside head."

She said, "I spoke with Alexei, and he said she is dead. No one knows anything about the American."

"Dead is my favorite kind of assassin."

Oxana smiled, and Volodya said, "Conspiracy to commit murder is serious crime, and I am honest businessman. I would never ask anyone to kill woman who lifted knife at dinner. But if someone brought to me pictures of her body in similar condition to man you killed in envelope, I would consider that person to be loyal friend to me."

Anya turned to Gwynn. "Show him."

Gwynn held up the knife the woman had wielded.

Anya said, "Of course you would never commit such crime. Obviously, you are honest businessman, but we are not same as you. Tell to me name you believe is hers."

Volodya leaned toward Oxana. "We know her name. We know everything about her."

"If this is true, you do not believe she will try to kill you. A big, strong man like you would crush tiny cockroach like her, or you would have men you trust do this."

"She's good," Volodya whispered to Oxana. "Are you suggesting you can make this woman disappear for Mr. Kalashnikov?"

"No, I would never suggest this. Such suggestion implicates Volodya in planning of crime. I am suggesting nothing. I am only telling you we can eliminate problem of our own free will."

Kalashnikov threw his napkin onto the table. "*Fignya*!"

Anya stood. "Is good for you to be doubtful. We are sorry to interrupt dinner. We will not do this again. When next time you see us, it will be in quiet and private place."

Gwynn lifted the woman's lipstick-stained napkin from the table, folded it neatly around the knife, and stood.

Kalashnikov watched the two women slip through the curtain as if they were ghostly spirits. He said, "What do you think they will do?"

Oxana laid a hand across his shoulder. "I think you just met the two best friends a man like you could ever have. Alexei told to me that she was trained sparrow but is much better killer than seductress. He is also certain she is dead. I believe he is wrong about one of those things. I suppose we shall know soon."

"This is all Alexei has to say?"

She slid a long, flawless leg across him and nestled onto his lap. As her tongue traced just beneath his earlobe, she hissed, "No, this is not all Alexei has to say. He said also that the Kremlin will pay five million U.S. dollars if we deliver this woman to them . . . dead or alive."

19

KTO ETA LEDI?
(WHO'S THAT LADY?)

After an exhaustive two-hour surveillance-detection route, Anya and Gwynn arrived back at Caesars Palace with their trophies in hand.

Dr. Celeste Mankiller held out her hands like a child reaching for candy. "Ooh, I can't wait."

Gwynn laid the knife and napkin in her waiting hands. "It's not much, but it's all we could get. I wanted the wineglass, but I couldn't figure out how to carry it out of the building without looking like I was stealing dinnerware."

Celeste held the knife up to the light. "You did steal dinnerware, but that's cool in this instance. Are you certain this was her knife?"

Gwynn chuckled. "Yes, we're certain. When we walked into the room, she handled it just like Anya would've. There's no question her prints are all over it."

Celeste slid the knife into a plastic evidence bag and examined the napkin. She pointed to the lipstick smear near one corner. "Also hers?"

"Yep."

The tech said, "It's not as good as lipstick—or drool—on Johnny's new shirt, but I think I can work with it. The knife is our best shot at an ID, but I'll have some fun with the DNA on the napkin, too."

Johnny Mac held up his phone. "Agent White wants a full report, no matter what time it is. Are you guys ready?"

Anya said, "Yes, put on speaker so everyone can enjoy. He is fun to mess with in middle of night."

Gwynn raised an eyebrow. "Oh, really? Do you spend a lot of time messing with our boss in the middle of the night?"

Anya feigned embarrassment. "I will never tell."

Celeste waved a hand. "I'm out, guys. If you need me, I'll be in the back playing with my new toys. I'll probably have some hits for you before you finish the briefing."

Johnny said, "All right, babe. We'll come get you if we need you."

Gwynn's eyes became beachballs. "Babe? Really?"

He said, "Cut it out. You two aren't the only ones who get to have a little fun on assignment. At least I didn't spend the night with an Air Force OSI officer."

Gwynn feigned offense. "Jealous much?"

Anya said, "I feel lonely. No one is calling me babe."

Gwynn rolled her eyes. "Oh, yeah, right. Tom came clean and told me he hit on you, but you shot him down."

"Why would he tell you this? I did not shoot him down. I told him . . . Oh, never mind."

Gwynn squeezed Anya's arm. "He told me exactly what you said, and that's the sweetest thing anyone has ever done for me. You have my permission to shoot down every hot guy you see. I don't mind picking up your crumbs."

"This is terrible thing to say—picking up crumbs."

Gwynn gave her arm another squeeze. "Don't worry. If your guy, Chase, ever hits on me, I'll send him down in flames and you can have my crumb."

Anya blushed. "You would not do this. He is beautiful man, and you could not say to him no."

Johnny said, "I thought Chase was married."

"Yes, this is true, but there was small time in past when I believed maybe I would be his wife. He is very happy with wife, Penny. I am sure of this."

Gwynn said, "I think we're getting sidetracked. Let's call the boss."

Johnny dialed the number, pressed the speaker button, and laid the phone on the table.

The line rang once, and Supervisory Special Agent Ray White growled, "It's about time. You better have something to report. This thing is already costing the taxpayers a hundred grand a day."

Gwynn began the show. "Hello, Agent White. It's Davis. We had a productive night, and the murder photos worked like a charm. We made solid contact with Kalashnikov, and I thought for a minute he might see through the ruse, but thankfully, I was wrong."

"You're wrong a lot, Davis. Let's not start celebrating those instances yet. Johnny Mac, what have you got?"

"We've got hard IDs on the chasers and their cars. The wonder twins over here did a slash-and-go on their tires, so I had plenty to work with. The FBI field office punched up the sheets on the drivers, and there's no surprises. It's just petty stuff . . . Some numbers, prostitution, and a couple assault and batteries. It was just what we expected. The FBI should've copied you on the report."

"They did, but I like to hear you talk, Johnny. How's your little cream puff doing?"

Johnny blushed blood red. "She's . . . I mean, um . . ."

White chuckled. "Relax, Johnny. I'm just busting your chops. Just don't make her live up to her last name."

Gwynn pulled Johnny from the hot seat. "Also, Agent White, we collected a napkin with possible DNA and a piece of silverware with definite prints. It looks like we found our first victim, but I'm not so sure she'll be willing to play ball with us."

"She?" White asked.

"Yes, sir. Volodya Kalashnikov believes she was sent to kill him, so Anya and I saw that as an open door to slide her to the top of our list. Dr. Mankiller is running the DNA and prints now. She thinks we'll have a hit tonight."

White said, "Hmm. I don't know. Let me chew on that one. We need to know who and what she is before we make a move. For now, I've got some more insight on Oxana Kozlova. She's the real deal. Her father was Nikita Kozlov, a former mid-level commie party guy and KGB officer. After the Soviet Union came crashing down around him, he found himself at the right place at the right time. It seems he made a bundle selling stolen military hardware to some of the breakaway former Soviet states."

Anya said, "I am certain Oxana was, or is, sparrow. It does not make sense she would be daughter of party official."

"Don't interrupt me. I wasn't finished. Kozlov either ran afoul of Putin or one of his trusted generals when he undercut them on an arms deal. He caught a Makarov round in the head after being forced to watch Mrs. Kozlova suffer a fate far worse than a bullet to the brain. I guess even Putin has a soft spot for kids. He didn't kill little Oxana. Instead, she became a ward of the state and wound up in State School Four, where she learned to make men melt in her hands . . . and every other body part."

Anya sighed. "I have theory. I believe Volodya is in love with Oxana."

Silence consumed the room until White asked, "Is the feeling mutual?"

Anya said, "A sparrow can make anyone believe she is in love with him, but sometimes they really do fall in love with target."

White softened his tone. "Yeah, I've got a nice thick file on just such an incident."

Anya lowered her head. "Yes, this is forbidden, but sometimes it happens. Maybe this is case with Oxana and Volodya. If she is only former sparrow, and not working now for SVR, this is okay, but if she is still officer in SVR or FSB, this is death sentence for her."

White thumbed through a file. "We're still not certain exactly who she is, but if she's still on the Russian payroll, she's doing a killer job hiding it."

Anya closed her eyes. "I know we do not do our job because of gut feeling, but I do not think Oxana is active Russian officer. I think she is *perebezhchik*, like me."

White clicked his tongue against his teeth. "Deserter?"

"Yes, this is proper English word, but in Russian, it is greatest of all sins."

Gwynn asked, "So, if Oxana is a former—or maybe current—Russian agent, and knife-girl is likely an active agent, we're getting into some dangerous ground. Should we call in the counterintelligence guys?"

"Not yet," White said. "If those guys get involved in this, they'll screw it up by the numbers. We may have to play ball with the CIA before this is over, but for now, it's our baby, and we'll feed it and change its diaper every time it cries."

"This makes no sense," Anya said. "There is no baby."

Gwynn whispered, "I'll explain it later, but for now, the case is ours until it gets out of hand."

Celeste burst from her room down the hall. "I've got her!"

"What was that?" White asked.

Johnny said, "Celeste, uh . . . Dr. Mankiller, seems to have gotten a hit."

Celeste pointed toward the phone. "Is that Agent White?"

Johnny said, "Yes, we're still briefing, but what do you have?"

She took a seat at the table. "The prints from the knife were perfect, but I couldn't find anything until I searched Interpol. Apparently, they have a match in their database, but I need a little muscle to open that door. Agent White, do you think you could give me a hand?"

"Sure, but it'll be tomorrow morning. I'm not waking up the attorney general unless somebody has a big gun pointed at my head."

"That's cool. I'll be waiting to hear from you in the morning."

Gwynn scanned the faces at the table. "So, do we have any kind of plan?"

White said, "Don't get ahead of yourself, Davis. We've got the fish nibbling at the bait, but he's not swallowed the hook yet. For now, we need to know who this mystery lady with knife skills is. If we can get her to play ball with us, we'll pursue that angle, but if she's really after Kalashnikov, maybe we should stay out of her way and let her do her thing."

Johnny Mac narrowed his gaze. "Is that legal?"

White sighed. "Davis, punch Johnny Mac in the throat so he won't ask any more stupid questions."

Gwynn pushed from her chair. "Yes, sir."

Johnny threw up his fists. "Don't you do it, Davis!"

White said, "Save it, Davis. Catch him when he's not expecting it. Does anybody else have anything?"

Anya cleared her throat. "Uh, I have something, but you're not going to like it."

"Spit it out," White ordered.

She hesitated before saying, "The Kremlin believes I am dead."

Gwynn and Johnny showed only confusion on their faces, but Celeste and White groaned.

"What?" Gwynn asked.

White answered before Celeste could open her mouth. "I hadn't considered that little rat's nest. If either Oxana or knife-girl is working for the Kremlin, we don't want you anywhere near them. In fact, until we know who these people are, I'm ordering you to stand down and stay out of sight."

Anya frowned. "No! This is terrible idea. We must keep working."

White cut in. "Anya, I wasn't asking for your opinion, and I wasn't talking to anyone except you. The rest of the team is still in play, but you're on the bench for now. It's not up for negotiation."

The Russian snatched the phone from the table, turned off the speaker, and stormed from the room. With the door slammed and still vibrating behind her, she shoved the phone against her ear. "I believed you knew what I am. I thought you understood I am not weak American woman. The Rodina tore weakness from inside me until nothing is left. Horrible men in cold, dark places, in forgotten forest beside frozen river carved innocence from little girl and made her a whore for country that is not capable of compassion. If I was ever human, that is gone. It can never be again. I do not fear what will happen to me. I gave to you promise to do what you want and capture—or maybe kill—evil men inside America."

White interrupted. "You don't under—"

"I am not finished. I am not junior government agent who is afraid of you like Gwynn and Johnny Mac. You are just man. You have only power because they give to you this power. I made to you promise, and I will always keep promise if you are beggar on side of street or president inside White House. Do not stop me from keeping promise I made to you. If I am captured and returned to Russia, I will escape again until they kill me. Volodya Kalashnikov is nothing. He is bug under shoe and nothing more. Oxana Kozlova is coward. I will laugh when I make her scream to a god she does not believe in. I am not coward, Ray White! I am—"

"Anya! Stop it! I'm not calling you off for *your* sake. Gwynn loves you, and I need you. Now, shut up and do what you're told for once in your life."

20

Mech Angela
(The Angel's Sword)

Oxana Kozlova reclined in her favorite chair and draped her hand across the arm as a young woman carefully manicured Oxana's nails. "I have feeling this girl, Anya, and her American friend, will be more valuable to us than every bottle of vodka in Las Vegas."

Volodya Kalashnikov stared back at her over the rim of his cocktail. "Perhaps you are correct, but is also possible she is far more valuable to us alive right here in America than delivered back to Moscow in box."

Oxana jerked her hand from the girl's grip. "Ouch! Be careful! These hands are worth more than your life, little girl."

In frightened, schoolgirl Russian, the young lady cowered. "I am sorry. I am sorry. Will not happen again."

Oxana returned her hand to the girl's labor. "I love you, Volodya, but if Kremlin learns this woman is alive and working for us inside United States, they will send whole platoon of assassins for us. We have comfortable life. We do not need to upset apple cart, as Americans say."

"You are right, of course," Kalashnikov said. "But consider possibility of having sparrow assassin at our disposal."

Oxana huffed. "You want her for your personal sparrow. I can see this."

He lowered his chin and glared at her. "I have my personal sparrow. What I want is fearless angel with fiery sword."

"And this is what you believe this woman to be?"

Volodya took a long, deep breath. "Perhaps, but we will know soon. When she agreed to kill Paulina Pavlova, she did not even ask for her name."

"What do you think that means?"

He leaned back and crossed his arms. "It can be only one of two things. First, she is supremely confident she can identify, find, and kill Paulina with no direction from us. If this is true, she is without doubt my sword-bearing angel. Other possibility is she already knows Paulina and is working with her to kill me, and perhaps, also you."

Oxana let Volodya's thoughts tumble through her mind for a moment. "If she is here to kill us, why would she kill the man she brought to club three days ago?"

"Maybe she did not kill him," he said.

"You saw pictures. Man in picture was surely dead, no?"

Volodya shrugged. "Maybe. I think we should put at least three men on her and follow her until we are certain she has killed Paulina."

"This will not work. She has eyes in back of head, and maybe also team of other people watching and protecting her. She cannot be followed without detecting followers."

Volodya ignored her. "What about the American woman?"

"What about her?"

"She does not speak, but somehow, she communicates with the woman who wants us to believe her name is Anya. You are smart woman. How does she do this?"

Oxana groaned. "I do not know, but I am not certain second woman is American. She is beautiful, maybe like someone from Spain or maybe France, but definitely not Russia or Ukraine. She moves like Anya, so perhaps she is her student."

"Perhaps, but maybe the woman who does not speak is assassin, and Anya is student."

Oxana pulled her hand from the girl, inspected her nails, and motioned for the girl to move to the other side. Once her left hand was well established under the girl's care, she said, "No, I think you are wrong about this. Anya is definitely sparrow. Is impossible for one sparrow to hide from another. We know. I know she is sparrow, and we will soon know what else she is."

* * *

Anya sat in defeated disbelief with the phone in the palm of her hand. "You need me?"

Ray White said, "Yes, Anya, I need you, but not just for the job."

"What else could you mean?"

He cleared his throat. "I also made a promise to you, even though I never said it aloud. I like you, Anya, and in some other universe, maybe I'd like you more than I should."

"Ray, do not do this. This thing you feel for me is not real. I am sparrow, Ray White. I have no choice. I am seductive because this is what SVR did to me. I am not capable of love as you see it and feel it."

"I didn't say love, Anya. I said I *like* you. When I only knew you from your file, I was terrified of you. That hasn't changed, with one exception. I've become intrigued by your humanity—something you believe you don't have."

She swallowed hard. "I am source of constant frustration for you. How can you say I have humanity?"

"Just look at Davis. She was a shy, quiet professional before you, and now, she's on her way to becoming a belligerent, deadly, supremely confident agent. You're doing that to her, but that's not where it ends."

"I do only for her what she asks of me. I do not force her to learn anything."

"I know. But before you came along, she went home every night, studied old case files, and came back to work early the next morning, every day. Now she runs off with you to the Caribbean to ride four-wheelers through the desert, and instead of studying old cases, she works out five nights a week, does yoga, and she must own a thousand knives. You took a woman destined to become an administrator and turned her into a warrior. She worships the ground you walk on. Imagine what it would do to her if you got sent back to Russia in a Ziploc bag."

Anya sat in silence remembering the first time she taught Gwynn to hold a knife. "Okay, I will do this being on sideline because I do not want to hurt Gwynn, but there is something you should know."

"I don't care why you do it. Just do it. And what's this thing I should know?"

"I think her name is Paulina Pavlova."

"Who?"

"The woman at table with knife tonight."

"Why didn't you say you knew her? That could've saved Celeste a lot of work."

"I did not remember her until you said things about Gwynn. I think she was *sekretar'* inside Kremlin."

"Why would a secretary from the Kremlin be in Vegas with a knife? You're not making any sense."

"I heard stories of this woman, Paulina Pavlova. She was attacked by two men with knives in darkness outside of apartment. She killed one man and hurt other very badly. She was never trained to do this. She was daughter of man who makes shoes and woman who is cook. After doing this thing, FSB took her from Kremlin and trained her to do these things."

"Why would the Federal Security Service grab her instead of the SVR?"

Anya said, "Think of FSB as maybe same as FBI, and SVR as American CIA, but not exactly. You are not FBI, but almost same, and you wanted me."

"You've got a point, but the FSB is internal security, right?"

"Yes, this is correct."

"Then why would they send this Paulina woman over here to kill Kalashnikov?"

"This would not happen, so I think maybe she is no longer working for FSB and is maybe working only for Vladimir Vladimirovich Putin now. He considers Volodya Kalashnikov to be national embarrassment, and he would kill him with hands if he could."

"So, what makes you think she's working directly for him and not for the SVR?"

"SVR has terrible taste left inside mouth because of me. I think will be many years before training for women is done inside SVR."

"Ah, I see," White said. "So, if this woman is who you think she is, do you believe her to be a threat to us, and specifically to you?"

"If she is Paulina Pavlova and working directly for President Putin, she is credible threat to everyone inside American government. Especially me."

"But you can . . . I mean, she's not—"

"Do not be afraid for me, Ray. I am not afraid of her, just like I am not afraid of viper. Both are deadly, but only in one direction."

"How can we know for certain if this woman is Pavlova?"

"Perhaps Celeste has found her inside database of Interpol but is waiting only for you to open locked door."

"Hold that thought, and don't hang up. I'll be right back."

The phone clicked, and Anya found herself alone and maybe ashamed. She thumbed the speaker button, pulled open the door she'd slammed, and returned to the living room of the suite. "I am sorry. I was angry with Ray. He is talking to Interpol to help Celeste with fingerprint. We have maybe theory."

Gwynn took the phone from Anya's hand and slid it onto the table. "Yeah, we could tell you were angry. You're loud and a little scary when you're mad."

Before Anya could speak, White came back on the line. "Are you still there?"

Johnny Mac said, "We're all here, Agent White."

White paused for a moment. "Uh, I wasn't on speaker the whole time, was I?"

Anya giggled, but Johnny said, "No, sir."

"Good. Here's what I have. Interpol is just transitioning from the midnight watch to the day watch, when the admin guys who think they're important get to work. Unfortunately, they're the guys we need, so I'll hopefully have some good news for you shortly. In the meantime, we have a working theory on who the mystery woman is. Anya will brief you on that while I keep ringing phones at Interpol."

Gwynn glanced between the phone and Anya. "A working theory, you say?"

Anya said, "Yes, I believe I know who this woman is."

Gwynn huffed. "You could've mentioned that last night before Celeste spent two hours glued to her computer."

Anya cocked her head and smiled at her partner. "Yes, but this was before I knew you loved me."

21

TEMNAYA OBLOZHKA
(DARK COVER)

Anya spent twenty minutes explaining her theory on Paulina Pavlova being the knife wielder. Doubt poured from Johnny Mac's face, intrigue from Celeste's, and anticipation exploded from her understudy's like a kid on Christmas morning.

"It sounds like a long shot to me," Johnny said.

Celeste pondered the possibility. "That could explain her prints being under lock and key at Interpol, but I'm with Johnny. I'm not ready to brand her just yet."

Anya smiled as Gwynn pulled the fighting knife Anya had given her from its sheath on her ankle.

Gwynn said, "Go ahead and doubt her if you want, but if Anya says this woman is Paulina Pavlova, I plan to watch her bleed."

Johnny stared up with terror in his eyes. "You know you're turning into Anya, right?"

Gwynn slid the knife back into its sheath, leapt to her feet, and kissed Johnny on his forehead. "Thank you! That's the best compliment I've ever gotten from anyone."

Celeste laughed. "I've worked with a lot of feds, but you guys are, by far, the weirdest. I never want to leave."

Johnny shoved Gwynn away and said, "Then don't."

Celeste smiled down at him. "Maybe I won't, but for now, I'm going to bed. It's two o'clock in the morning."

Everyone checked their watch, and groans filled the air.

Before turning away, Celeste pointed a finger at Gwynn. "Knife or no knife, that better be the extent of your lips being on Johnny's face."

Gwynn recoiled. "Ooh, yuck! That's like kissing my brother. Don't worry, Science Girl. He's all yours."

Johnny tapped on the table. "All funny business aside, everyone keep your ringers on high. We don't want to miss a call from Interpol or DC."

Lights were doused, and heads hit pillows, but Johnny's admonition had been right on target. Thirty minutes later, Celeste's and Anya's phones rang in unison.

Anya pulled herself from unconsciousness and lifted her phone. "*Da.*"

Ray White said, "What do you mean, *da*? You're an American now. Try answering the phone like one."

Anya licked her lips. "Okay. I suppose *this* is how American answers phone at three in morning . . . What do you want?"

"That's more like it," Ray said. "It's time to wake up your little friends at your sleepover. You were right. It's Pavlova, but Interpol says the prints can't be fresh."

Before Anya could answer, Celeste beat on her door. "Anya! Get up. We got a match."

Anya pulled on a pair of shorts and a T-shirt. "I am coming." She turned back to the phone. "Apparently, Celeste has also telephone call from Interpol."

White said, "Good. Listen to her briefing and call me back. Got it?"

"Yes, Ray. I have very good memory. I can remember to call you when briefing is over."

"Remember what you said about being a constant source of frustration for me?"

"Yes, I remember this."

"Well, you were right. If you don't call me back, I'm calling the Kremlin myself, and telling them where you are."

"Do you need phone number for President Putin?"

"Goodbye, Anya."

Anya wiped the sleep from her eyes and joined the rest of the team in the room that had apparently become their conference room.

Celeste still held her phone to her ear, and her eyes said she was listening intently. A moment later, she said, "Hang on. I'm putting you on speaker."

She thumbed the button and laid the phone on its back in the center of the table. "Okay, can you hear us?"

A voice came through the tiny speaker in a decidedly British tone. "Yeah, I can hear ya bloody well, but who are ya? I can't go about handin' out information willy-nilly."

Celeste said, "You know me. The rest of us are . . ." She pointed to Johnny.

He said, "Special Agent Johnathon McIntyre, DOJ."

Gwynn said, "Special Agent Guinevere Davis, also DOJ."

Then to everyone's surprise, with no discernible accent, Anya said, "Special Agent Ana Fulton, DOJ."

"Jolly good, then. I'm Chief Inspector Clyde Rafferty, so let's get on wif it. I don't fink you'll be likin' what I have to say too much, but it's the best I can do, I'm afraid. Are ya sittin' down?"

Johnny said, "Come on, Inspector. Let's have it. It's the middle of the night over here."

"That's chief inspector, and 'twas your agency who called me, so keep your shirt on. Like I told your superior, them prints o' yours, they come back on a set we've logged over at Interpol, but they ain't likely to tell you nuffin'. It's MI-Six you need to talk to, but I can tell you this much . . . Them finger-prints ain't no livin' person's prints. I saw the list meself, and I reckon they set off all sorts of bells and whistles 'round here, they did. Ever heard of a lass named Paulina Pavlova? Like Pavlov, the guy wiff them slobberin' dogs?"

Celeste held a finger to her lips. "That name isn't ringing any bells in this room, but on behalf of the U.S. DOJ, we appreciate you getting back to us so quickly."

"Sure thing, but there ain't need to be saying nuffin' about me telling you that lass's name. That was off the record."

Celeste reached for the phone, "What name, Chief Inspector? You didn't give us nuffin'." She ended the call and shoved the phone into the pocket of her oversized sweatshirt. "Is that good enough?"

Anya nodded, but the other two agents shook their heads.

Celeste laughed. "It seems there may be some discrepancy in what qualifies as 'good enough' to our Russian contingent and our Yankee Doodle Dandy duo over here."

Johnny Mac said, "It's not enough to get a search warrant, or even enough to initiate an immigration investigation."

Anya gave Gwynn a wink. "Paulina Pavlova is not under arrest, and we do not wish to search her home. We wish to challenge her to fight, and for this, we have enough."

"That's not how any of this works," Johnny said.

Anya pulled out her phone. "We will see."

Seconds later, Ray White's voice came over the speaker. "Will miracles never cease? You *did* call me back. How'd it go with Interpol?"

Anya and Johnny spoke at the same time until White ordered them down. "Hey! Only one person at a time. Let's start with the only sane person in the room."

Anya said, "This is good choice."

White said, "No. Not you, Anya. I was talking about Johnny Mac."

Johnny spoke up. "It wasn't Interpol. It was a chief inspector from Scotland Yard, and he couldn't give us any official answer. He did ask if the name Pavlova rang any bells, and of course we said no. He said we need to talk to MI-Six. I'm of the opinion this doesn't give us any actionable information."

White said, "Okay, Johnny, you can stop talking now. I just got off the phone with MI-Six, and their official position is this. The prints are definitively those of Paulina Gregorovna Pavlova, who was killed while on a hiking trip on the Lake Baikal Trail near the village of Listvyanka. Her body was never recovered, and it's suspected she was either attacked and killed by a bear, or she fell into the deepest lake on the planet and never resurfaced."

Anya smiled. "This is common story and stock of laughing inside SVR."

Gwynn said, "I think you meant laughingstock."

Anya ignored her partner. "This means Pavlova is no longer officially recognized by Kremlin. She is now *temnaya oblozhka*. I do not know English phrase for this. Perhaps Gwynn knows since she is now language specialist."

Davis chuckled and scowled at her friend and partner, but White said, "Dark cover."

"Yes, this is correct. Forgive Gwynn for not correcting me. I still love her."

Gwynn's mouth fell open, and she made eye contact with everyone in the room. "Did you hear that? She said she loves me. Somebody write down the date and time."

Anya rolled her eyes. "Back to work at hand. Pavlova is dark cover, so she is working directly for only one of three possible people—president, prime minister, or chief of line KR in SVR."

"Which do you think it is?" Ray asked.

"I have no way of knowing, but if only guess, it is president. Putin has special kind of hatred for Volodya Kalashnikov. To have descendant of Russian national hero leave for United States is disgrace to Putin. There is one thing only that does not make sense to me inside all of this."

Everyone around the table leaned in as if it were story time, and Anya said, "If Paulina Pavlova is such expert in *mokroye delo*, why has she not killed Volodya already?"

Gwynn blurted out, "I know that one. It's wet affairs, or what we call wet work."

"This is correct," Anya said. "It is from having hands wet with blood. When someone is under dark cover, this person should be invisible and silent. Killing should be done privately with no witnesses, but this person is working into inside circle of Volodya Kalashnikov, very much same way like we are doing. This does not make sense to me."

Johnny Mac said, "Maybe she faked her own death and she's trying to get inside Volodya's organization because she needs a job."

Anya nodded. "This is good theory, but we might never have chance to ask her. We must try to capture and interrogate her, but I have first question for Supervisory Special Agent Ray White."

White didn't let the use of his full title and name slip his detection. "Is this like when your mother uses all three of your names? I get the feeling I'm in trouble."

Anya frowned. "You are not in trouble, but I need truth. Is Paula Pavlova working also with American government like me?"

White pondered the question. "I can't answer that question with certainty. I can, however, say unequivocally that she is not working for me or anyone else directly at the DOJ level. I understand your concern, and it's well justified. I'm asking the same question. To my knowledge, she is not working with the U.S. government, but I will put the question to the attorney general."

Anya said, "Thank you for honesty. I think you should also ask director of Central Intelligence and commander of FBI organized crime taskforce."

White answered without hesitation. "The FBI falls under the AG, so she'll know if Pavlova is working for them in any capacity. I don't have direct access to the DCI, but even if I did, I wouldn't expect him to tell me the truth. He's not in the business of divulging anything resembling the truth."

Gwynn jumped in. "Does this mean our mission objective has changed? Are we going after Pavlova instead of Kalashnikov?"

"No, our objective hasn't changed. It's expanded. We're going after both. If Pavlova is who we think she is, we've stumbled onto one of the highest intelligence value targets in the world, and I want her in our bag, not the CIA's."

Gwynn looked like a kid who just lost her balloon. "Does that mean I'm not allowed to kill her?"

White scolded her. "That's not what we do, Davis."

Gwynn turned to Anya, and the Russian whispered, "Do not listen to him. He is bureaucrat."

"I heard that!"

Anya covered her mouth. "He is bureaucrat with excellent hearing."

"All right. That's enough," White said. "We're still after Kalashnikov, but temporarily, Paulina Pavlova is our primary target. Find her, take her into unofficial custody, for God's sake don't mirandize her, and then put her in a room alone with Anya."

Gwynn perked up. "Then can I kill her?"

White sighed. "Yeah, probably, but not until we suck out every piece of intel she has inside her head."

Anya said, "This means also I am no longer on bench, yes?"

"I'm probably going to regret this, but yes, you're back in the game. Now, go catch a dead woman."

22

VVEDITE SHKIPERA
(ENTER, THE SKIPPER)

Anya leapt to her feet as if shot from a cannon. "We must go!"

Gwynn reached up for Anya's arm. "Calm down, you little Russian jumping bean. We've been awake for twenty-two hours. We're not going anywhere except to bed."

"But I am no longer on bench."

Johnny said, "Just because you're not riding the pine doesn't mean you have to run onto the field with your hair on fire. Gwynn is right. Get some rest. Besides, Pavlova is a night creature. We've got all day to catch up on our sleep. We'll get her, but not right now."

Anya glanced from Johnny to Celeste. "You will not sleep, yes?"

Celeste shrugged. "I'm a little like Pavlova when it comes to being a night owl. I do my best work while everyone else is sleeping."

"This is very good. I will help you."

Celeste held up a hand. "No, Anya. Owls work alone. Get some sleep. I'll find her for you, but I'll do it with my fingertips and keyboard. If this woman is half as good as you say she is, you'll need to be well rested."

Anya let her shoulders slump. "When they taught us about Americans in school, they told us all of you were lazy and rich. Now I am also American, and this is only half of truth."

Johnny frowned. "Wait. What? Are you rich?"

Anya smiled and laced her arm around Gwynn. "I am rich because I have all of you for friends. Especially Gwynn."

Celeste waved a backhand. "You guys can hold hands and sing campfire songs all you want, but I'm going to work."

As the team rose to head for their beds, Anya quietly slipped into the hallway and pulled her phone from a pocket. Exhaustion kept anyone from noticing, but if the phone call yielded results, it would be impossible to keep it a secret.

* * *

Sleep came, but Anya rose with the sun, and the teapot was soon whistling its morning cry. She curled her long legs beneath her on a chaise lounge overlooking the mountains west of the city. Tranquility isn't a sense associated with the city of Las Vegas, but in that moment, Anya felt exactly that—tranquil.

The tea steamed, and her brain pulsed inside her head. Just like millions of warriors had done through countless ages, Anya fought the coming battle in her mind before stepping onto the field.

The endless hours spent inside dilapidated rooms with a small wooden stick in her hand poured through her memory. The training officers wielded razor-sharp, gleaming blades of their fighting knives while the students tried in vain to defend themselves with eight inches of wood and their wit. Some of the fighters she trained with had been instinctual, seeming to know what the instructors would do next and avoiding their slashing lunges. She sipped her tea and stared down at the scars crisscrossing her forearms, where she'd learned to attack around the instructor's jabs instead of directly into them. Her methods had never been based on instinct. The skill she ultimately developed and maintained was tempered by determination and unending practice. The punishing but shallow wounds inflicted by the cadre of trainers taught her the brutal reality and inescapable truth of a knife fight: No matter who starts or ends the fight, everyone bleeds. The victor is the warrior who bleeds less than her opponent.

Gwynn's soft morning voice drew Anya from her trance. "I thought I'd find you out here. Want some more tea?"

164 · CAP DANIELS

Anya looked up and could almost feel the affection pouring from her partner and friend just as the steaming water left the pitcher and cascaded across the teabag.

"I am glad you are here. We must talk."

Gwynn perched on a chair across from her and took the first tentative sip of her tea. "Okay, let's talk."

Anya cradled her mug between cupped hands. "This woman, Paulina Pavlova, is dangerous person."

Gwynn tried to lock eyes with her mentor, but the Russian wouldn't look up. "Everything I have taught you has been technical fighting, and with this type of fighting, you are more deadly than almost everyone in street fight."

Gwynn leaned in, and Anya continued. "When I showed you how to anticipate attack because of position of feet or direction of hips, this is fighting with science, and you are very good at this. But there is another type of fighting I have not taught you."

Gwynn placed her mug on the balcony floor and focused on Anya's voice. "This woman does not fight the way I have taught you. She has ability to feel what will happen next instead of seeing with eyes. She is deadly because her mind and body work together perfectly."

Before she realized she'd opened her mouth, Gwynn said, "Are you afraid of her?"

Anya finally met Gwynn's eyes. "I have never been afraid of dying. I am human and must die sometime, but I have now something I have never had since I was young girl."

Gwynn furrowed her brow. "What are you talking about?"

"I have you, Gwynn, and I love you. You are my heart, and I do not wish to leave you."

"What do you mean? Why would you leave?"

Anya sighed. "Please do not fight with this woman. If I cannot defeat her, you must escape."

Gwynn leaned back in her chair and put on a confident smile. "Anya, I'm a special agent of the United States Department of Justice. I carry at least one Glock nine-millimeter and usually two everywhere I go. If you can't defeat Paulina Pavlova, I will drill holes in her until you can see through her. But what did you mean about leaving me?"

Anya turned her attention to the floor again. "I mean that I am now afraid of dying because I will be without you."

Gwynn sat in shocked disbelief for a long moment before asking, "So, *are* you afraid of Pavlova?"

Anya whispered, "Is not fear, but respect."

* * *

By midafternoon, everyone had reclaimed the rest their bodies and minds so desperately needed, and the war room was called to order.

Celeste straightened a stack of papers and began her briefing. "Here's what I found, and I'm quite disappointed in myself. I'm used to mastering everything I undertake, but this Pavlova woman is hard to nail down. There was a warrant issued by the International Court of Justice in The Hague back in two thousand three, but since she supposedly died, that warrant is no longer enforceable. Although we now know she did not, in fact, die in two thousand six, there were only three reported sightings of her from the time the warrant was issued until now."

"Who keeps track of reported sightings?" Johnny asked.

Celest pointed at him. "That's a great question, and I don't have an answer. What I do know is that Interpol had these three sightings on file. The sightings don't really matter except to confirm what we already know—that she's alive and well."

Anya held up a finger. "I would like to know where and when she was reported."

Celeste shuffled through the stack of papers. "Uh, the first sighting was in Vancouver two months after the warrant was issued, but she evaded capture."

"Who spotted her?" Gwynn asked.

"That's the weird thing about it," Celeste said. "A Norwegian businessman whose name I can't pronounce called her by name when the police arrived."

Gwynn made a rolling signal with her hands. "Come on, Celeste. Lay it out for us. What happened? How and why were the police involved?"

Celeste sighed. "Sorry. I'm a little frazzled. This isn't really my world. I'm not an analyst, I'm a scientist, but here's what I found out. This Norwegian guy is a big muckety-muck in the commercial fishing and processing business. He's worth a billion bucks or something like that. He was in Vancouver on business when his two bodyguards and one of his sons were attacked inside a limousine. It was screwy timing. Fisherman-guy stepped out of the limo, apparently to take a call from a mistress, and didn't want his son to hear. When he returned to the car, he saw Pavlova running from the scene. One of the bodyguards bled to death in seconds. The other lived long enough to get to the hospital, but no longer, and the son . . . well, that's where it really gets weird. She cut out his tongue, and he almost drowned on his own blood. Weird, freaky stuff."

"How did we not hear about that?" Johnny asked.

Celeste shrugged. "I guess when you've got enough money, you can keep almost anything out of the media's hands. Here's the real kicker, though. Fish Guy died a year later from acute radiation poisoning."

Gwynn said, "Died? You mean, he was murdered."

"Yeah, of course, but either way, he's still dead."

Anya narrowed her gaze. "Did son with no tongue inherit business?"

THE RUSSIAN'S LUST · 167

Celeste shuffled more paper. "I don't know. I didn't go down that rabbit hole. I told you this isn't my thing, but I'm doing the best I can. We should really bring in a professional analyst."

Gwynn lifted her phone, but Anya laid a hand against it. "Do not call Ray. I have already analyst working on this. She is maybe better than anyone Agent White could task."

Gwynn froze. "You didn't!"

"I did."

"Agent White is going to be furious with you, Anya. You can't just arbitrarily call outsiders into an investigation. That's not how we do business."

"Is no longer investigation. Is now life and death, and I trust her when life is on line."

Johnny threw up his hands. "Do you want to let the rest of the class in on your private little game? Who are we talking about here?"

Anya pulled the phone from Gwynn's palm and laid it on the table. "Her name is Elizabeth Woodley, but she is called Skipper."

Gwynn palmed her forehead. "Oh, boy. Here we go. If Agent White doesn't kill us, he's going to make us wish we were dead."

Anya thumbed a button on her phone. "If we do not have help from Skipper or someone like her, we will not have to worry about White killing us. Pavlova will do it for him."

The line rang twice, and Skipper's faint Southern drawl poured from the speaker. "I've been expecting the phone to ring. Let me guess. Your guy couldn't get a grip on our girl, Paulina?"

Anya said, "Is not guy. Is girl. But you are right. She found some information, but nothing to help us find her. Please tell to me you have good news."

"How often do I call with bad news?" Skipper asked.

Anya held up a finger. "Yes, this is true, but this time, you did not call. You answered."

"You've got me there, Kremlin Katerina, but I do have some information that might be just what you need."

"Kremlin Katerina? This is not someone I know. Who are you talking about?"

"Relax, Anya. It was just a joke. Are you ready for the info?"

"Yes, we are ready, and your joke is not funny."

Skipper paused. "You just said *we*. Who's *we*?"

Gwynn said, "Hey, Skipper. It's Special Agent McIntyre and me, along with Dr. Celeste Mankiller from tech services."

"Mankiller? That's a little ominous, but whatever. Here's what I know. Pavlova is one hundred percent alive and well. They did finally pull a body out of Lake Baikal and *officially* declared it to be her body. I hope you could feel my air quotes around the word *officially*."

Anya said, "This is not surprising. If Kremlin said sun is coming up in morning, I would not believe them."

Skipper continued. "Yeah, we all know that, but lucky for you guys, I don't base my information on official Kremlin news releases. I found an old photograph of Ms. Pavlova. Okay, actually, I found several, and I put together a composite and compared it against the FRCs in a bunch of the big casinos."

Anya jumped in. "Wait! What is FRC?"

Four voices answered in unison. "Facial Recognition Cameras."

Skipper said, "Hold your questions 'til the end. I'm working pro-bono on this unless the DOJ wants to cut me a check for my standard hourly rate of two thousand an hour."

She paused, but no offer came. "That's what I thought. Just as you might expect, I got thirty-one hits on the FRCs. I yanked the photos from the databases out there in Vegas and ran a scrutinization program to tighten our hits and discard our losers. After all of that, my computers—which are a lot better than the DOJ's—spit out four matches, and all four were . . . wait for it . . . Paulina Pavlova in the flesh. I must say, she looks great for someone who's been dead for a while."

Gwynn said, "That's great news, but it's just confirmation of what we already knew from the fingerprint hit. If you're really worth two grand an hour, I suspect you have more."

Skipper said, "Ding! Thanks for playing, and you are right. I have a bunch more, so get out your pencils, boys and girls. You'll want to jot this down. She's staying in a rented house in Boulder City."

She rattled off the address, and Gwynn wrote almost as fast as Skipper could talk. When she'd finished writing, she asked, "How could you possibly know where she's staying?"

Skipper huffed. "Remember my hourly rate? I'm worth more than I charge."

Celeste said, "Seriously, how did you figure it out? I'm Celeste, by the way."

"I figured. Nice to meet you, Dr. Mankiller. Awesome name, by the way. You get Mankiller, and I get branded with Skipper. Anyway, I figured it out by paying attention. The cams at a lot of the big casinos record the valet drop-off and pick-up for insurance reasons. I watched Paulina get into a cab with an ID number stenciled on the door. I pulled the GPS tracking data from the cab company for that particular car, and poof!"

Gwynn's phone chirped, and she picked up and groaned. "It's Agent White."

Celeste said, "Don't worry. What he doesn't know won't hurt him. Answer it, and put him on speaker. I'll give him an earful."

Anya lifted her phone. "We will call you back, Skipper."

"No need," she said. "I just emailed you and Gwynn everything I have. Tell Mankiller she can take all the credit. See ya!"

The line went dead, and Gwynn punched the green button. "Good afternoon, Agent White."

White growled. "It better be a good afternoon. Tell me what you've got."

Gwynn said, "Celeste was just briefing us on what she pieced together."

White said, "Then why are you talking? I want to hear what the good doctor has to say."

Celeste cleared her throat. "Hello, Agent White. Through various sources, including FRCs, local cab company GPS databases, and some old-fashioned data mining, we now know for sure that our target is, in fact, Paulina Pavlova."

"We already knew that. You better have more than that."

"We do," she said. "We have the address of the house where she's staying down in Boulder City."

White sighed. "I knew you'd figure it out. Well done, Doctor. See, guys? That's the kind of work real professionals do. You two should take notes. Dr. Mankiller obviously has her priorities in order."

"Oh, we've been taking notes," Gwynn said. "But you know how Celeste is . . . She won't take any of the credit. She keeps saying it's a team effort."

"She's right about that," White said. "When are you going to hit the house?"

Johnny Mac asked, "Should we get a warrant and have the hostage rescue team back us up?"

Anya didn't wait for White to answer. "No! We cannot do this. No warrant, and no hostage rescue team. Gwynn and I will do this. If we survive, Pavlova will not. And also opposite is true."

Johnny leaned back. "I don't like it."

White said, "Get over it, Johnny. This isn't white-collar law enforcement. We're going after one of the world's deadliest assassins, and the next time the Kremlin declares her *officially* dead, it'll be because we delivered her body to their door."

23

Logovo Zmei
(Den of Vipers)

Anya sat patiently sharpening a pair of knives while the rest of the team devoured a duo of pizzas. "We need common car."

Gwynn wiped sauce and cheese from her chin. "Ooh, you're right. The Porsche isn't what anybody would call inconspicuous."

Johnny looked up. "Maybe the hotel has a car service."

Anya momentarily stopped passing the blade across the stone. "Perhaps, but that would involve driver, and we do not need witnesses. Maybe we should rent a common sedan."

Gwynn dipped a piece of crust into a tiny plastic cup of garlic butter. "Or, better yet, maybe we could get one from the Air Force."

Celeste rolled her eyes. "Oh, you'd love that, wouldn't you? Maybe your lover boy can deliver it in uniform."

Gwynn shrugged. "I hadn't thought of that, but now that you mention it . . ."

Anya chuckled. "I think you would prefer him to deliver car without uniform."

"He does look good without his shirt," Gwynn admitted.

Anya blushed. "This is not what I meant. I didn't mean he should be naked, only that he should not be in uniform. You are terrible."

Gwynn wasn't listening. She already had the phone stuck to her ear. "Hey, it's me. Got a minute?"

"Always for you. What's up?"

"We need a car—one that looks like every other car and doesn't stand out. Do you have anything like that?"

Captain Tom Elsmore said, "You called the right guy."

"Oh, trust me. I know."

He chuckled. "I meant for the car, but I like the way you're thinking. I just happen to have four such cars in the motor pool with civilian plates. We use them for undercover work. When do you need it?"

Gwynn turned to the team. "Hey, guys. When do we need the car? Tom has four of them."

Anya checked her watch. "Now."

Before Gwynn could relay the message, Tom said, "I'm on my way. I'll be there as soon as traffic will allow."

Gwynn said, "Don't wear your uniform!"

"It's been so long since I've worn a uniform, I doubt if I remember how to put it on."

Gwynn bit her lip. "I bet you look crazy hot in blues."

Tom laughed. "I don't know about that, but I'll see if I can find a set when all of this is over, and we can test your theory."

"Oh, yeah."

He said, "Okay, I'll be there within an hour, hopefully. This time of day, it's probably faster to walk to Caesars from the base than drive, but I'll see you soon."

"Just come on up when you get here. There's no reason to call."

She hung up and licked her lips. "He's on his way."

Anya gave her a smile. "It looks like maybe you are also on your way. Do not lose focus. I need your full attention tonight."

Gwynn took a long breath. "Sorry, it's just that—"

"Do not be sorry. I saw him also without shirt, so I understand, but tonight is not going to be easy for you and me."

* * *

Tom knocked on the door of the suite a little over an hour later, and Gwynn yanked it open. "Hey! Come on in. We're just about to brief the mission."

He let his hand brush against hers a little longer than necessary as he slid the keys into her palm. "Your chariot, my lady."

Gwynn laid the back of her hand against her forehead in a feigned swoon.

Anya eyed the duo. "Stop this! If you are distraction, you cannot stay."

Tom threw up his hands. "Sorry. I didn't mean to . . ."

Anya frowned. "I once heard person say, 'Do not be sorry. Be better.' This is what we need now. Come inside if you want, but do not distract Gwynn."

Tom froze in place. "This sounds serious. If I can help, I'm all in, but if I'm in your way, I'll disappear."

Anya eyed the man standing several inches taller than Johnny Mac and carrying at least thirty more pounds of lean muscle. "Do you have gun?"

Tom raised an eyebrow. "Yeah, but unless I'm on an official operation for the OSI, I don't have any jurisdiction off base."

The Russian huffed. "I did not ask about jurisdiction. This is not important. The four of us staying alive is all I am concerned about. Do you have gun?"

"I have a gun."

"Is at least nine-millimeter with also extra magazines, yes?"

"Yes."

"Good. You will come inside and sit down, but not beside Gwynn."

Tom followed Anya's order and settled into a chair well away from the focus of his affection.

Anya stared at Johnny Mac. "Give to me arm."

Hesitant but obedient, he slid his arm toward the Russian. She drew a knife and clamped her hand against his wrist. He yanked away, but she held fast. Before he knew what happened, Anya ran the newly honed blade across his flesh, slicing a quarter-sized collection of dark hair from his forearm. "Is sharp enough. You must work on trusting skills. I will not hurt you."

Gwynn laughed. "Don't believe her. She's kicked my butt more than once, and it hurt every time."

Johnny Mac dusted off his arm and slid away. "Next time, let a guy know what you're doing with that knife. You're scary sometimes."

She ignored the accusation. "Tonight will be a dangerous and probably deadly night. Is possible we will be able to capture Paulina Pavlova, but she will fight."

Anya's words drifted off, and silence befell the room. The remaining hair on Johnny's arms stood on end, and goosebumps claimed the remaining flesh in the room.

Anya pressed her lips into a flat, horizontal line before whispering, "I am very good fighter, but Paulina Pavlova is better."

Gwynn shivered. "That can't be true."

"Is completely true, and do not think otherwise. She will fight like great wounded animal, and she will not stop fighting until everyone is dead or she is unconscious. Do not believe you are stronger, faster, or more dangerous than she is. This will only get you killed."

Johnny fidgeted in his seat. "I still think we should call in the HRT."

Gwynn glared across the table. "If you don't want to be here, there are a hundred outbound flights tonight, and you can be on any one of them. If you're in, you're all the way in, and nothing less."

He puffed his cheeks and blew out a long breath. "Okay, I get it, but if this thing goes bad—"

Anya knocked twice on the table. "Do not worry, Johnny. If this goes badly, we will not be alive to deal with fallout."

He closed his eyes and slowly shook his head.

Anya motioned toward Tom. "You will drive to house in Boulder City. We will study property for ingress and egress, and you will drop us."

Johnny said, "Wait! Who is *we* and *us*?"

Anya eyed Gwynn, and she nodded barely visibly. Anya paused only momentarily before continuing the briefing. "I am sorry. I was not clear. Tom, Gwynn, and I will survey house, and he will drop us at position I choose. Celeste and Johnny Mac will be operations center here in hotel in case it is necessary to call in hostage rescue team at moment's notice. This is good plan, yes?"

Everyone nodded, but Gwynn and Tom shared a knowing glance.

Celeste let her gaze linger on Johnny for a moment before turning to Anya. "I have six sets of communication gear in my goody bag if you think it would come in handy."

"Yes! This is excellent idea."

The Russian pointed toward Gwynn. "I think maybe we should have also Skipper watching during operation."

Gwynn nodded. "I like that idea. Do you think she'll do it?"

"Yes, she offered already. I will tell her yes."

Tom cocked his head. "What exactly is going to happen after I drop you two off at the house?"

Anya said, "This depends on many things, but plan is for Gwynn and me to hide on darkest side of house while you make commotion to draw Pavlova outside. I do not wish to fight with her inside house. She will have too many advantages in house she knows, and we would not survive this. Is much better outside."

Johnny asked, "What makes you so sure she's going to fight?"

Anya hissed. "You cannot step into den of viper and not get bitten."

The revelation sent chills down every spine in the room, and hung in the air like an ominous cloud, until Johnny Mac slammed his palm on the table, leaving everyone, except Anya, startled. "Look. I owe everyone an apology and an explanation. All of you deserve better than you've gotten from me on this mission."

Everyone leaned in, hanging on his every word. "I've not had my head in the game, and for that, I'm sincerely sorry. I had a talk with Agent White before all of this began, and he led me to believe I'm being considered for promotion to supervisory special agent. It's never been a secret that I want to move up, but I've allowed the prospect of promotion to distract me from where my head *should* be. We're a team, and I've been skirting the edges and trying to keep my reputation and record spotless. Looking at all of you around this table reminded me of the dark, ugly realities of what we do. We're not making traffic stops and writing speeding tickets. We're taking nasty animals off the street, and dealing with those types of people leaves our hands a little dirty, and I'm okay with that. I'm sorry I've been distracted and selfish. I'm all in, and I can't sit here in this hotel room while the three of you are diving into the viper's den—as Anya so eloquently put it. Snakes don't get to bite my partners and survive."

Celeste was the first to smile, and hers looked more like pride than relief. Gwynn closed her eyes for the briefest of moments, silently thankful to have Johnny back on track.

Anya showed no outward reaction, but she was relieved and silently shared Gwynn's feeling. "This is good. We are now whole again, and it is important to know we are not on killing mission. We will take Pavlova into custody, if possible, but she will fight, and people will be injured. If I believe she will kill any of us at any moment, I will destroy her."

In unison, Tom, Gwynn, and Johnny Mac said, "Me, too."

Anya continued. "When she determines we are willing and able to kill her, she may run. There is only one direction to run from Boulder City. This is into desert. If this happens, we must be prepared." She eyed Tom. "Car you brought . . . It can run inside desert, yes?"

Tom shook his head. "No, not far. If the sand is soft, there's no chance, but I have an idea."

Anya raised her eyebrows. "Do not keep us waiting. Tell to us idea."

"The OSI at Nellis just commandeered a pair of rail buggies."

Anya furrowed her brow. "What is rail buggy?"

Tom said, "Sorry, that's what they called them on the paperwork. They're dune buggies especially built for use in the desert, and they're fast. Really fast."

Gwynn grinned like a kid at Christmas. "I just happen to have some recent experience in offroad vehicles with a friend of mine who owns some toys in the Caribbean. If the viper leaves her den, I don't think we'll have any trouble catching her with the Air Force's newly acquired rail buggies."

"I'll make the call," Tom said.

After he hung up, he said, "They'll be staged and waiting."

Anya stood and peered through the curtains and onto the veranda. "Sun will be down in less than one hour. It is time for us to go to work."

24

Ch'ya Krov'?
(Whose Blood?)

Just as it had done since the den of iniquity sprang up out of the desert—thanks in part to Bugsy Siegel's ambition and Meyer Lansky's ill-gotten fortune—the sun kissed the city goodnight and fell behind Red Rock Canyon. The lights of Las Vegas greedily replaced it in the nightly ritual that seemed to usher in drops of darkness that hadn't existed the night before and would never surrender their hold on the light.

Captain Tom Elsmore lifted his phone from the seat beside him and passed it to Special Agent Gwynn Davis, who studied the text message closely. "The rail buggies are in place, and they're in a great spot if Paulina runs like Anya predicted."

The Russian said, "I did not predict this. I only said if she runs, it will likely be into desert. More likely, she will not run, but stand and fight."

From the back seat, Johnny said, "Whatever happens, we'll be ready."

The communications check had been perfect, and to Anya's delight, Skipper was only a whisper away in the state-of-the-art operations center at Bonaventure Plantation in Coastal Georgia.

Tom motioned through the windshield. "Okay, guys. Here comes the address. It's the second house on the right."

Every eye stared through the darkness at the unlit house resting fifty feet off the gently curving street. No cars were in the driveway, and no sign of life shone through the windows.

"It looks like nobody's home," Gwynn said.

"This is exactly what she would have you believe, but is too early for her to be on street already. She is inside house. I can feel this."

Gwynn pressed her face against the window of the car as she tried to feel the same presence as her mentor. "How do you know?"

"I cannot teach to you this feeling. It will maybe come in time, but I have no doubt she is here."

Tom said, "There's a house under construction just ahead. We can ditch the car there and move in on foot."

"Yes, this is perfect plan, but before we stop, remove bulbs from lights that will come on when doors open."

Tom threw up a hand. "It's already been done, but that's not all. I also have a switch to turn off the brake lights so we don't draw attention when we slow to a stop."

Anya didn't acknowledge anything the Air Force officer said, but instead kept her gaze focused on the house where Paulina Pavlova waited before her nightly prowl.

Tom parked the car, and the four crossed the empty street, moving silently and remaining covered by shadow.

Anya held up a finger. "This is as far as you go, Tom. We cannot risk getting you injured. If it becomes necessary to flee for hospital, you must be driver."

Tom nodded and took a knee well inside a row of hedges.

Anya took Johnny Mac's arm. "Give us five minutes to get into position, then knock on door and ask to use telephone."

"I got it," he said. "Let me know when you're ready."

She said, "When you do this, keep bulk of door between you and Pavlova. If we startle her, she will know you are part of game and possibly move to kill you. Do not let this happen."

Johnny shook his head. "Don't let her kill me . . . I'll try to keep that in mind."

"Yes, but also do not kill her unless is absolutely necessary. Is much better to have her alive and under control, but this may not be possible."

For the next ninety seconds, Anya and Gwynn crept across rocky, grassless terrain, toward the unlit house.

Gwynn felt her partner's hand on her shoulder and focused on Anya's whisper. "There is motion detector on light above."

Gwynn slowly raised her eyes to meet the barely visible sensor. "I see it."

"Good. Move directly toward light in slow, steady motion, but do not move sideways. Is infrared, and our bodies are same temperature as air, so if you move slowly, it will not turn on light."

Gwynn nodded and did exactly as her mentor instructed. The light didn't draw its sword of revelation, but if the night played out as Anya expected, lights would be the least of the team's concern.

Pressed against the stucco exterior of the house, they moved in silence toward the back door.

Without checking her watch, Anya whispered, "We have only two minutes. Move more quickly, but stay against wall."

They quickened their pace and situated themselves near the back door. Anya drew a pouch from her pocket and pulled out a pair of small tools. She slipped the tensioning arm into the deadbolt and applied light pressure to the arm. With the curved pick, she felt for the pins inside the barrel of the lock. Seconds later, she spun the tensioner, and the deadbolt retreated from the jamb and into the housing. She then applied enough pressure to the knob to feel the resistance. Repeating the picking sequence, she had the knob unlocked almost instantly and looked up at Gwynn.

The special agent swallowed hard and gave a nod, so Anya spoke softly into her mic. "We are in position and ready."

"Roger. Ringing bell."

Almost before he finished his response, he cursed. "The light came on when I rang the bell."

Anya whispered, "Is okay. Continue."

With his heart pounding in his chest, Johnny Mac listened for movement inside the house. Finally, a voice came from the small speaker built into the doorbell housing. "Who are you?"

"Uh, my name is Johnny, and um . . ."

"What do you want, Johnny?"

"I uh . . . my car. I'm having car trouble, and my cell phone is dead. I really need to use your phone, please."

Listening through their earpieces, Gwynn said, "He's doing well."

Anya only nodded.

The angry, Russian-accented voice said, "I do not have phone. Go away."

"Not even a cell phone? I'm really sorry to bother you, but I'm in a bad situation. You see, I'm in the Air Force, and I'm going to miss curfew if I don't get back to the base. I just need to make a call . . . please."

The disembodied voice said, "Go away. Find other house with phone, or I will call police."

Anya gripped the doorknob, turned it slowly, and lifted upward to take the weight of the door off the hinges. "If alarm sounds, we attack. Otherwise, we move slowly."

Anya pressed the door inward. It cleared the jamb, and the pair scanned the edge of it for sensors, but saw none. She moved the door another foot and felt it touch an object inside. Anya paused, knelt, and slid one hand around the door to feel for the object. "It is chair. Can you fit through opening?"

Gwynn eyed the space and nodded as Anya slipped to the side, giving her partner room to squeeze into the house. She drew her Glock and held it tight against her side as she held her breath and slipped into the abyss of the rented home. Gwynn blinked quickly in an effort to clear her night vision as a silhouette appeared on the chair. She steadied the object and lifted the chair, moving a foot to the right. After placing it back on the floor, Gwynn covered Anya's hand still wrapped around the edge of the door and pulled it inward.

The Russian drew two fighting knives and moved through the opening like an apparition. With the heel of her hand, she directed Gwynn behind her.

It took several torturous seconds for their eyes to grow accustomed to the darkened interior. When they moved, the duo did so in perfect, practiced unison as if sharing one body. Anya led their slow, measured progression, testing each placement of her leading foot before allowing her weight to transfer. Any sound would likely alarm Pavlova, giving her a greater advantage than she already had.

To their surprise, the doorbell rang again, followed closely by repeated pounding blows to the solid wooden door. The commotion gave Anya and Gwynn the cover they needed to move more quickly through the interior. They arrived at the opening into the front room, and Anya leaned ever so cautiously, exposing nothing more than one of her scanning, vigilant eyes. Her continued movement into the space told Gwynn the room was empty of waiting threats.

Johnny Mac continued calling into the hidden microphone. "Come on! Just let me use your phone for one minute."

The break Anya hoped for finally came when Pavlova spoke into the intercom. "I said go away, or I will call police."

Gwynn could almost feel her mentor's relief as she quickened the pace across the floor. The woman's voice had clearly come from the end of the hallway. Anya pressed the back of her hand against Gwynn's hip and nudged her into a small recess beside the opening into the hallway, then she positioned herself opposite her protégé.

Anya whispered into her mic as Johnny continued his relentless pounding and bell ringing. "Make her come to door. We are ready for her."

Johnny thumbed the bell again. "You know what, lady? I think your neighbor beat you to it. I just saw the cops turn onto the street. I'm pretty sure I smell marijuana, or maybe that's the smell of somebody cooking meth in there. I believe I'll flag them down and make them come get a whiff."

The sound of Johnny's ploy working like a charm came in the form of rapidly approaching footsteps in the hall.

In mumbled Russian, Pavlova growled, "I will kill this man, whoever he is."

The footsteps kept coming, and Gwynn's pulse raced. Anya's heart rate never changed, but she shifted slightly, placing the bulk of her weight on the balls of her feet in anticipation of the coming clash of SVR-trained assassins.

Gwynn felt sweat form between her palm and the grip of her Glock.

Suddenly, the approaching footsteps ceased, and the world turned crushingly silent. The unmistakable sound of a blade leaving its sheath hissed through the darkness, and Anya Burinkova, former Russian operative turned American agent, stepped through the opening into the hallway and threw a massive front kick to Pavlova's gut, sending the woman stumbling backward on her heels. Anya lunged forward, throwing a fist into her opponent's face. The collision of knuckles on cheekbone sounded like lightning.

Gwynn followed Anya into the hall and raised her pistol, flipping on the weapon's powerful light. Instantly, the hallway was illuminated with a beam of light so brilliant, it rendered Pavlova temporarily blind, but she crushed her eyelids closed and covered her face with a raised forearm.

Anya pounced like a jungle cat with a blade raised high above her head and cascading downward in an elongated, powerful arc, but when the blade struck, it was a harmless blow, leaving the tip of her blade buried in the hardwood floor where Pavlova had been less than a second before. The woman's speed was like nothing Gwynn had ever seen.

Anya yanked at the blade, but the oak flooring wouldn't surrender the weapon. The blinding speed with which Pavlova moved gave her no time to fight with the stuck knife. Instead, she abandoned the weapon and moved the remaining knife from her left hand to her right. Pavlova captured full advantage of the instant by throwing a leaping kick toward Anya's skull. She raised an arm and dived away to block or avoid the kick, but was too slow. And Pavlova was too well trained.

The kick landed on the back of Anya's arm with such force, she was thrown into the wall with enough violence to knock her fighting knife from her grasp and temporarily leave her shocked. The strike that would've disabled most fighters wasn't enough to stop Anya's attack.

She shoved herself from the wall and toward Pavlova, who was recovering her balance after the flying kick. The woman lunged toward Anya, wielding her knife like a knight's lance. Anya threw a punch to the inside of Pavlova's elbow, deflecting the attack and sending the woman into a quarter turn to her right. Anya slid a foot between Pavlova's legs and laced her arms around the woman's neck and head. She locked the chokehold in place and clamped down with all her strength. Her foe had only seconds to continue standing if she could keep the hold in place without Pavlova finding her femoral artery with her flailing blade.

Gwynn's light danced across the walls and ceiling as she tried to find an angle to fire. "Get in here, Johnny!"

Anya dodged several slashing attempts at her legs, and Gwynn yelled, "Give me a shot!"

Anya heard her partner's plea, but releasing Pavlova to allow Gwynn to get off a pair of rounds wasn't in the cards. The instant she released the deadly assassin, she would spin, gutting Anya with slashes too quick to see.

The explosion of Johnny's boot against the front door sounded like thunder clapping overhead, and a second beam of light from his pistol illuminated the space, turning the hallway into Broadway.

Finally, the chokehold accomplished what it was designed to do, and Pavlova wilted in Anya's arms as her knees buckled beneath her own weight. Anya continued the hold and took advantage of the light to search for blood from either of her legs. She saw none and released her lock from the woman's head and neck.

As Pavlova's arms fell limp at her sides, Gwynn saw the woman's hand still gripping the knife. "Don't let her go! She's not out!"

The potentially fatal mistake had already been committed, and Anya fumbled in a desperate attempt to reclaim the hold she'd released. Her power and superior position wasn't enough to overcome Pavlova's speed.

The woman slammed her palm against the floor and thrust with her heels, pushing her body backward toward Anya. Gwynn watched in horror as her partner was driven back and onto her heels. Still trying desperately to get an angle from which she could put at least two rounds into Pavlova's torso, Gwynn jockeyed, only to be blocked in every direction by Anya's body.

Johnny yelled, "Dive! Give us an angle!"

Frustrated and unable to wait for a shot, Gwynn holstered her Glock and lunged forward. She contacted Anya's back just between her shoulder blades and stopped Pavlova's forward progression. Crushed between her partner and her foe, Anya fought for the woman's weapons, but Pavlova's arms thrashing in razor-like blades of gleaming steel made Anya's efforts futile at best.

In desperation, Gwynn redrew her pistol and elevated it across Anya's shoulder, hopefully bringing the muzzle to bear on the woman who was clearly bent on killing them at any expense. Gwynn yanked the trigger too many times to count, sending supersonic lead from the muzzle and scalding hot brass from the ejection port.

Gunshots, blood, and cries of agony filled the air, rendering Anya deafened by the explosions only inches from her ear and blinded by the blood in her eyes. She expected Pavlova to slump to the floor in a bloody, lead-filled heap, but the battle raged on.

Is the blood mine? Anya questioned as her survival instinct continued fueling her trained body in the fight of her life.

She wiped the blood from her eyes and sent a powerful elbow strike to the woman's temple, sending her opponent backward one stride and giving Anya the space she needed to again draw her knives. With Gwynn's weight no longer pressed against her back, the Russian retreated with her left foot to gain a solid fighting stance. She was an instant away from being face-to-face with one of the few knife fighters on Earth who could match her skill . . . or perhaps surpass it.

As Anya slid her foot backward, instead of finding purchase on the bloody floor, her heel met a solid object, and she knew instantly the fight was over. She fell backward across the object, and Pavlova remained poised in place with her knife leaving the tips of her fingers and beginning its flight toward Special Agent Johnny Mac McIntyre.

Johnny's pistol echoed its thunderous report until the killing point of Pavlova's flying blade pierced his shirt just above his heart. As the knife buried itself an inch past the fabric of his shirt, Johnny retreated one stride and took a knee.

Training demanded that he keep firing at Pavlova, but instinct and desperate yearning to survive sent his eyes to the embedded knife in his chest. He grabbed the blade and looked back up barely in time to see the woman who'd thrown the knife diving through a window at the end of the hallway.

Knowing unconsciousness would take him in only seconds, he yelled into his mic, "At least two officers down inside residence. Maybe three. Suspect is fleeing to the south. She's armed and extremely dangerous."

Unhurt, Anya crawled to her feet over Johnny and Gwynn. Their weapons' lights still illuminated the space, and she took inventory of their condition. Blood pooled around Gwynn's right side, and a Russian fighting knife protruded from Johnny's chest. Her mind raced as she made a thousand decisions in an instant.

Anya planted her foot in the center of Johnny's chest and grabbed the knife, thrusting with her foot and yanking until the knife left its temporary home. She threw the blade at the floor, sticking its tip into the oak planks.

With both hands, she tore at Johnny's shirt and slid her hand into the spot where blood should be gushing from his chest. "You are not hit," she yelled, the words rattling in her head like echoes through a canyon. "Your vest stopped knife. You are okay. Take care of Gwynn. Do not let her die!"

Johnny pawed at his chest until his fingertips sank into the layers of Kevlar where Pavlova's blade had come to rest. Instantly relieved, he forced himself forward to triage Gwynn's injuries as Anya bounded toward the demolished window.

25

KROV′ PUSTYNI
(THE DESERT'S BLOOD)

Anya dived through the remains of the window and rolled to her feet on the sand and stones beneath. Checking to ensure her mic was still in place, she said, "Skipper, you are there, yes?"

The analyst two thousand miles away in the security of her operations center at St. Marys, Georgia, swallowed the lump in her throat. "I'm here, Anya. It sounds bad."

"Is very bad and becoming worse." Her words came in staccato as she sprinted toward the abyss of the waiting desert.

Skipper said, "I tasked an NRO satellite, but it's not online yet. What else do you need?"

"I need to know where Pavlova is going."

"I'm working on it."

A roar came through the comms, and Tom's voice boomed above the noise. "I can help with that one. I'm in pursuit of a motorcycle heading due east. I have the horsepower to keep up, but I can't catch up."

Anya said, "Report changes. I am inside desert buggy now. Keep lights on."

The rail buggy started at a touch of the key, and desert sand flew into an expanding rooster tail as Anya accelerated into the relentless darkness.

Tom said, "Roger. Lights on."

Using the skills she mastered on the island of Bonaire, Anya pushed the buggy to its absolute limits and soon caught intermittent glances of Tom's lights. Whether it was her one-hundred-pound weight difference or Tom's lack of skill in the machine, Anya passed the Air Force officer and slowly closed on the fleeing motorcycle.

Pavlova had every light extinguished, making herself and the machine a challenge to keep in sight, but Anya's solitary focus on her target penetrated the darkness and distance until she was within feet of the bike. She angled slightly away, planning a crossing clip of the rear tire. At the same instant she cut back toward the bike, Pavlova swerved ninety degrees and disappeared from the beams of Anya's headlights. A pair of massive boulders appeared in front of the buggy where the bike had been an instant before, and Anya braked hard as she cranked the wheel to its limit.

The front tire missed the boulder, but the wider wheelbase at the rear caused a back tire to collide with the enormous stone. The combination of the vehicle's momentum and angle sent the buggy tumbling forward, throwing Anya through the rail frame. She landed on her side, tightly tucked to roll and absorb the energy of the crash. When her body finally stopped moving, she was shaken, scratched, and filthy, but unhurt. Tom slid his buggy to a stop beside her, and she ordered, "Move over!"

Tom unbuckled his harness and slid to the other seat.

Anya assumed command of the vehicle and accelerated toward the north. "Did you see where she went?"

Tom yelled over the wind and engine noise. "No, but the cavalry's on its way."

"What cavalry?"

He motioned to the sky ahead. "You'll see. There they are now."

The massive searchlight beneath the spinning rotor of an Air Force H-60 Pave Hawk lit up the desert like a full moon. The pilots pushed the airframe through the steamy air less than fifty feet above the desert floor, leaving a sandstorm roiling in its wake.

Anya pointed toward the rapidly approaching chopper. "You did this?"

Tom gave her a nod, but she was laser-focused on catching her prey one more time.

The H-60's searchlight scanned the desert until it fell on the motorcycle and Paulina Pavlova still coaxing every last ounce of speed from the machine. The helicopter didn't struggle keeping up with the assassin, but Anya's machine didn't have the horsepower of the massive piece of military hardware. She and Tom closed the distance on the bike just in time to watch the Pave Hawk pilots prove their mettle. They maneuvered the chopper in front of Pavlova and rained down a flood of light in an obvious effort to blind the fleeing warrior.

The effort worked, but only partially. Pavlova changed directions faster than the heavy helicopter could copy. Changing tactics, the crew brought the chopper directly over the bike and boiled the sand around it into a torrent of tiny rocks and grinding sand. The actions of the flight crew gave Tom and Anya exactly the break they needed to regain their position.

Tom worked the pivoting searchlight mounted high on the windshield frame, studying every exit Pavlova might take to escape the man-made sandstorm.

"Watch out!" Tom yelled. "She's coming right at us."

Anya looked up to see the outline of the bike exploding from the wall of sand ahead. Instead of braking as Tom expected, she continued toward her target, closing at breakneck speed. Seconds before the front tire of the bike collided with the buggy, Pavlova yanked the handlebars and spun the throttle, sending a spray of sand from her back tire across the windshield.

Anya tapped the brakes and cut the wheel hard. The right front tire collided with the rear wheel of the bike and sent it and Pavlova tumbling across the sand. Anya was out of the buggy before it came to a stop and running toward her target.

The Pave Hawk crew brought the helicopter to a high hover above the scene and trained their spotlight on Pavlova. She tucked her arms tightly against her body and rolled to a stop in the center of the searchlight's beam.

Tom watched in disbelief as Anya leapt into the air with a knife in each hand like a cougar pouncing on its defenseless prey.

Pavlova, although on her back, disoriented, and battered from the crash, was anything but defenseless. Seeing Anya flying through the night air like a descending angel of vengeance, she drew a knife of her own and sent both feet into the air. A foot caught Anya's hip, and the other landed squarely in the center of her chest. The twin blows sent Anya rolling to the left and colliding with the desert floor, unsure if her blades had begun their awesome destruction. Tom heard the thud of Anya's body striking the earth over the chopper's whirring blades, and he ran toward the fight.

Anya leapt to her feet and yelled, "Stay back!"

By the time Tom stopped in his tracks, Pavlova was on her feet and circling Anya. Each fighter eyed the other with destruction in their eyes. Anya flipped the knife, gripping it perfectly before launching it through the air like a missile, directly at Pavlova's chest. As the flying blade raced through the air, Pavlova spun and leaned back just enough to allow the missile to pass only centimeters from her flesh.

Anya took full advantage of her opponent's instant without balance to lunge toward her with her remaining knife leading the charge like a soldier's bayonet. The first cut entered Pavlova's flesh just above her hip bone, and she bellowed like a wounded beast.

Anya let her momentum carry her behind the woman far enough to wrap her arm around her neck. Arching her back, Anya pulled Pavlova from her feet and drew her arm into a powerful arc toward the Russian's gut.

Even at a clear disadvantage and wounded, Pavlova was far from out of the fight. She slashed at Anya's wrist as the blade drew ever closer to her body. The slashing blow deflected Anya's attack, but the razor-like weapons opened the flesh of each woman's hand.

Both groaned in pain, but neither surrendered. Anya tried to throw her opponent to the ground, but Pavlova reached over her head and grabbed a handful of Anya's hair, forcing her to the ground with her. As they hit the dirt, Anya pressed the point of her knife into the back of Pavlova's thigh, sinking the blade to its hilt. The wounded warrior opened her mouth to bellow in pain, but Anya sent an elbow to the back of her head, silencing her cry with her face driven into the sand.

Having never seen a knife fight, Tom stood in awe of the scene unfolding in front of him. He watched Anya carefully pull the knife from the woman's thigh, and the realization occurred to him that Anya wasn't trying to kill the other Russian . . . yet. She was punishing her.

Anya stuck a knee in Pavlova's back and gripped the back of her collar, using the neck of her shirt as a makeshift garrot. As the assassin twisted and struggled beneath Anya's weight, she flailed wildly with her knife, aiming at nothing, and obviously hoping to strike some part of Anya's body hard enough to escape her grasp. With every wild swing, Anya caught a tiny piece of Pavlova's flesh with the edge of her already blood-soaked knife. None of the wounds were life-threatening, but all were enough to diminish her will to continue the fight.

Finally, after several seconds, Anya stood and yanked the woman to her feet. She threw a devastating side kick to Pavlova's knee, sending her back to the ground, the wound above her hip still seeping blood and the slices to her forearms glistening in the artificial light.

"Get up!" Anya demanded.

Pavlova pressed a hand against the desert floor and forced herself back onto her feet.

Anya lowered her knife and stepped in front of the woman, then growled in angry Russian. "You were supposed to be legendary fighter. You are only coward who runs instead of fighting."

Anya motioned toward the pool of blood forming behind Pavlova's foot from the deep wound to her thigh. "The blood that was yours now belongs to desert, and your life belongs to me."

Pavlova ignored the blood and the pain and the chides of the woman who'd once been her fellow Russian comrade, and she raised her knife like a sword. Anya laughed and raised a foot to kick the blade from her hand, but she immediately realized she'd fallen directly into the woman's trap.

Pavlova withdrew the knife and stepped around the kick. When the blade sank into flesh, it was Pavlova's knife and Anya's calf. Fighting through the pain and potentially deadly mistake, Anya pulled her leg away from her opponent and landed a fist on the bridge of Pavlova's nose. Blood poured from her face, and she sent a hand flying to the wound to wipe her eyes.

Disoriented, in agony, and nearly defeated, Pavlova became a wild animal consumed by her anger, fear, and will to survive. She growled like a bear and lunged toward Anya with her blade slashing through the air with complete abandon.

Anya watched the woman approach and timed her strike perfectly. The point of her knife impacted the back of Pavlova's knife hand and separated the flesh and bones until the knife was forced from her pierced hand. She jerked the wounded hand away, pinning it against her side, and continued forward with blood and spittle exploding from her mouth and demolished nose.

Anya let her come, but instead of raising her knife to meet her attack, she sent a powerful claw to the woman's throat and raised her to her toes until they were eye to eye. Tom stepped closer, unsure what was coming, but certain both women would need his help and the attention of the medic he prayed was on the hovering chopper.

As he grew nearer, he heard Pavlova groan. "You are better than they said you were."

Anya narrowed her gaze and hissed, "For hurting my friend, you will die." Tightening her grip on the woman's throat, she forced Pavlova to her knees and lifted the knife she'd dropped from the sand at her feet. "And for running like coward, you will die by your own knife."

26
Bol'she ne Tvoy Boy
(No Longer Your Fight)

Captain Tom Elsmore stood in mortified disbelief at the scene in front of him as Anya Burinkova knelt and wiped blood and sweat from her face. "You must take photograph."

Tom swallowed hard but found himself unable to take a step. "Anya, this is wrong. This isn't what we do."

The Russian said, "Come to me and take picture. Is absolutely necessary."

He took a stride on trembling knees and finally reached the gruesome scene. He studied the tableaux at his feet but couldn't bring himself to raise the camera.

The Pave Hawk crew landed the helicopter a hundred yards away, and a pair of flashlights approached from the storm of wind and sand.

Anya watched their approach and looked up at Tom. "You still have radio, yes?"

Tom patted his pocket and felt for his mic at his throat. He nodded but didn't speak.

"Good," Anya said. "You will report status to Skipper and also ask if Gwynn is alive."

Tom took a step back and turned away just as the two airmen from the helicopter approached.

Anya pointed toward Tom. "Take from him cellular telephone and take picture for evidence."

The first of the two crew pulled off her helmet and laid it on the sand beside Anya's boot. "Okay, ma'am. Sergeant Pelham will do that, but you have to let me take a look at that wound on your leg."

Anya glanced down to see blood oozing from her wound. "Cut is not fatal. You can do this after picture."

Sergeant Pelham motioned toward Tom. "Did you say for me to get his phone?"

Anya nodded. "Yes, and hurry. Is most important thing. Take from him telephone and make picture, now!"

Pelham shook his head. "But that's Captain Elsmore. You want crime scene photos on his personal cell?"

"Do it, now!"

Pelham jogged toward Tom and returned with his phone seconds later. "Am I supposed to get you in the picture, too, or just her?"

"Both of us. Take many shots from everywhere, but only me and this woman in pictures."

"Okay. Whatever you say, ma'am."

Pelham took a dozen shots and returned the phone.

Anya pulled Pavlova's knife from her body, wiped the blood from the blade, and stuck it behind her belt. She pocketed another object Pelham couldn't identify.

With Anya back on her feet, and the evidence sealed inside Tom's cell phone, the medic took Anya's arm. "Come with me, ma'am. I really need to get a look at that leg. Are you cut anywhere else?"

Anya pulled her arm away and headed for Tom. "Gwynn is alive, yes?"

"Yes, she's alive, and she's going to be okay. She's demanding to know if you're okay."

"Give to me radio."

Tom pulled off the comm gear and passed it to Anya.

She pocketed the transceiver and pulled the mic to her mouth. "Gwynn, you are there, yes?"

Instead of her partner's voice, Skipper's tone filled her ear. "Gwynn is going to be fine, Anya. She's getting some stitches and probably some pretty good painkillers. Is it done?"

"It is," she said. "Pavlova is dead, but mission has only just begun. We must now find Kalashnikov."

Skipper said, "That can wait, Anya. We've got to get you to a hospital. Tom says you're cut badly."

"Is only small cut. Paramedic from helicopter will clean and put in stitches."

Skipper chuckled. "Yeah, that's not really what they do. He may clean it a little, but he's going to package you for shipping. He's not a doctor, so he won't do your stitches."

"*He* is not man. Medic is woman, and *she* has strong stomach. She will give for me stitches if necessary."

Skipper said, "Whatever you say. Oh, and as far as finding Kalashnikov goes, I think Celeste has that covered, but there's one more eight-hundred-pound gorilla in the room."

Anya frowned. "There is no gorilla."

"It's just a saying, Anya. Relax. We—and by *we*, I mean *you*—have to do something with the body."

"We will put inside body bag and keep for Kalashnikov to see. After this, we will deliver her to Kremlin with nice little note."

"That's up to whoever you're working for, but my bet is that none of that will happen. Anyway, I don't think you need me anymore. I'll keep my phone on, though. If something comes up that's too much for the federal government to deal with, let me know, and I'll do what I can."

"Thank you for doing this for us. I trust you."

Skipper said, "Yeah, trust . . . that's it. Good night, Anya."

"Wait. Before you go, please tell to Chase—"

"No, Anya. I'm not telling Chase anything from you. Good night."

When Anya turned around, a second pair of crewmen from the helicopter were zipping the black body bag.

Anya focused on the buggy. "Put body inside there, and you may now see my leg."

The medic led Anya to the helicopter. "Do you want me to cut your pants off, or do you want to take them off?"

She kicked off her boots, unfastened her pants, and pulled them off.

The medic grimaced. "That's a big laceration, but it looks like a surgeon's incision."

"Knife was very sharp. You will make stitches, yes?"

"That's not really my thing. I'm a flight nurse. It's my job to stabilize the patient while the pilots get us to the hospital."

"But you are soldier, no?"

"No, I'm an Air Force first lieutenant."

"If this happened in combat and you were there, but no doctor and no hospital, you would let patient bleed to death?"

"No, of course not, but we're like five minutes from the hospital."

"There is no time for hospital. Make stitches, or give to me suture kit and I will do it, but no hospital."

The nurse shook her head and sighed. "I've worked with a lot of feds, most of them men, and I've never seen any of them take an injury like this without throwing in the towel. You're my kinda woman, ma'am. This is going to hurt like hell unless you want me to hit you with some morphine."

Anya shook her head. "No, I will be okay with pain. No morphine. I must go back to work."

The nurse searched her kit and the cabin of the chopper and finally handed Anya a strap hanging from overhead. "This is a cargo strap. Roll it up and stick it between your teeth. If you don't, you'll bite your own tongue off, and I'm not stitching that back together."

Anya did as she was told and bit down on the nylon webbing.

Five minutes later, the nurse put away her tools and bandaged the wound. "Well, it's not pretty, and it's still going to bleed for a while, but that's the best I can do. Change the bandage when it soaks through, and please go see a doctor as soon as possible."

Anya spat out the strap and inspected the work. "You were right."

"About what?"

"It did hurt, but even after pain, I am still alive, and she is not."

"You're right about that, ma'am, but I need to check your hip for a wound I must've missed in the initial assessment. The pocket of your pants is soaked in blood."

Anya laid a hand on the nurse's arm. "Do not worry. Is not my blood. Thank you for stitches, and I think you should be doctor."

"From your lips to God's ears," she said. "Whoever you are, I'm glad you're on our team."

Anya and Tom stood in the relative silence of the open desert as the Pave Hawk disappeared to the north.

Tom finally spoke. "You'll have to forgive me, but I've never seen anything like you just did. It was amazing and absolutely horrific at the same time."

Anya sighed. "Is sometimes necessary, but is also terrible for me. Maybe this is American feeling. When I was SVR officer, I did not have thoughts such as these."

"I don't think it's uniquely American, but I'm happy to hear you don't take pleasure in . . . this."

"There is no pleasure in killing. Only sadness and sometimes relief."

"Relief?"

She lowered her chin. "Sometimes, options are only kill or die. If I do not die, this is relief for me."

"I get it, but I hope I never have to make that decision."

She stepped closer. "I hope this for you, as well, but our work is not over. We must take Pavlova to Kalashnikov."

"What? We can't run around Las Vegas with a dead body."

"We have no other choice, and we are police officers, so help me put her into buggy."

They situated the body bag behind the seats and climbed back aboard the rail buggy for the run back to Boulder City. The western sky was ablaze with the artificial life of Vegas, and they made the trip in less than half an hour.

A quarter mile from the house where the night began, Anya rolled to a stop and peered through the windshield. "We cannot go back to house. Police are everywhere."

"You're right, but back there in the desert, you said we were police, too. Besides, Johnny Mac is still the incident commander, unless the attorney general showed up while we were playing in the sandbox."

She turned in her seat and glanced at the body bag behind them. "My mother told me when I was little girl, '*Vorovat' arakhisovoye maslo nekhorosho, dazhe yesli vas ne poymayut.*'"

Tom let his eyes turn skyward as he tried to unscramble the part of his brain that knew Russian. "Peanut butter?"

Anya smiled. "Yes, when I was little girl, I loved peanut butter, and inside Soviet Union, it is not so easy to find. Once, I stole it from inside government locker and my mother made me give it back to soldiers. Stealing peanut butter is wrong, even if you do not get caught."

"I'm sure this story has a moral somewhere, but I'm a little too rattled to pluck it out. Can you give me a clue?"

She tapped the thick plastic of the body bag with her fingertips. "Carrying dead body in front of policemen is wrong, even if we do not get caught."

He chuckled and pointed to the north. "Head up that way about a mile. That's where they unloaded the rail buggies. I'll meet you there with the car."

Without another word, he leapt from the buggy and sprinted away as if he'd been desperately seeking any excuse to put some distance between himself and the carnage the desert night had produced.

Running dark, Anya turned to the north and carried two bodies and one soul to the new rendezvous point. The empty lot where Tom's Air Force troops offloaded the rail buggies lay in black shadow, making it the perfect place to transfer Pavlova's body from the desert vehicle to Tom's innocuous-looking staff car.

He backed the car to the edge of the lot with the lights disabled, and Anya positioned the buggy by the trunk. They hefted the bagged body into the trunk and closed the lid on the night's phase one before settling onto the front seat of the car more determined than ever to put Vladimir "Volodya" Kalashnikov exactly where he belonged.

Tom wiped the sweat from his brow. "What now?"

Anya stared through the windshield at the glowing night sky of Las Vegas. "Now, you take me to Gwynn, and you return to your world inside safety of Air Force Base. But first, give to me your phone. This is no longer your fight."

27

Iz-za Protsessa
(Due Process)

Captain Tom Elsmore gripped the steering wheel and eyed the former Russian assassin in the passenger seat. "Is that sanctioned?"

Anya asked, "Is what sanctioned?"

"What we . . . Well, what you just did out there in the desert."

Anya stared at the roof of the car for a long moment before Tom asked, "You know what the word *sanctioned* means, right?"

"Yes, I know this word, but I do not know how to correctly answer question. I am not exactly typical federal police officer. I have badge and ID, but I did not go to training academy. Maybe you could say I was grandfathered into program. You know this word, *grandfathered*, yes?"

Of all the reactions he expected to have, laughter was not one of them, but it came anyway. He sat, shaking his head. "I think it's safe to say you're not the typical anything. I don't pretend to understand exactly what you and Gwynn and the rest of them do, but what just happened out there . . . That's not due process."

Anya cocked her head. "Why is this funny?"

"It's not. I think that was just my brain having no idea what else to do, so I laughed."

"You are correct. Tonight is not due American process, but the situation is not only American. Paulina Pavlova was not American citizen. She was international fugitive and assassin for hire. She may have been here to kill Volodya Kalashnikov, but we will never know. When we determined who she was, we could not let her escape. She made decision to fight and die."

"What would've happened if we couldn't catch up with her tonight?"

Anya shrugged. "This depends on who she is working for. If for Kremlin, she would continue mission no matter what sacrifices she had to make.

I think this is reason she tried so hard to escape, but I do not know this for sure. If she was working for someone else, she would forfeit payment and disappear. I do not think she would risk fight with me for only money."

He said, "Normally, that would sound a little arrogant on your part, but after seeing what you're capable of, it makes perfect sense."

"Arrogance is most deadly of all character flaws."

"Before tonight, I might have argued that point with you, but not anymore."

"Okay, this is enough talking. You will now take me to Gwynn."

"There's just one more thing before we go."

"What is this one thing, and why can we not discuss it on way to Gwynn?"

He shifted the car into gear and pulled onto the street, turning away from the melee still underway at what had been Pavlova's rented house. "I want an introduction to your boss, Special Agent White."

"He is not boss for me. We have agreement, but he is boss for Gwynn and Johnny Mac. You have one thing wrong, though."

Tom screwed up his face. "What do I have wrong?"

"He is not special agent. He is supervisory special agent. This is what makes him boss. But why do you want to meet him?"

"I may need a job when I leave the military, and if I keep hanging around with your team, something tells me the Air Force isn't going to be too happy with me."

"Yes, of course I will do this for you, especially since you got for us the helicopter tonight."

"About that . . ."

Anya drove a finger through the air. "More driving! Not so much talking."

They pulled into the driveway of a modest, southwestern-style house a mile from the main gate of Nellis Air Force Base, and Anya said, "Gwynn is here?"

"No, she's not here, but there's a shower and clean clothes here. You can't run around inside the hospital covered in blood, no matter whose blood it is. Now, come on. We're wasting time."

She followed Tom through the front door, and he pointed down a short hallway. "The bathroom is down there. I'll lay your clothes on the sink while you're in the shower."

She scanned the room. "Whose house is this?"

"It's my sister's house. I'm staying with her until I can get a place of my own, and she's about your size."

To his surprise, Anya giggled.

"What's so funny?"

"I think you will have to tell lie to your sister because she will not believe truth."

He joined her in laughter. "I guess you're right, but thankfully, she's not here."

Fifteen minutes later, Anya emerged from the bathroom wearing a pair of jeans one size too big and a UNLV T-shirt. "How do I look?"

"Definitely not like my sister."

"Maybe I am Russian sister from other mother, no?"

"I don't think so."

She glanced back into the bathroom. "You have plastic bag, yes?"

"We're not keeping your clothes. We're burning them."

"Is not for clothes. I need only small plastic bag, maybe size of hand."

He disappeared and returned with a tall kitchen garbage bag and a much smaller sandwich bag. "Put your clothes in this one, and the other one is for whatever."

On the way out the door, Tom dropped the bag of bloody clothes into a rolling garbage can, and they climbed back into the car. He said,

"You know, this is my first time driving around with a dead body in the trunk."

"You will get used to this. It happens more than you think."

"That's terrifying."

They pulled into a restricted parking zone outside the Air Force hospital, and Tom pulled down the visor with his OSI placard. They found Gwynn sitting on the edge of an exam table, checking her watch.

"It's about time the two of you got here. I've been waiting for an hour. I hear you caught our girl."

Anya stepped in and took Gwynn's hands. "You are okay, yes?"

Gwynn squeezed. "Yeah, I'll be fine. I lost some blood, but thanks to Johnny, I didn't lose enough to take me out of the game. Now, tell me about Pavlova."

Anya stared down at her friend. "I was afraid for you, and I have for you gift."

"A gift? What are you talking about?"

Anya produced Pavlova's fighting knife and laid it in Gwynn's palm.

"What's this?"

Anya closed Gwynn's fingers around the handle. "This is knife Pavlova used to stab you, and also knife I used to kill her. Is now yours."

"You killed her? With her own knife? That's cold, but I love it."

"You are welcome, friend Gwynn. Is now time for telling and showing."

Gwynn giggled. "I think you mean show-and-tell."

"Yes, this is same thing. You are coming, yes?"

Gwynn peered down a long hallway. "If I can get the doctor to release me, I'm coming. Otherwise—"

Anya interrupted her. "You are in hospital, not prison. You are coming."

* * *

On the ride to the Red Square inside Mandalay Bay, Anya detailed the events of the night Gwynn had missed and concluded her story by thanking Tom again for scoring the helicopter.

He said, "You don't understand . . ."

"Yes, I understand this perfectly. Without helicopter, Pavlova would have escaped, and we would be no closer to Kalashnikov."

When they arrived, Tom said, "I'll stay with the car. I don't like the idea of anyone snooping around and finding our friend in the trunk. How long will you be in there?"

Anya checked her watch. "I think only short time. Maybe fifteen or twenty minutes."

"I'll be waiting."

Gwynn and Anya strolled into Red Square, completely ignoring the hostess, and continued toward Kalashnikov's personal corner of the lavish restaurant. They found their man sitting with his back to the wall and a crowd of adoring fans enraptured by some tale he was telling in Russian.

Anya pushed through the gathered crowd. "It is done."

Kalashnikov eyed his guests and then Anya. "What is done?"

She pulled Tom's cell phone from her pocket, opened the best of the twelve pictures, and placed it in his hand.

He glared down at the screen, and his stomach convulsed at the scene of Paulina Pavlova bloody, missing one ear, a fighting knife plunged beneath her chin, and the blade—though unseen—penetrating upward into what had once been her brain. He closed the picture, composed himself, and handed the phone back to Anya. She took it, and with the skill of a sleight-of-hand magician, slipped the severed ear into his palm.

The cold, blood-covered flesh sent him reeling, and he threw the ear to the floor. "Go! All of you, go away."

The gathered guests formed a retreating phalanx, leaving Kalashnikov alone with Anya, Gwynn, and the ear.

"Why would you do this? Why would you come in here with"—he pointed toward the floor—"*That*? What is wrong with you?"

Anya ignored the question. "You were correct. She was here to kill you, but she had plan to get you alone and make video call to Moscow so Putin could watch you die. We saved you from this fate. You will now come see body."

"No! I do not want to see the body."

Anya leaned in close. "What is matter? You have soft stomach, Volodya?"

He raised a hand to shove her away, but she landed the flat side of her knife against the back of his hand. "You will never touch me unless I tell to you I want this. I do not allow anyone to put hands on me and keep hands. You understand this, yes?"

He carefully lowered his hand, moving it slowly around the glistening blade. "Fine. I will not touch you. Forgive me. What is it you want from me? Payment for killing that woman?"

Anya sheathed her knife and took a seat across from him. "We do not want payment for her, but for next person you wish to be dead, you will pay us instead of others who worked for you in past. You want private *ubiytsa*, yes?"

He swallowed hard. "Yes, a private assassin is exactly what I want, and I have finally found you."

"You did not find us," Anya said. "We found you, and this is better. Is very good for you that we came here. Paulina Pavlova would have killed you in next few days. You are alive only because we saved you. This means rest of life is gift from us to you. You agree with this, yes?"

He groaned and mumbled something in a voice that sounded neither Russian nor English.

Anya said, "Relax, Volodya. We are now your friends, and is very good to have friends like us. You will now come and see body of woman who believed she was one of best assassins in all of world. I proved to her, and now I will prove to you, that we are better."

He shook his head violently. "No. I don't need to see it. I believe you."

"You have no choice. Pavlova was personal killer for President Putin, and we are giving her dead body to you. Is rude to refuse gift such as this."

He paused and furrowed his brow. "She was sent by Putin? How do you know this?"

Anya never looked away. "I was trained in same places and by same people as Pavlova. She was legendary assassin and believed to be dead. Is no longer belief. Is fact, and you can show Putin you did this."

Kalashnikov almost smiled. "Photographs and video can be faked. I will give to you one million dollars to deliver body to Moscow."

Anya shook her head. "This is not possible. We make dead bodies. We do not deliver them."

"This is not true," he said. "You delivered Pavlova's body to me here tonight, so you have proven you do this. I am only asking you to do this across ocean."

"I cannot do this. I will be captured or killed if I return to Moscow for any reason. I will do, instead, next best thing. I will deliver body to *rezident* inside Russian embassy in Washington."

He squinted. "What is *rezident*?"

Anya looked surprised. "You really do not know this?"

Kalashnikov raised both hands. "I am businessman. How would I know these things?"

"*Rezident* is commander of all SVR officers inside embassy and also inside United States. He is same as American CIA station chief inside embassy in Moscow."

Kalashnikov leaned back and turned his eyes to the ceiling. "Maybe this is almost as good as dropping her on Putin's desk."

Anya turned to Gwynn, who stood somber and silent behind her, and she gave Anya a barely perceptible nod.

"This I can do, but not Moscow. I will do this for you, but you will give to us every job for one year. This is deal?"

Kalashnikov narrowed his gaze. "Why knives?"

Anya smiled. "Because they are silent. Only sound is dying breath leaving body. We have deal, yes?"

"How much?"

"This depends on difficulty of target. For simple person, one quarter million. For protected person with only one layer of security, one half million. And for layered security person, is at least one million, maybe more."

"If I wanted you to kill prime minister of Russia, you would do this for one million dollars?"

Anya locked eyes with him. "You will pay expenses plus one million American dollars. Deposit half now, and other half when we bring to you proof of death. I can give to you account number, and we will begin tomorrow."

He squeezed his eyes closed and shook his head. "No, do not kill prime minister. It was just example."

"Do not give to me example. Give to us jobs."

He took a long swallow from an elegant tumbler. "I don't have a job for you right now."

"You will come with us now to see Pavlova's body, or we will bring her inside restaurant for you to see. You choose."

He threw up his hands, "Fine. I will come with you, but—"

"There is no but. You will come."

He stood and followed Anya through the door as Gwynn silently slipped in behind him.

Tom spotted them approaching the car and popped the trunk from the button inside while silently praying the trunk lid wouldn't fly open. It didn't, and Anya lifted the lid. Kalashnikov shrank away, but Gwynn planted a hand on his shoulder, encouraging him to move closer. He resisted, but when he saw the black plastic of the body bag instead of the carnage from the photo, he exhaled a long sigh of relief.

Gwynn planted a foot behind his heels, and Anya unzipped the bag. The muscles of his stomach convulsed again, but this time, he was unable to keep his most recent meal inside his body.

Anya pulled a rag from the trunk beside the body and tossed it to Kalashnikov. "This is what we do. And now, we do it for you."

28

SERDTSE D'YAVOLA
(THE HEART OF THE DEVIL)

Twenty-four hours later, Volodya Kalashnikov sat in a secluded office in the back of Club Gedo with Oxana Kozlova sitting on the corner of his desk. "She is more than simply a killer," he said in his native tongue.

Oxana said, "How are you certain she killed Pavlova?"

"I saw her body! It was the most horrifying thing I've ever seen. She is either a psychopath or the SVR-trained assassin you suspect her to be. Maybe both, but that's not what frightens me the most. It's her partner who never says a word. She makes my skin crawl."

Oxana considered his words. "We must now decide if she is more valuable working for us or as bargaining chip with Moscow."

"Perhaps both."

Oxana raised an eyebrow. "I like it when you get that look, Volodya. What are you thinking?"

"I think I will have this woman and her silent friend pay a visit to Anthony Lucchesi."

"Lucchesi? That is close to home, but I like it."

Volodya put on his ice-cold smile. "Then, I will call my uncle Nikolay."

Oxana slid from the desk and ran her hands through his hair. "This is why I love you, Volodya. You have mind of genius and heart of devil."

* * *

Supervisory Special Agent Ray White stepped through the door of the Bellagio suite with only a briefcase in hand. "I hear the two of you had quite the outing last night."

Gwynn said, "Welcome to Vegas, boss. Have a seat, and we'll tell you all about it."

Anya leapt to her feet. "Ray White, I want you to meet Captain Tom Elsmore. I promised to him I would make introduction, so now is done, and I will make tea."

White shook Tom's hand, untied his necktie, and settled into the chair he thought would be the most comfortable in the room. "Okay, let's hear it."

Gwynn spent five minutes detailing the operation right up to the point when Pavlova made her exit from the rented house. Anya returned with tea just in time to finish the story.

White listened intently and even had to force back a smile at least twice. "It sounds like a party to me. So, did Kalashnikov buy it?"

Anya said, "Yes, and we made deal, but I see deception in his eyes."

"Deception," White said. "What do you mean?"

"He believes he is smartest person in every room, and even though he knows we are dangerous, he is planning to . . . I think phrase is *double-cross* us."

"Double-cross you? How?"

"This I do not know yet, but we will find out soon. I think he is licking lips and excited about having killing team like friend Gwynn and me at his disposal."

White said, "We'll deal with the double-cross when and if it happens. Until then, stick to the playbook. He'll hire you to kill somebody soon, and when he does, that's when it gets good. We'll get the intended victim alone and pull him, or her, in. We'll fake another assassination, collect another fee from Kalashnikov, and lock him up."

"Yes, of course," Anya said. "This has been plan all along, but I must tell you something."

White rolled his hand through the air. "Spit it out."

"Captain Tom wants to be federal police officer like us, and I think you should hire him right now. He does not have house or wife yet. This would be perfect time for him to change job."

Tom said, "Anya, this isn't the time for this."

"I promised to you I would make introduction. Now I have done introduction and also recommendation for you."

"This really isn't what I meant when I asked for an introduction."

Anya huffed. "But is what you said."

White said, "Forget it, Tom. She does this all the time. You just have to learn to ignore her. We'll talk about the job when this is over, but fraternization between Department of Justice employees is forbidden unless they work in separate divisions. I just thought you should know."

Tom blushed. "Thank you, Agent White."

"Relax, Tom. I've been a cop a long time, and that means I notice things other people miss. I'm sure you know what I'm talking about."

"Yes, sir. I do."

White sipped his coffee and leaned toward Tom. "The way Davis looks at you is how she used to look at Anya, so you've got some pretty big shoes to fill."

Tom stared at Anya and then back at Gwynn as disbelief consumed him. "You mean you two were . . . I mean, I didn't . . ."

Anya slid onto the arm of Gwynn's chair and brushed her cheek with the back of her hand. "Yes, Gwynn and I do not technically work in same division."

Tom swallowed hard and stammered until everyone in the room except him burst into raucous laughter.

Anya kissed Gwynn's cheek and gave Tom a wink. "We are only playing joke, but if you are mean to friend Gwynn, I will not kill you in sleep. Instead, I will wake you up to kill you." Tom didn't laugh, and Anya didn't

214 · CAP DANIELS

take her eyes from him until she said, "We must now do something with body."

"Don't worry about that," White said. "I've got a pair of hot-shot, young CIA case officers who can't wait to drop Paulina Pavlova's body on Evgeny Kuznetsov's desk in the Russian embassy." He checked his watch. "In fact, they should be picking up her body from the Air Force morgue as we speak. Thank you, Tom, for arranging cold storage for our 'guest.'"

"My pleasure," Tom said.

Anya rubbed her hands together. "This means is time to go to work, yes?"

Gwynn looked up. "Work? What are you talking about?"

Anya said, "Volodya has been thinking of who he wants us to kill for twenty-four hours. I am certain he did not sleep last night, so must now go and give to him what he wants."

"I like it," Gwynn said. "I'll be ready in half an hour."

She rose and headed for her room, and White turned to Anya. "What do you need from me?"

"I need nothing right now. I have upper hand with Kalashnikov, but he does not know this, of course. I will let him believe he is in charge of every-thing inside his world until we are ready to take him down. That is when I will need for you to have people to do this."

White slid forward onto the edge of his seat. "Listen close, Anya. When this is over, you are not slipping away. There are too many global forces col-liding. I'm not willing to lose you if this thing turns sour, so I need you in-side the country and under my thumb until we know for sure the smoke has cleared."

Anya sighed. "This is not what we agreed, Ray. I promise to always be available for mission, but you will not control me between missions. This is agreement."

"Yeah, I know, but this time is different. We're thumbing our noses at some pretty powerful players on this one. I want to be able to protect you."

Anya let out a chuckle. "You believe you can protect me better than I can do alone? This is laughing funniness. When I am alone, I am invisible. I am ghost, and no one can touch me."

"You were alone when my team pinned you up in that alley in St. Augustine. You weren't a very good ghost that night."

Anya scowled. "This is different."

"Yeah, it is. This time, there's an entire government who wants to put your head on a pike in Red Square, and I'm not going to let that happen."

Anya stood. "Maybe we will discuss this again before mission is over, but for now, Gwynn and I have work to do."

White growled. "You're the most frustrating human I've ever met."

"Thank you. This is high compliment from man like you. Do you have for us address?"

"Yeah, I've got Kalashnikov's address, but your typical game of fast-and-loose isn't going to work on this one. It's one thing if you get yourself captured or killed, but if you let something happen to Davis or Johnny Mac, our agreement is over, and that doesn't end well for either of us. You're part of a team now, and the lone-wolf mindset of yours has to go."

Anya reached down for Ray's cup, and he slid it into her hand. "I will not agree to living beneath your thumb, but I will protect friend Gwynn and Johnny Mac."

He grabbed her wrist. "Be careful, Anya. We've still got a lot of work to do, and we can't do it without you."

She glared at his hand wrapped around her wrist. "You are one of very few people I will allow to do that without cutting off hand. Would you like more tea before Gwynn and I go?"

He released her wrist and produced a small slip of paper. "No, thank you. Here's the address. Oh, and there's one more thing."

"What is this one more thing?"

White leaned back and crossed his legs. "Leave Skipper out of this. She's a civilian."

Anya froze. "How did you know . . . ?"

White held up his credentials pack. "Read the top line. It says Supervisory Special Agent. It means I see everything, hear everything, and know everything before it happens with my team. Don't forget that."

Anya stomped to the kitchenette and deposited the cups into the dishwasher.

White turned to Tom. "By the way, I forgot to thank you for the helicopter last night. That was excellent thinking on your part."

"I've been trying to tell Anya all day that I'd love to take the credit for the chopper, but that wasn't me. I don't know who dispatched it, but I'm glad it happened."

Anya peered into the sitting area and directly at Ray White. "Do you still want me to promise to leave Skipper out of operation?"

29

Znay Svoikh L′vov
(Know Your Lions)

Gwynn emerged from her room in jeans, a black T-shirt, and hiking boots.

Anya surveyed the look. "Is perfect. Now we must make house call."

White said, "Not so fast, you two. We've got a new player in the game. Skipper isn't the only analyst with magic fingers. We have a warehouse full of analysts who can do anything she can do, and probably more."

Anya rolled her eyes. "I doubt this is true."

White opened his briefcase. "Doubt it all you want, but this one stays in-house. I sent a number to both of your cell phones. The analyst's name is Bryan Wells. He's dedicated to this case and this case alone. He'll manage the security cameras at Kalashnikov's condo and make sure you have any asset you need tonight."

Anya pulled out her phone and stored Bryan's number.

Gwynn did the same and said, "If he's better than Skipper, he wouldn't be working for the government."

White shot a pointed finger at Gwynn. "Stop letting your crazy Russian friend get in your head."

In the elevator on the way down to the parking garage, Anya said, "I am driving."

Gwynn looked up from her phone. "Are we taking the Porsche?"

Anya smiled and dangled the key fob from her fingertips.

Gwynn snatched the key before she could withdraw. "Too slow. I guess that means you've got shotgun."

Forty-five minutes later, after a drive that should've taken less than ten, they pulled to the curb one block from Kalashnikov's high-rise.

Gwynn said, "I guess it's time to get Bryan, the super analyst, on the phone."

Anya thumbed the speed dial and speaker button and waited. "Operations, Wells."

"Is Anya and Special Agent Davis. You are analyst, yes?"

"I've been expecting your call. I'll open the garage when you pull up. Drive to the second level and all the way to the back. There's a pair of orange traffic cones blocking spot number two eighty-one. It's for you, and I'll have the elevator waiting for you about twenty yards away."

Anya covered the phone. "He is good so far."

Gwynn eyed her. "Better than Skipper?"

Anya snickered. "Not yet."

Just as Bryan promised, the spot was reserved, and the elevator doors were open.

Inside the elevator, Anya turned off the speaker and stuck the phone to her ear. "We are inside elevator and going to wireless earpieces. Stand by for comms check."

They inserted a pair of small devices into their ears to act as both microphones and receivers, and in turn, performed comms checks with Bryan.

With comms checks complete, he said, "Here we go, ladies. I'll take you to the top, and the doors will open into Kalashnikov's foyer. If this guy is half as good as he should be, the comms will go dead when you enter the penthouse but should recover when you leave. Your earpieces are recording devices, but if he insists on you taking them off, there's not much we can do. Just keep your stories straight when you come out. Your testimony may be the only record of the meeting."

"We understand," Gwynn said. "Keep the elevator at the top for our exit . . . if you're good enough. I don't want to stand in the foyer waiting for a ride if this thing falls apart in there."

"I'm already on it," he said. "I've isolated the elevator car, and I have full control. I won't leave you stranded up there, but from Kalashnikov's perspective, it will look and sound like the elevator has left the building."

The doors opened, revealing a muscular man less than two feet outside the elevator car with a pistol aimed at Gwynn's head. In a motion too fast for the armed man to process, Anya stepped toward him, grabbed the pistol, and moved the slide a fraction of an inch to the rear, rendering the weapon useless before stripping it from his hand. Continuing her motion forward, she planted a knee in his crotch and hooked a heel behind his leg. A second later, the man was on his back, groaning in pain with his own pistol pointed at his head.

"You are terrible bodyguard. I should kill you for being stupid."

Volodya Kalashnikov stepped into the foyer wearing a black silk robe with a glass in his hand. "I should have known you could override security locks on elevator, but I did not expect you to disable my guard so quickly. You must forgive me for underestimating you."

Anya dismantled the guard's pistol into a dozen pieces and pocketed the firing pin. She sprinkled the pieces of the weapon across the guard as he continued rolling on the floor. "Do not point gun at us ever again, or you will die where you stand. Are you smart enough to understand this?"

They stepped around him and into the opulent penthouse. "You have job for us, yes?"

Kalashnikov motioned for them to follow. "Come inside and have drink. We will discuss situation."

"We do not drink while working, and we prefer to talk here inside foyer."

"I'm sure you do," he said, "but I have electronics to disrupt recording and transmissions inside. Out here in foyer, not so much. I am sure you understand."

Anya moved to follow him. "Of course. We will talk wherever you feel safe, but having us working for you is ultimate safety. You will soon learn this. No one is stupid enough to hurt you if they know they will die horrible death for only trying."

He led them to a sitting area with a low table and two sofas facing each other. "Please sit. Are you sure you will not have drink with me?"

Anya ignored the question, and Gwynn remained as silent as the dead.

"Okay, then. Straight to business it must be. There is man named Anthony Lucchesi. He is . . ." Kalashnikov paused and shrugged. "Maybe he wants to be called businessman, but he is not. He is dinosaur from days when American mafia controlled Las Vegas. He makes, shall we say, trouble for me. But he has money and security."

Anya surveyed the room. "It is obvious you have same, but man at elevator was not very good security. We can teach your people to become proper security for you if you want."

"Perhaps, but first, we must deal with Lucchesi."

"Is up to you, of course. What you say, we will do."

He shook his glass, rattling the remaining ice. "Are you sure you do not want drink?"

"We stay alive because we have rules we do not break."

He stood and poured himself a second vodka. "This man, Anthony Lucchesi, he is called—"

"Father Tony."

Kalashnikov froze. "You know of him?"

Anya raised her chin. "If you go to Africa without understanding lion, you will never leave savanna alive. Same is true for Las Vegas."

He raised his drink. "Where have you two been all of life? Maybe I should call you lion killers."

Gwynn and Anya shared a knowing glance. "Lucchesi will not be first lion for us. We have long history of leaving carcass of lions for vultures to clean bones."

He pondered Anya's statement for a moment. "Italians do not understand things in same way as Russians like us. They make threats and then have what they call *sit-down* to discuss problem. I am not kind of man to discuss compromise, and I think you understand this. You already know who and also what this man is, no?"

Anya said, "He is leftover from days when American mafia was strong in this city. He is now using chessboard for his silly game of checkers, and he is fly buzzing around your head. You are important man who cannot be bothered by such pesky insect."

"I like how you understand my world. I cannot deposit two hundred fifty thousand dollars into account if I do not have account number. Two hundred fifty is correct, yes?"

Anya nodded and handed him a slip of paper with a U.S. government-owned offshore account. "You are brilliant man. Lucchesi is man with one or maybe sometimes two layers of security. He will be no problem, but there will be collateral damage. You understand this, yes?"

"Of course. But you understand I do not pay for this collateral damage."

"We have understanding," she said. "Is only extra fun for us. Is still only one half million when finished. What do you want to see?"

He furrowed his brow. "What do you mean?"

"We must bring to you proof Lucchesi is no longer alive. Tell to us what you want. You have ear of Paulina Pavlova. We can bring to you heart of Lucchesi inside silver bowl if this is what you want."

Kalashnikov chuckled. "How long have you been in America?"

"This is strange question. Why does this matter?"

He said, "American saying is, *on silver platter*, not *inside silver bowl*."

"Yes, I know this saying, but is terrible to deliver round heart on flat tray. Is much better inside bowl. But if you want tray, for one half million dollars, you will have heart on tray."

She and Gwynn rose in unison, and Kalashnikov said, "Where are you going?"

Anya cocked her head. "You will transfer money, and we will go to work. This is what we do. For next forty-eight hours after transferring money, have always with you someone for strong alibi."

He stood, leaving his drink behind, and followed them to the waiting elevator. "I really do not need or want to see Lucchesi's heart. If he is found dead, it will be on every news channel."

Anya spun on a heel. "If you want his body to be found, this is two hundred fifty thousand more. We do not leave bodies to be found. Forensic investigation in America is very good. If no body . . . no autopsy and no evidence. Is up to you."

Kalashnikov froze and studied Anya's face. Slowly, he moved toward her, and Gwynn closed the distance between herself and Anya's side.

He ignored her and stepped within inches of Anya until their eyes were locked on each other's. "If you look into my eyes and tell to me Lucchesi is dead, I will believe you until I find out you have lied. Then I will send a dozen men to send you to Hell. Lying to me is a death sentence. Never forget this."

As promised, the elevator car waited at the touch of a button, and the pair backed into their mirrored stainless-steel chariot.

"That was amazing!" Gwynn almost squealed.

Anya smiled. "Yes, it was, and part when you stepped close to me when Kalashnikov tried to be threatening? That was favorite part for me. You are very good at this."

Back in the Porsche, the adrenaline slowly drained, and Gwynn asked, "How did you know about Lucchesi?"

"Same as I told to Kalashnikov. I do not go to dangerous place without knowing who and where are lions."

30

DAVAYTE SDELAYEM STAVKU
(LET'S MAKE A BET)

When Gwynn and Anya returned to the suite at Bellagio, they found Supervisory Special Agent Ray White sitting on the floor with Dr. Celeste Mankiller three feet away, hovered over a chessboard.

Gwynn studied the scene and turned to her partner. "Did you know he played chess?"

"This is wrong question. Good question is, did you know we had chessboard inside room?"

"That's why we're great together," Gwynn said. "We look at everything from every possible angle."

Anya touched a finger to her chin. "Since we are in Las Vegas, I will make with you bet for one hundred dollars."

"If you're going to bet me that Agent White wins, I'll take that bet, girl, and you will lose."

"No, this is not bet. Bet is Celeste can stand without using hands, but Ray cannot."

Neither of them stood, but White said, "Pretty nice job tonight, ladies. I have another bet for you. I'll bet you a thousand bucks that I can tell you the manufacturer and model of the pistol you stripped from Kalashnikov's bodyguard. That was an extremely impressive move, by the way."

Anya considered the offer. "I think this is not possible, so I will make with you this bet."

White lifted his queen and moved her six spaces across the board. "Checkmate, and it was a Sig Sauer P-two-two-six with a stainless slide and threaded barrel."

"This is not possible. How could you know this?"

Celeste huffed. "Hey! That's not—"

White gave her a wink. "Fair? Is that what you were about to say?"

She knocked over her king. "No, that's not what I was going to say, but it's true."

White looked up at Anya. "Remember Bryan Wells, the analyst who turned off the security cameras in Kalashnikov's penthouse?" He didn't give her time to answer. "He only turned them off for Kalashnikov. He kept the feed running for us on Celeste's laptop, but that's not all."

Anya scowled. "What else?"

White raised both hands above his head as if surrendering, and he stood without touching anything. "That'll be eleven hundred you owe me."

Anya rolled her eyes. "I think I agree with Celeste. That is not fair."

White shrugged. "Hey, a bet's a bet, but you wanna hear something even better?" He paused and then said, "I'll take that as a yes. Not only did Bryan steal the camera feeds, deliver your elevator twice, and find rockstar parking for you, he also blocked Kalashnikov's jammers with a program he wrote and installed on your cell phones."

It was Gwynn's turn to doubt. "He's never had possession of our cell phones, so he couldn't have installed a program he wrote—or any other program for that matter."

White mimicked Anya's Russian accent. "This is not possible. Is that what you're thinking?"

"Exactly."

White smiled. "He may have never held your phones in his hands, but you stored his contact information when I sent it to you. The program was playing a little game of piggyback, and we have flawless audio of every word you and Kalashnikov spoke. Oh, and we got some pretty cool audio of the bodyguard calling you every Russian curse word he could groan."

Anya fell into a chair like a balloon whose air had leaked out. "This is terrible way for mission to end, and I do not like it."

Gwynn followed suit. "I hate to admit it, but I agree. These things usually end up with dead bodies everywhere and explosions no one can explain. By comparison, this is pretty dull."

Johnny Mac spoke up. "This isn't *Law and Order*. It's real life. We're cops. We build cases, deliver evidence, and make arrests. It's up to the prosecutors to piece it all together and present it—making a case beyond a reasonable doubt. It's what we do, and this is exactly how it's supposed to work. You've been running around with Red Sonja too long. Good cases end in good convictions—not in a smoking pile of dead bodies. That's how our system is designed to work."

Gwynn suddenly perked up. "Wait a minute! That video and audio is fruit of the poisonous tree. We don't have a warrant to tap his security cameras. Nothing we did tonight is admissible in court."

A shrill whistle blasted from the kitchen, and White said, "Oh, look. Our tea is ready."

He headed for the kitchen while Johnny sat, pondering Gwynn's point. "Wait, though. We don't need a warrant to record the audio on your earpieces. We just need a sworn affidavit from both of you that the voices on the recordings are yours and Kalashnikov's. With the tapes and affidavits, any federal judge in the country will sign our warrant, and we can collect all the audio and video we want."

Anya perked up when Ray delivered a steaming mug. "Thank you, Ray. Is very sweet of you. This means mission is not over, yes?"

He nodded. "That's exactly what it means. Davis is right about the inadmissibility of what we gathered tonight, but Johnny is right about the federal judge. With a pair of affidavits from the two of you, we'll have our warrant as soon as we wake up a judge."

Anya took her first sip and looked up with mischief in her eyes.

White froze, "What? What are you thinking? I know that look, and I don't like it."

The Russian said, "Johnny will write affidavits, and we will sign, but do not wake judge tonight. Is late, and judge will be less grouchy in morning after breakfast."

White lowered his chin. "No, that's not all you're thinking. Spit it out."

"If we wait until morning to have judge sign warrant, this will give to us six hours to kill Anthony Lucchesi."

"Hold on!" Johnny said. "You don't get it. None of this is real. You're not killing anybody."

"You mean anybody *else*," Anya said.

Johnny ignored her and continued. "This case isn't about Lucchesi. It's about Kalashnikov, and that's it. Nobody else. We pin Kalashnikov to the floor and send him to federal prison for the rest of his life. That's what we're here to do."

Anya cocked her head. "Aw, you are so innocent. Is cute, but you did not listen. Nothing from tonight is admissible. We have to finish job and give to Kalashnikov Lucchesi's heart in silver bowl."

White sipped his tea. "Watching you two fight like jealous siblings makes me feel like a proud poppa. But none of your opinions matter. You do what I tell you, and nothing more. That's how this works. You're both right, but Anya's answer is more complete. Johnny, you write up the affidavit from the video and audio feeds. And you two, tell me about Lucchesi."

Gwynn said, "I'll confess. I didn't study the lions in Vegas before we came out here, and I'm ashamed of that. It won't happen again."

Anya said, "Plan is simple. You can get for us propofol or ketamine, yes?"

"What?" White said.

Celeste joined in. "Yes, we can get either or both. How much do you need?"

"This depends on how many people are between us and Anthony Lucchesi."

Celeste grinned. "I like this plan already. Give me two minutes."

White said, "Slow down. It's almost midnight, and we can't plan an all-out assault on a mafioso before the sun comes up."

Anya said, "This is waste of time. When sun comes up, we will be asleep, and mission will be almost over. Planning is finished. Is all inside my head."

"It may be in your head," White said, "but I'm not authorizing it until it comes out of your mouth and I understand it and approve it. So, start talking while Celeste is ordering your party favors."

Anya took another long sip of tea. "We will need . . ." She froze and studied the room. "Where is Tom? We will need very good driver, and he is exactly this."

White threw a thumb down the hall. "He crashed a couple hours ago, but Johnny can drive."

"No," Anya insisted. "Johnny is too good with paperwork. He must do affidavits. Tom is driver I want."

"Okay, okay. If I like your plan, we'll wake him up. We did get lucky and score a couple extra cars while you were gone. The FBI field office is dying to get at least an honorable mention if we pull this off, so they're giving us whatever we ask for."

"This is good," Anya said. "They can send two or maybe four agents to cover us and get us out if plan goes badly, yes?"

White nodded. "Oh, yeah, they'd love that, but keep talking. I'm not sold yet."

Anya continued laying out her plan in exquisite detail for the next ten minutes. When she paused to take a breath and a sip of tea, Celeste yelled out, "Got it, but it's even better than what you ordered. It's a cocktail including propofol, but our chemistry class is made up of ambitious over-achievers. This stuff will put a gorilla on the ground in thirty seconds."

"Thirty seconds is too long," Anya said.

Celeste stuck her hands on her hips. "I said thirty seconds for a gorilla. Even the biggest human you find in there will hit the deck in five seconds after you stick him with this stuff."

"This is perfect," Anya said. "But we must first know Kalashnikov made deposit into account."

Celeste's fingers flew across the keys. "Bingo! It's there."

Anya detailed precisely how the night's operation would end if everything went as planned.

When she was finished, Ray leaned back and checked his watch. "It's genius, and I wish I had thought of it. Get the drugs, get the FBI on the line, and get Tom out of bed."

As the suite became a beehive of activity, White snapped his fingers. "I almost forgot. You still owe me eleven hundred bones, so don't get yourself killed out there."

Anya tried snapping her fingers, and White laughed. "You look like a drunken monkey. Do you really not know how to snap your fingers?"

Anya growled. "Is silly, unnecessary skill, but I need one quarter of a liter of your blood inside bag for mission."

White took a step back. "What?"

"You have same blood type as Lucchesi, and we need to leave behind bloody evidence."

"How? How could you know that?"

"I know blood type of everyone on team. If we are injured on mission, this is important."

"I get that, but how do you know Lucchesi's blood type?"

"Always know more about enemy than enemy knows about you."

"Is that Sun Tzu?" White asked.

"No . . . is Anya Burinkova."

31

SEREBRYANAYA CHASHA
(A SILVER BOWL)

Just as Ray White predicted, the local FBI agents were more than willing to pitch in. They met Tom, Anya, and Gwynn a mile from the gated entrance to Anthony Lucchesi's estate. The all-male team of agents looked like fourteen-year-old boys vying for Gwynn's and Anya's attention during the briefing, but the Russian reined them in.

"What we are doing is very dangerous, and we need all of you to focus." Anya paused long enough to offer a hint of a smile. "If this goes well, there will be plenty of time for Gwynn and me to get to know all of you a little better."

Gwynn thought, *Her finesse works almost as well as a fighting knife.*

"If we give to you signal of three times saying *abort*, you are to get us out as quickly as possible. You can do this, yes?"

The senior agent said, "Don't worry, ma'am. We'll be there before you can get the third word out of your mouth."

"No! This is not what you will do. You will wait until we give full command before moving. You understand this, yes?"

He sighed. "Yes, of course. It was just a figure of speech. We won't move until we hear the signal. If we see something we don't like outside, though, we'll give the same signal, and you'll halt and retreat."

Anya glanced at Gwynn, and they both giggled. "You do not understand. This is not what we do. When we are inside house, we will not come out until we make decision to do so. You will not call off mission under any circumstances."

"That's not how this works, ma'am."

White had been listening in through their comms and kept silent until that moment, but he couldn't hold his tongue any longer. "This is my op, boys and girls. Anya, Gwynn, and I are the only three who can call it off or on. Ours are the butts on the line if this goes south. Theirs—quite literally —and mine, professionally. This is not a contest to see who can pee over the highest wall. It's an operation to get a dangerous man off the streets. Any questions? Good. I didn't think so."

Anya pulled Gwynn aside. "You are okay with everything, yes?"

"I'm good."

"This is first time for something like this for you, yes?"

Gwynn nodded. "Yeah, it's my first time, but I understand, and I'm ready."

Anya squeezed her hand. "Needle, knife, knockout, in this order. No guns."

"I'm ready, Anya. If I weren't, I'd tell you."

"Is time now to go to work."

Bryan Wells spoke through the comms. "Okay, boys and girls. The lights are out. Go have some fun."

Anya and Gwynn slid onto the back seat, and Tom hit the gas.

He glanced up at them in the mirror. "I've got a question before this night turns into a three-ring circus. Are all DOJ agents as insane as the two of you?"

Gwynn met his eyes in the mirror. "Only the good ones."

Tom killed the headlights, flipped the switch to disable the brake lights, and pulled to a stop at Lucchesi's gate. The look in his eyes turned sincere. "Don't get hurt in there, and I'll be here when you come out."

They slid from the car and bounded across the gate as if it weren't there. The solitary man in the guardhouse never looked up, and the two moved silently through the night. The cactus-lined, curving drive wound its way to the impressive house situated on a sandy piece of soil a few feet higher than everything else.

The man on the front door melted into Anya's arms seconds after she injected the first syringe into the muscle of his upper arm. She laid him against the railing and almost envied the sleep he would enjoy for the next half hour.

She picked the lock, pushed the door inward, and whispered into her mic. "Doorman is down, and we are inside."

It took their eyes thirty seconds to adjust to the deepened darkness inside Lucchesi's mansion, and they spent the time listening for signs of life in the cavernous interior of the palace.

The echoing voices of at least two men filled the darkness. As their eyes adjusted, Anya pointed across the foyer, and Gwynn followed. They moved in silence toward the voices until reaching a short hallway to the kitchen. Anya held up a syringe, and Gwynn did the same.

A nod of Anya's head sent them through the opening, where three men stood enjoying something they couldn't stop shoving into their mouths. Gwynn moved with lightning speed to the left and had the first man on the floor before the other two could react. Anya threw a crushing punch to one man's throat, and he grabbed at his neck in choking disbelief. The Russian sank a needle into his neck, and he wilted to the floor. The third man watched and drew his pistol.

The thought of a pistol shot exploding through the relative silence was not a reality either woman was willing to face, so Anya drew another syringe and stepped toward the giant of a man. He turned to face her with determination in his eyes. His turn toward Anya gave Gwynn the opening she needed to lunge toward the massive target. Her syringe landed in the back of his right arm, and he spun with remarkable speed, yanking the needle from his flesh before she could depress the plunger. Anya took full advantage of the instant to thrust her needle toward his back. The beast of a man spun again and landed a mighty fist beneath Gwynn's jaw, knocking her onto the table with stars circling her head.

Believing Gwynn was no longer in the fight, the man squared his shoulders with Anya and braced for the fight of his life. She dropped her syringe and drew her knife. The man laughed as he pulled a pistol from his belt. Anya focused on the weapon and moved in to remove herself from the line of fire. She threw a fist to his gut, but it was like punching a rock wall. The man didn't flinch, and when she raised her blade, he grabbed her wrist with a powerful claw, eliminating the threat.

Wrapped in his powerful grip, Anya struggled to free herself. She pawed at the pistol, trying desperately to keep the muzzle pointed away from herself and Gwynn, but the man's strength was like wrestling with a bear.

Gwynn shook the stars from her eyes and leapt from the table. Seeing her partner battling the man, she reacted by instinct and drew the knife Paulina Pavlova had used to try to kill her two days before. She left the surface of the table and landed the piercing tip of the blade on the side of the man's neck and watched the steel disappear into his flesh. With the knife firmly embedded inside his neck, Gwynn gripped and shoved until the glistening blade reemerged from the front of his neck, having severed the trachea and rendering the man incapable of sound. The final noise he would ever make was his three hundred pounds collapsing to the floor.

Anya gave a nod of respect and appreciation but never said a word. They moved in unison to the massive, curving stairwell leading to the second floor. The double doors to the master suite swung inward without a sound, and the two stepped into the room, where the most delicate piece of the puzzle awaited.

Anya pointed to the right, and Gwynn followed her finger to the side of the waiting bed. Anya moved to the left and knelt beside Anthony Lucchesi, who lay snoring with his mouth hanging open. Gwynn slid a hand across the mafia boss's wife's mouth and slipped a needle beneath the skin of her arm. The pain of the needle woke the woman, but only long enough to register confusion on her face and drift into a narcotic absence.

Anya pressed Lucchesi's chin, closing his mouth, and covered the lower half of his face with her palm. The man stirred, and his eyes exploded open.

Anya hissed, "You do not have to die, but you will if you do not cooperate. Capisce?"

The seven decades Anthony Lucchesi had spent on Earth had taught him two things: nothing was as important as staying alive, and strange women in his bedroom were the epitome of trouble. With that knowledge foremost in his thought, he drew a long breath and surrendered. "Just don't hurt my wife."

"She is fine. We have given her a drug to make her sleep, but we have not hurt her. You will come with us, and we will not hurt you, either."

He shucked the cover away. "Let me put on some pants. For God's sake, don't rob me of that dignity."

She took a step back, allowing him to stand. He reached for his trousers hanging across the valet and withdrew a pistol barely larger than his meaty hand.

Gwynn saw it first and said, "Gun!"

Anya reacted by throwing a punch to the back of his hand. He yanked the trigger, sending orange fire belching from the muzzle. The bullet landed harmlessly in the plush mattress, but the threat was far from over. Gwynn bolted from beside the bed, never taking her eyes from the pistol. Anya fought with Lucchesi for control of the weapon, but she did so only as a distraction to allow her partner to sink her needle into his hip. Soon, his grip failed, along with his knees, and he collapsed to the floor.

"Are you hurt?" Anya asked.

"No, I'm fine. Are you okay?"

"I am also fine. You must lead, and I will carry him."

Gwynn helped her partner heft the man into a fireman's carry, and she headed for the staircase.

Anya said, "Do not forget blood."

Gwynn withdrew the plastic bag and tore away the tab. She allowed Agent White's blood to pour over the sheet beside the sleeping woman.

"Tom, we're coming out, but we need you at the house."

"Roger," came his instant reply.

Bryan, the analyst, said, "Give me thirty seconds, and I'll have the gate open, but you're on your own with the guard."

Tom slid from the car and moved silently through the darkness to the gate. By the time he reached the hinges, the ornate metalwork was swinging inward.

The guard from inside the small shelter stepped through the door and thumbed his flashlight, illuminating the drive. "Who's there?" he demanded, but Tom never moved.

As the guard approached, Tom pulled his Air Force Office of Special Investigations cred-pack from his pocket and held it up in front of him. "I'm sorry to bother you, but I'm the local animal control officer, and we've had several reports of one of the escaped tigers from the Las Vegas Zoo being seen in this area. Would you mind if my officers and I have a look around? It's important that we recover this particular tiger before he hurts anyone else."

The guard approached hesitantly. "What are you talking about? I ain't heard nothin' 'bout any tiger escaping. Who are you, really?"

"Here, have a look at my credentials. You'll see that I am who I say I am." He lunged toward the guard, shoving the cred-pack into his face and capturing his still-holstered pistol with his other hand.

With the guard stumbling backward, Tom pressed the retention release on the holster and slid the pistol free while simultaneously hooking a heel behind the guard's knee. They ended up on the ground together with the guard staring straight into the muzzle of his own pistol, while Tom slid a hypodermic needle into the man's belly and crushed the plunger.

The guard groaned. "Hey! What was that? Who are you?"

Tom applied enough pressure with his knee to keep the guard pinned to the ground. "Good night, John-Boy. I hope you dream of tigers and Italian beauties."

The man shuffled in a useless effort to free himself of Tom's weight and the tranquilizer's coming trance. He failed on both attempts, and Tom dragged his body into the guard shack, where he could spend the next hour getting the best sleep of his life.

"The guard is down, and the gate's open. Keep coming. I'll meet you with the car."

Hearing Tom's transmission, Gwynn said, "We're thirty seconds from the gate. Don't pull inside. It'll only cost time turning around. Have the back door open and waiting at the gate."

Anya struggled under Lucchesi's weight but kept moving toward the waiting car. With the gate in sight, Anya huffed into her mic. "You . . . still . . . have . . . control of . . . cameras . . . yes?"

Bryan said, "Yes, I have all cameras and alarms. Continue."

Gwynn rounded the rear of the car, threw open the right-side door, and reached in for Lucchesi as Anya shoved him from her shoulder and onto the back seat. She followed him into the car as Gwynn pulled from the other side until both were in and the rear doors were closed. Tom and Gwynn slid onto the front seat, and he hit the gas.

Anya's breath came hard as she recovered from the labor of carrying Anthony Lucchesi's limp form. "Close . . . gate."

"It's already done," came Bryan's reply.

Gwynn reported, "The team is clear of the compound. No friendly casualties. One casualty inside the house, but it was unavoidable."

Ray White said, "Nice job, everyone. I'll meet you at the FBI field office. It's time to find a silver bowl."

32

POKHISHCHENIYE
(KIDNAPPING PARTY)

Inside the FBI's Las Vegas field office at 1787 West Lake Mead Blvd, Anthony Lucchesi opened his eyes and shook his head in a desperate effort to clear the cobwebs from his head. "Where am I, and who the—"

White slapped Lucchesi's cheek. "Watch your mouth. I'm Supervisory Special Agent Ray White, and you're on a gurney in protective custody of the Federal Bureau of Investigation."

"Protective custody? FBI? What the f—"

White slapped him again. "I told you to watch your mouth."

Lucchesi sat up and squinted against the light of the interrogation room. "I ain't sayin' nothin', and you ain't got nothin' on me. I want my lawyer."

White handed him a steaming cup of black coffee. "Relax, Mr. Lucchesi. You're not under arrest, and you don't need your attorney."

He stared down at the FBI crest on the coffee cup. "Ha! FBI coffee, in an FBI cup, on a hospital bed in 'protective' FBI custody."

White raised his mug in salute. "It's been a hell of a night, Mr. Lucchesi, and you're probably going to need several more cups—and maybe a shot of bourbon—before we finish telling you the story."

Lucchesi glared across his cup. "If I find out you hurt my wife, I don't care if you're the president. I'll tear you in half and feed you to the buzzards."

"Your wife is perfectly fine. In fact, she's having the best sleep of her life. We'll let you talk with her in a couple of hours."

"Let me?" Lucchesi growled. "What do you mean, let me? If I'm not under arrest, you can't stop me from talking to her right now."

"Let us explain to you what's going on, and then you can decide what you want to do next. Do you know a man named Vladimir Kalashnikov?"

"Of course I know that piece of Russian dog—"

"Language, Anthony. We're all civilized adults here. There's no need for vulgarity."

"So, what about Kalashnikov? What's he got to do with any of this?"

White took another sip and paused to remind the Italian who was in charge. "Mr. Kalashnikov paid one of the deadliest assassins in the world one million dollars to kill you."

"So what? I got some of the best bodyguards around. I ain't afraid of no assassin that Russian piece of crap can hire for any price. If he thinks a million bucks is enough to kill me, he's drinking the wrong vodka. You know what I'm sayin'?"

White took a seat and motioned for another chair a few feet away. "You don't have to sit on that gurney, Anthony. You can sit in a chair, and we can even get you some clothes if you'd be more comfortable out of your pajamas."

Lucchesi looked down at his blue and white pinstripe pajamas and laughed. "I guess I do look pretty ridiculous, huh?" He slid from the gurney and cautiously made his way to the chair. "What'd you give me?"

"It's a proprietary cocktail we whipped up especially for this occasion. It'll wear off in a couple of hours, and you'll feel as good as new. We gave your wife a dose, as well, but hers will last a little longer since she's half your size."

Lucchesi positioned himself in the chair and looked for a place to put his coffee. "What? This place ain't got no side tables?"

"We'll get you one. But first, let's talk about your bodyguards. They didn't do such a good job tonight."

"You're tellin' me. But when I get home, you can bet your ass there's gonna be some heads rollin' over this thing tonight. So, I'll ask again.

Who's this so-called assassin that's so good for a million bones, huh? Where's he at?"

White threw a thumb toward the two-way glass. "*She* is on the other side of that glass, and *she* works for me."

Lucchesi laughed. "Oh, you're a funny guy, Ray White. A million-dollar *she*-assassin. You should've been a comedian instead of a fed. I thought we were levelin' with each other, and you come in here with this kinda crap. Get outta here with that stuff."

"I can bring her in if you'd like. I'm pretty sure her face will ring a bell for you when the drugs make their way out of your system."

"What are you sayin'? This assassin of yours is the chick who ran the little kidnapping party tonight?"

"That's what I'm saying, Anthony. Wanna meet her?"

"We've already met. And I didn't like her none the first time."

"Have it your way, but let me tell you the rest of the story."

Before White could continue, the door opened, and Gwynn came through the door, rolling a metal cart. She positioned it beside Lucchesi. "There you go, sir. This is the closest thing we had to a side table."

She turned to leave, but he caught her arm. "You ain't her, are you?"

Gwynn smiled, pulled her arm from his grip, and left the room.

"Was that her? 'Cause I remember the chick in my house being blonde."

"Maybe she just looked blonde in the dark. Who knows?"

"So, that was her? That scrawny little babe? She's your assassin? You feds are a bigger joke than I ever knew. Tony and Franky ain't never gonna believe this."

"Let's get back on track. I'm running a sting operation to take down Vladimir Kalashnikov. One of the tentacles of that operation turned out to be a hit on you. Apparently, good ol' Volodya sees you as a serious threat."

Lucchesi raised his mug. "He *better* see me as a threat. That vodka-drinking, caviar-eating son of a—"

"Let me finish," White said. "We took the upfront money for the hit, and we're getting the rest when we deliver your heart to Kalashnikov on a silver tray."

Lucchesi flushed pale. "What do you mean, my heart on a silver tray? That ain't funny, G-Man."

"It's obviously not going to be *your* heart, but it'll look a lot like yours. The Vegas morgue is full of overweight sixty-year-old guys with bad hearts. We'll pluck one of those out and drop it in Kalashnikov's lap."

"My god, man. You people are worse than the Sicilians. That's some sick stuff."

"Stop interrupting me. I'm a busy man." White checked his watch. "In about an hour, your wife is going to wake up with a nasty headache—a lot like the one you've got right now—and she's going to see your side of the bed empty, except for a pint of my blood."

"Your blood? What's wrong with you?"

White showed him the Band-Aid on the inside of his left arm. "It turns out you and I have the same blood type. Go figure. Anyway, she's going to see the blood, and she's going to lose her mind. Ten minutes later, the story is going to be all over the streets, and word will get back to Kalashnikov right about the time I have my favorite blonde assassin deliver your heart."

Lucchesi pointed at White. "I knew she was a blonde, you sneaky mother—" He stopped himself this time.

"What can I say? I'm a slimy G-Man, but I am sorry for the few minutes your wife is going to be scared out of her mind. As soon as word hits the street, we'll put you on the phone with your wife, and you can calm her down."

"Calm her down? Are you some kind of maniac? Have you ever tried to calm down an Italian woman who thinks her old man is cut to pieces? Huh?"

"That's up to you," White said. "You're a free man. You can walk out of here and call her right now if you want, but that means Kalashnikov gets the word this was all an elaborate set-up, and he walks away scot-free."

Lucchesi licked his lips and swallowed the last drink of coffee. "So, you're tellin' me if I do this thing for you, Kalashnikov goes down, and I get to go home, no strings? Is that what you're saying . . . Special Agent?"

White finished his coffee. "It's *Supervisory* Special Agent, but yeah, you've got it right."

The mobster lifted his mug. "Bring me some more coffee, and I'll think about it."

White rose, took the mug, and walked out of the room, leaving the door slightly ajar to reinforce the message that Lucchesi was free to go at any time.

Anya met White just beyond the door and whispered, "I can go inside, yes?"

White considered the idea. "Wait until I get back with his coffee, and you can take it in."

Anya took the pair of mugs from Ray. "In this case, I will go for coffee."

She vanished down the hall, and White strolled back into the interrogation room.

"Where's my coffee, G-Man?"

White nodded toward the door. "It's coming. What have you decided?"

"I've decided I'm waiting for my coffee."

White crossed his legs and examined a fingernail. "Fair enough."

After three minutes of tortured silence, Anya came through the door and handed White his mug. He took it and said, "Thank you," but she ignored the courtesy.

Anya stepped between the two men, giving Lucchesi ample time to size her up before placing his mug on the makeshift side table. She leaned down and spoke barely above a whisper. "You are very fortunate man I am now

American girl. If I were still Russian girl, blood in bed would have been yours."

Anya closed the door behind her as she left the room, and Lucchesi exploded.

"I knew it! I knew it wasn't that scrawny brunette. I don't know what kind of cop you are, Ray White, but you ain't no FBI agent."

White took a tentative sip. "I never said I was."

Another long moment of silence followed until the mobster said, "Okay, I'll do it, but you've got to keep that woman out of my house forever. Capisce?"

"No more visits from my Avenging Angel. You've got it, Lucchesi."

33

SERDTSE TRUSA
(THE COWARD'S HEART)

Volodya Kalashnikov sat on the veranda of his penthouse, overlooking the fishbowl of depravity below. The city provided the perfect setting for his lust for more of everything, and fulfilling that lust with the blessing of the Kremlin, some ten thousand miles away, made the potential even more alluring.

The bodyguard who'd fallen victim to Anya's speed and violence of action during the previous night's visit saw the inside of the penthouse for the last time and had been replaced by four former Russian Spetsnaz soldiers waiting for the former Russian SVR officer and sparrow to deliver the promised prize to Kalashnikov. She would be no match for the former Eastern Bloc special forces soldiers trained to eviscerate targets with extreme violence and absolute prejudice. Delivering Anastasia Robertovna Burinkova's body to Sobornaya Square inside the Kremlin's walls would launch Vladimir Kalashnikov, the grandson of one of Russia's greatest heroes, back into the good graces of the blue-eyed former KGB officer who sat on the president's throne at the heart of Moscow.

* * *

Celeste came through with a donor heart, just as promised. "It came from the chest of a sixty-seven-year-old victim of cardiac arrest. I couldn't find a real silver bowl, so this stainless-steel version will have to do. It was a gift from the Vegas morgue."

Ray White ignored Celeste's contributions and stuck a finger in Anya's face. "Something doesn't feel right about this whole thing. None of us knows what's going to happen in Kalashnikov's penthouse this morning, but if you get my agent hurt, or worse, you better hope somebody in that penthouse throws you through a window, because what I'll do to you is a lot worse than a fall from a skyscraper."

Anya sighed. "I agree with your feeling. Something smells funny, and it is not that heart."

"Have you got any ideas?" he asked.

"I think maybe he will try to negotiate price down from million dollars. He probably believes if we could do job so quickly, it is not worth so much money."

"I hope you're right," Ray said. "But whatever it is, you can't carve him up. We need him to go to trial or at least cut a deal. He can't do either if you filet him up there, so keep your knife in your pocket, or wherever you keep it, and don't get Davis hurt."

Anya stuck out her bottom lip. "You care only about Gwynn getting hurt, but not me?"

"Why do you have to be so . . . whatever you are. Of course I'm worried about you, too. As mad as I get at you sometimes, I still like having you around. It's nice to have a sparring partner who won't pull any punches."

She grinned. "But I *am* pulling punches. Otherwise, you would lose even more quickly."

He gave her a playful shove. "Get out of here and go to work. The same four FBI agents from last night will be one floor beneath you, and Bryan will have the cameras and elevator."

Anya's grin turned ominous. "I have better idea than same elevator trick. In case bodyguard wants to get even, I think it would be safer and scarier for Kalashnikov if Gwynn and I rappelled from roof onto balcony where he always has breakfast."

White waggled a finger in the air. "You've got to stop coming up with better ideas than me. I'm starting to get a complex."

244 · CAP DANIELS

He turned to Gwynn, who'd been busy inspecting the heart. "Davis, how long has it been since you've done any rappelling?"

"I've only done it once, and that was at the Academy. Why?"

"Oh, it's just another of Anya's harebrained ideas. I don't think you'll like it, but that's the beauty of being the boss. I don't care if you like it. Do it anyway."

* * *

They collected the gear they'd need from the FBI agents and climbed the service stairs to the room of Kalashnikov's building. The flat, gravel-covered roof offered more than a dozen options for securing their rope, so they peered over the knee wall until locating a spot directly above Kalashnikov's balcony, where he sat with a newspaper in one hand and a cup of coffee in the other. Across the table from him sat Oxana Kozlova, staring out over the city from her perch.

They backed away from the edge, secured their lines, and situated their rope bags on the back of their harnesses.

"Remember, there is only one hundred feet of rope inside bag. If you miss balcony, you do not have enough rope to make it to bottom. You must land on balcony. There is no other option. Are you ready?"

"I'll be honest," Gwynn said. "I don't love this idea, but it'll definitely be dramatic."

"Yes, it will. Let's go!"

They stepped atop the knee wall, side by side, and each woman gave a nod. With the rope paying out of the bags, there was no line dangling beneath to warn Kalashnikov and Oxana they were coming. They each bounded off the wall and began their short descent to the penthouse balcony. The street five hundred feet below offered no comfort and left

Gwynn's heart racing, but they landed in perfect unison—Gwynn beside Oxana, and Anya only inches from Kalashnikov.

Oxana screamed, and Volodya dropped his coffee. When the commotion was over and both women were clear of their gear, Anya reached inside her shirt and pulled out the small bowl. It hit the table only an instant before the lifeless heart of the nameless victim landed mostly inside the receptacle.

Kalashnikov recoiled. "My god! What is that?"

"I told to you I would bring heart of Lucchesi inside silver bowl. I have now done this, and you will now pay other half of agreed price for this."

"I told you I didn't want to see that thing!"

"Yes, this is what you said, but I did not believe you. You heard what was done, yes?"

He turned away from the table. "Yes, all of world knows Anthony Lucchesi is dead. What did you do with his body?"

"I will tell you this only after remaining balance is paid."

He threw up both hands. "Of course. I will get laptop from inside, and you can watch me do transfer, okay?"

"Is that a human heart?" Oxana asked, almost choking on the words.

"Yes, is part of promise to Volodya. He told you about this, yes?"

She shuddered. "No, he did not tell me anything about someone's heart in a bowl. What is wrong with you?"

Anya leaned down, almost touching Oxana's face. "Many things are wrong with me, but if I promise to bring to Volodya someone's heart, it will always be done, and there will never be excuse."

Kalashnikov reached for Oxana's hand and led her into the penthouse. "Wait here. I will bring out laptop, and please do something with that thing."

The instant the two vanished into the interior of the plush penthouse, four men poured from the door in perfect formation. Two turned toward Gwynn, and two directly at Anya. The two women retreated to separate corners of the veranda and drew their weapons. Anya sank her blade beneath the lead man's ribcage and scrambled his entrails with a whipping motion of the deadly knife.

The first attacker collapsed to the floor, and Anya stepped across his corpse. The second man drew a pistol from his waistband, raising it to center on Anya's chest. Before he could complete the first pull of the trigger, Gwynn's Glock sounded its thundering report, and the man collapsed, having drawn his final breath.

With the number of attackers cut in half, the fighting became one-on-one affairs, and both women were more than capable of destroying singular opponents. Anya grabbed the rope that had delivered her to the balcony and wrapped it twice around the neck of the man standing closer to her. The man pawed at the rope at his neck, and Anya led him around like a leashed dog until he was only inches from the rail.

Gwynn retrained her aim onto the last man and squeezed the trigger. To her amazed disbelief, the man lunged for her, catching the Glock in a meaty hand before she could get off a shot. Believing the more powerful man could rip the pistol from her grip, she thumbed the magazine release, dropping the remaining rounds onto the deck, and leaving only one round in the chamber.

Consumed by her own fight, Anya spun her opponent around, wrapped a length of the rope around his legs, and hefted him over the railing. He fell several feet before the rope came taut and suspended him over four hundred feet above the street below and quickly suffocating the life from his body.

Gwynn, still in the fight of her life, twisted and yanked to recover her pistol, but the odds on the balcony had been cut in half, and the ex-Spetsnaz warrior had just unwillingly become the deadly focus of a woman who'd once been his countryman.

Anya delivered a crushing side kick to the man's knee, bending it backward as he collapsed to the floor as the sounds of breaking bones and torn ligaments echoed through the morning air.

Gwynn reclaimed her pistol, retrieved a replacement magazine from her belt, and slammed it home into the pistol's hollow mag well. She planted a booted foot on the man's right wrist and shoved the muzzle of her pistol into the base of his nose.

As he roiled in pain from the broken knee, he said, "We are only here for her, not you."

Gwynn pressed hard against the flesh of his nose. "You said *we*, but from where I stand, it looks like you're all alone. That means you've got ten seconds to tell us everything about what's going on here before I drill an enormous hole through your skull."

"I told you! We are here for her, not you."

"That's a terrible answer, and bad answers get bad rewards." She pulled the Glock from beneath his nose and pressed it against his single remaining knee. "Don't worry, Boris. This will only hurt for the next fifty years or so . . . if I let you live. Tell me what's going on, and don't make me reencourage you to spill your guts."

The man spat at his tormentor and snatched a small, formerly concealed pistol from beneath his shirt. Gwynn watched the muzzle rise, and she retreated until her back collided with the railing, knocking most of the breath from her lungs. Before she could send a pair of nine-millimeter rounds into the threatening Russian, Anya sent a thundering boot to the man's face and drew her knife through the air faster than Gwynn could focus. Blood filled the air above the supine warrior, and his pistol bounced off his stomach and harmlessly to the floor.

Gwynn recovered her breath and threw herself forward, yanking her belt from her waist. She holstered her pistol and threw the belt around the man's arm, just below his elbow. A second later, the makeshift tourniquet was tight, and the bleeding from his wrist slowed.

"Your fight is over, comrade. You've got one knee and one hand left. Your only remaining choice is to tell us what we want to know, or you can bleed out right here. It's your decision."

The spirit of the previously hardened soldier melted into that of a man clinging to the remains of his life. "Kalashnikov hired us to capture or kill"—he turned his attention to Anya—"her, and deliver her body to Moscow. This is all I know. Nothing more."

Anya turned for the door and into the penthouse. "Let him die."

Gwynn retrieved the final syringe remaining from the previous night's mission and rocked the defeated warrior to sleep. With the belt cinched in place, she followed her partner inside and into a scene beyond description. Four suited FBI agents stood in a practiced formation with pistols drawn and trained on Kalashnikov and Oxana.

Volodya held his grandfather's greatest creation at waist-height, with the muzzle swinging wildly between Oxana and the federal agents. His trembling finger vibrated against the arch of the trigger.

"Put down the weapon!" one of the FBI agents ordered.

But Kalashnikov, wrought with fear and desperation, could only hear the pounding of his own heart and the terrible roar of his empire crumbling beneath him.

Gwynn drew her pistol, leaving her trigger finger pinned to the slide and well away from the trigger. She trained the weapon on a space between two of the FBI agents.

Continuing the charade Gwynn began, Anya leapt behind Kalashnikov and drew her knife. "Tell me what to do, Volodya. There are only four of them. We will keep you alive."

Confounded by confusion and racked with fear, Vladimir Kalashnikov turned to his only apparent ally in the room. "If they take Oxana, you must kill her. Do not let her talk."

He grabbed Anya's arm and yanked her between the agents and himself. She took full advantage of his brief instant of imbalance and captured his wrist, twisted his hand, and sent him to his knees in agony. The butt of the AK-47 slung around his shoulder and neck bounced from the floor, and Anya placed a boot on the rifle, essentially pinning her victim to the floor by the very weapon his countrymen had used to slaughter millions of lives through decades of war and oppression.

The mortified look of realization fell over Oxana's face, and she turned her attention and her weapon on Anya. Her first shot flew high and wide, exploding an Asian vase on a pedestal. Anya released her grasp of Volodya's hand and vaulted over his body, sliding her left arm beneath the sling of his rifle as she went.

Gwynn slid her finger from the slide of her Glock and onto its trigger as she abandoned her ruse and turned her muzzle on Oxana at the same moment Anya ripped the rifle from Kalashnikov's hand. She thumbed the selector to full auto and crushed the trigger, cutting Oxana Kozlova to the floor with a flurry of 7.62-millimeter projectiles. In the time it took the AK to dispatch a dozen killing rounds, Gwynn squeezed off two shots into the woman's back.

Every eye in the room, except Volodya's, watched the formerly beautiful Russian sparrow wilt into a bloody, unidentifiable mound of flesh. Volodya's eyes were trained on his only remaining option. As the thundering commotion waned, Kalashnikov stumbled to his feet and ran for the still-open door to the balcony, where at least three pistols rested on the floor.

Gwynn's position put her directly in the line of fire between the agents, Anya, and Kalashnikov. Praying they wouldn't fire, she spun and followed the Russian through the door, and to her horrified disbelief, he didn't reach for any of the discarded weapons lying rife for the picking. Instead, he bounded over the railing as if taking flight.

Instinctually, she lunged for him and caught one foot as his body crossed the only barrier between himself and certain death four hundred feet below. Gwynn dug her heels into the deck and leaned back in a desperate effort to arrest his fall. She bellowed in pain as the stitches holding her knife wound closed gave way and the flesh parted. The force of the man's flying body overtook her, and her feet left the floor. Time froze as the realization of her fate consumed her mind. Instead of releasing the man whose momentum was dragging her to her death, she abandoned reason and tightened her grasp on his ankle.

The collision came in explosive contact as Gwynn felt her body trying to implode around her soul. Her death grip on Vladimir Kalashnikov's ankle grew ever tighter as Anya laced her body around her partner, pinning her to the railing and bent in half at the waist.

The man kicked and yelled like an animal caught in a steel trap until four more sets of hands laced themselves through the railing and took control of the body that should've been spread over the street.

As the men struggled to pull Kalashnikov back over the rail, Anya collapsed on the floor with Gwynn still in her arms.

"What were you thinking?" Anya said.

Gwynn quivered in Anya's embrace. "I don't know. I don't know what I was doing, but I know you saved my life . . . again."

Vladimir Kalashnikov landed on his back beside them, with four FBI agents groaning and catching their breath.

Anya released her partner and pulled her credentials from her hip pocket. She unfolded the leather wallet, shoving her badge and DOJ identification within inches of Volodya's face. In growling Russian, she said, "You are under arrest, and you have right to remain silent, but you are coward, so you cannot."

He narrowed his eyes and clenched his teeth. "Why couldn't you let me die?"

Anya smiled, lifted the heart from the floor, and placed it on Kalashnikov's chest. "Because I made to Anthony Lucchesi promise you would go to prison, and he can now live inside your penthouse in return for his co-operation."

EPILOG
(EPILOGUE)

Supervisory Special Agent Ray White sat behind his two-acre desk with his tie undone and hanging loosely from his neck. "Well done, boys and girls. Have you seen the *Times* this morning?"

Anya, Gwynn, and Johnny Mac shook their heads in unison, and White read the article aloud.

"The Federal Bureau of Investigation in Las Vegas, in cooperation with other agencies, have arrested Vladimir Mikhailavich Kalashnikov, the grandson of famed Russian weapon designer, Mikhail Kalashnikov, on charges of conspiracy to commit murder, attempted murder of a federal officer, money laundering, forgery, and other undisclosed offenses.

"According to a spokesman from the Agency, agents of the FBI conducted one of the most elaborate undercover operations in the history of the Bureau to apprehend Kalashnikov and his coconspirator, Oxana Nikitovna Kozlova, who was killed during the resulting arrests and rumored to have once been an operative of the Sluzhba vneshney razvedki Rossiyskoy Federatsii (SVR), the successor to the Cold War–era KGB, specializing in seduction, blackmail, and espionage.

"The Russian embassy refused our attempts to obtain an official statement and has remained silent about the arrest, as well as the rumors surrounding Kozlova. Kalashnikov is scheduled to be arraigned in federal court tomorrow morning and is expected to remain in federal custody awaiting trial."

Johnny Mac shook his head. "We should've known the FBI would take all the credit. It's just like those guys to ride in when the work is done and grab all the glory."

White let his feet fall from the edge of his desk. "How did you want it to go down, Johnny? Did you want Anya and Gwynn plastered all over the front page of every newspaper in the world? The FBI didn't grab the glory. I gave it to them with a nice little bow on top."

White drew a circle in the air with his finger. "What we've got right here, this is too valuable to show the world. We're just getting started, Johnny, and if you want to remain inside this little circle, you need to get your mind right and start playing ball by the pitches I call instead of looking for your name in the headlines."

Johnny bowed his head, and Anya said, "I was pleased to have Johnny Mac on mission. I trust him to do what is right when time comes."

Both White and Johnny stared with blank expressions at the last person either expected to be the voice of reason at that moment.

Anya rewarded the pair with a sparrow's smile. "I have idea. We should celebrate as team. I know wonderful place in Caribbean where sun is hot and daquiris are cold. Best of all, is my treat. And before you ask, yes, Tom and Celeste can come, too."

ABOUT THE AUTHOR

CAP DANIELS

Cap Daniels is a former sailing charter captain, scuba and sailing instructor, pilot, Air Force combat veteran, and civil servant of the U.S. Department of Defense. Raised far from the ocean in rural East Tennessee, his early infatuation with salt water was sparked by the fascinating, and sometimes true, sea stories told by his father, a retired Navy Chief Petty Officer. Those stories of adventure on the high seas sent Cap in search of adventure of his own, which eventually landed him on Florida's Gulf Coast where he spends as much time as possible on, in, and under the waters of the Emerald Coast.

With a headful of larger-than-life characters and their thrilling exploits, Cap pours his love of adventure and passion for the ocean onto the pages of the Chase Fulton Novels and the Avenging Angel - Seven Deadly Sins series.

Visit www.CapDaniels.com to join the mailing list to receive newsletter and release updates.

Connect with Cap Daniels

Facebook: www.Facebook.com/WriterCapDaniels
Instagram: https://www.instagram.com/authorcapdaniels/
BookBub: https://www.bookbub.com/profile/cap-daniels